Extreme Malice

J. T. Tierney

CURTISS STREET
PRESS

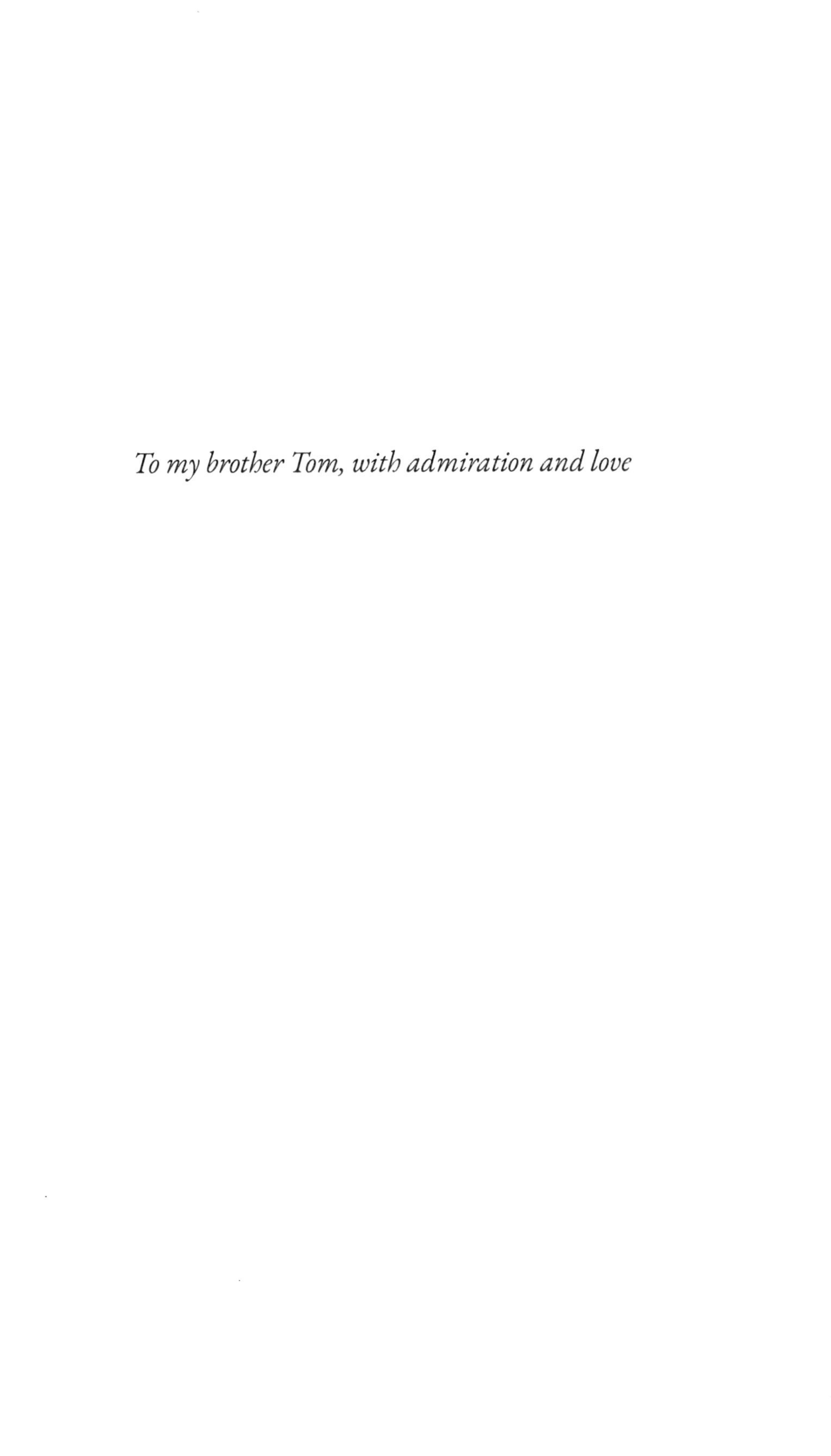

To my brother Tom, with admiration and love

Chapter One

August, 2021

Amy Wilson

Her Moms for Liberty T-shirt rides up, exposing flesh that bulges over black leggings. Crescents of sweat bloom under her arms as she lurches toward my son, her teeth bared, her eyes fever-bright. She snarls at him. "Your mother is an evil bitch. She hurts people." Each syllable slashes through the air like a blade, and I watch helplessly as my boy flinches under her assault. The words seem to leave physical wounds—I can almost see them cutting into him, drawing blood visible only to a mother's eyes.

Matt shrinks into himself as he hurries from the school building, shoulders curved inward like a shield. Each step seems to cost him. Watching him try to make himself invisible tears at my heart. My knuckles bleach white on the steering wheel. Every maternal instinct screams at me to leap out of the car, to place myself between this woman and my child. But I know better. These people are like sharks—the smallest drop of confrontation sends them into a feeding frenzy.

When Matt finally reaches the sanctuary of our car, the woman turns her fury from him to me. She slams against my window, her face so close I can count the flecks of spittle on the glass. Her fingertips leave greasy smears as she jabs the window again and again. "We're comin' for you!" The hatred twisting her features transports me back to those infamous photos from Little Rock, 1957—the same raw malevolence carved into the faces of segregationists as they screamed at Black children seeking an education.

"Wait 'til you see what we have in store for you," she shouts. Her mouth contorts around the words, and I realize only three inches and a pane of glass separate me from pure, distilled hate.

I slam the accelerator, a savage satisfaction flowing through me as gravel sprays from my tires back toward her. In the rearview mirror, her figure grows smaller but no less menacing —still stabbing the air with accusing fingers, still spewing hate into the autumn afternoon. Only when she vanishes from view do I dare look at Matt. The sight of him breaks my heart: face drained of color, lower lip quivering like he's seven years old again.

"Oh, sweetie, I'm so sorry." My hand finds his knee, seeking connection, trying to anchor us both in this storm. "You should never have had to face that."

"What the fuck was that about?" His voice cracks, and I hear the little boy beneath the tween's anger.

"Language, Matt." My rebuke slips out automatically, a mother's reflex, though cursing seems a reasonable response to what he's just experienced. I draw a shaky breath. "She's upset about the school board's Covid policies—like closing schools last spring, and the mask mandates. She thinks all that is hurting children." I swallow hard. "And she's convinced we're going to force vaccines on everyone."

He strips off his mask, looking at it between his fingers like it's a puzzling artifact. "What's the big deal? Most days I forget I'm even wearing it."

I force steadiness into my voice, though my hands still tremble on the wheel. "It's not really about the mask, honey." I pause at a red light, watching mountain bikers glide past, my eyes darting to the rearview mirror—checking, always checking now. "For these people, it's about control. About not wanting to be told what to do."

"But ..." Confusion furrows his brow. "We're told what to do all the time." His arm sweeps outward, encompassing the world beyond our car windows. "Stop at red lights. Go to school. Wear seatbelts." He tugs at his shoulder strap for emphasis. *What's the big deal?* his face seems to ask. *That's just how things work.*

My heart swells and breaks simultaneously. I drink in every detail of his profile—the sandy blonde hair that needs cutting, the lean planes of his face where baby fat once dwelled, those startling blue eyes that see straight through adult pretenses to the truth beneath. In eighteen short months, my little boy has transformed into someone who can slice through grown-up nonsense with devastating precision. Yet he's still my child, still so achingly young. Guilt sears through me like acid—my choices, my stands for what's right, have dropped him into this maelstrom of adult hatred. What kind of mother does that make me?

"You're right," I say, carefully choosing my words while my mind still churns with the confrontation. "But when these health requirements collide with politics, everything gets twisted—and ugly." I'm doing my best to sound like the calm, rational mother he needs right now, even as my stomach still churns from that woman's hate-filled face at my window.

"What does politics have to do with any of it?" His genuine bewilderment makes my heart ache.

I glance at him, seeing both the child who needs protection and the young man who deserves honest answers. "I'm about to oversimplify something incredibly messy, but here goes." I take a deep breath. "Politics is fundamentally about conflict—about how people with different beliefs decide to live together. Some people, like me and the other board members, believe the government has a duty to protect public health through things like mask requirements. We think that's as basic as maintaining roads or providing clean water." I pause, wondering if he's absorbing this. "Others believe government should back off completely, that these choices should be purely personal—even during a pandemic. And right now, that disagreement has turned toxic."

Matt's baby blues now have glazed over. I should've kept my spiel shorter, boiled it down to its essence: *Some people just love to fight.* He's now tuned me out, fingers tapping his phone to pull up BTS. The Korean pop washes over us as we drive through the tunnel of bur oaks that mark our neighborhood, their branches weaving a green canopy overhead. Beyond them, Grand Mesa rises like a sentinel, its flat top scraping the

Colorado sky at 10,000 feet. The late afternoon sun paints its sandstone cliffs deep red, the vertical grooves like ancient scripture carved by giants.

Mesa Vista has always felt like paradise to me. This small city on the Western Slope of the Colorado Rockies evolved from a mountain-man rendezvous point into a refuge for people seeking escape from Front Range congestion. The Utes had known its magic first. Now it draws outdoor enthusiasts, adventure seekers, and increasingly, people looking to reshape it in their own image.

"Holy shit, Mom!" Matt's cry shatters my reverie, as I pull the car into our cul-de-sac.

I follow his gaze to our front lawn, where someone has burned "EVIL" into the grass. Each letter is two feet wide, the dead grass brown against the green, like a giant scar across our property.

The rage comes first—hot, electric, overwhelming. Fear follows more slowly, a cold undercurrent beneath the anger. My muscles tense, my teeth grind. I don't truly believe they'd hurt us physically. But then again, I hadn't believed they'd terrorize my child or vandalize my home.

All this—the vandalism, the threats, the harassment—terrifies me. I've never gone through anything like this before. Four years ago, when I ran for school board, I thought I was signing up for budget meetings and curriculum reviews. Board service hadn't seemed political at all. The elections were non-partisan, the issues straightforward. It fit my middle-of-the-road pragmatism perfectly. A way to serve my community while maintaining my occupational therapy practice. Now it feels like I'm at ground zero of a culture war I never signed up to fight.

Mesa County was never exactly progressive, but we used to know how to disagree. The mix of retirees, young families, college students, and multi-generation locals once made this place feel like a living, breathing community. Then came Covid. First, the fights over school closures and remote learning, then masks and social distancing. Now it's about fear over vaccinations. Each issue strips away another layer of civility, revealing something ugly underneath—more rage, more threats, more people willing to burn their hatred into your front lawn.

Now, I stand at the kitchen window, staring out at those brutal letters burned into my lawn. I hear Dad's walker before I see him—that distinctive squeak-thump rhythm that's been the background music of my life since he moved out here from Denver. He appears in the kitchen doorway, silver hair caught in the afternoon light, his left leg swinging slightly as he makes his way to me. The polio that struck him in 1954 left its mark on more than just his muscles. It shaped his worldview, made him the pragmatist who raised me to believe in science, in facts, in solving problems methodically. Now that same belief system has painted a target on my back.

I point out the window. "They must've run out of Roundup—or gas, or whatever the hell they used—before they could add 'BITCH,'" I say, trying to joke but hearing the tremor in my voice instead.

Dad reaches for his phone with his free hand, the other gripping his walker. "I'm calling Frank."

"Chief Duffy won't do anything. Just like with the sapling, the letters ..." The list of recent incidents stretches behind us like breadcrumbs leading to this moment.

"Maybe not." Dad's broad forehead creases, the worry lines

deeper than they were a month ago. "But the police should have a record of it" He retrieves his honey-sweetened green tea from the fridge, the routine of his actions somehow emphasizing how abnormal everything else has become. "Any new ideas who's behind all this?"

I tell him about the woman at school, her face contorted with rage as she screamed about indoctrination and evil agendas. "But she's just today's version. There'll be someone new tomorrow."

"We should get security cameras," he says.

A sparrow lands on the wounded lawn, pecking at the scarred earth. "Yeah. Even if we don't catch anyone, it might help us feel safer." The word 'safer' tastes bitter in my mouth.

"I'll stop by Best Buy before meeting Jack for dinner."

"Say hi to my favorite uncle." I watch Dad maneuver his walker toward the hall, his determination visible in every labored step. The post-polio syndrome that emerged twenty years ago has been stealing his strength piece by piece, but it's never touched his resolve. "Be careful out there."

"*You're* the one who needs to be careful, sweetie. Board meeting tonight, right?"

"Yeah." My stomach tightens at the thought.

"Courage, kiddo." He pauses, turns back. "You know, you could resign. No one would blame you."

The suggestion hangs in the air between us. I think about Matt's face when that woman confronted him outside school, the fear that's becoming as familiar as breathing. Then I look at my father—the man who taught me never to quit, who showed me how to face problems with logic and reason instead of fear. The irony burns: his pragmatic approach to solving problems, so deeply ingrained in me, is exactly what's made me a target.

The late afternoon sun throws Dad's shadow long across the floor as he turns away. Outside, those crude letters glare up at me, demanding my surrender. But I'm my father's daughter. These people want me gone? They'll have to try harder than this.

Chapter Two

Marty Stauffer

The wind whistles through the open windows of my parked car as I study the education department building across the street. The "Masks Required" sign in the window catches the late afternoon sun, a beacon of everything wrong with this town. The school board is an absolute mess. But it isn't only the school board—all of Mesa Vista's government bodies have lost their way. Run by crazy people. The city council is a disaster, too. The county public-health department is full of tyrants. But this school board, with their endless parade of Covid restrictions, has crossed a line that makes my blood boil. Each restriction is another chain around people's necks.

I take another sip of cooling coffee and smile, thinking about our movement's growth. What began as scattered resistance has swollen into something unstoppable. Moms for

Liberty, Stand for the Constitution, Patriots United—they're our public face, our ground troops. Let them fill board meetings with their righteous anger, flood social media with their outrage. Like the Soviet army grinding down Hitler's forces, they'll wear down the enemy with sheer numbers.

But my team? We're different. We're more like Special Ops Forces. Like Navy Seals. While the troops march in daylight, we move in darkness, in the shadows. We bring the kind of pressure that makes people question whether they're cut out for public service after all. Amy Wilson's just the first. She thinks she's tough, thinks she can weather the storm. She hasn't seen anything yet.

My phone buzzes. An encrypted text from Ray, confirming the date of our next team meeting. Ray's a peculiar guy, a technology savant, a bit of a recluse who doesn't much like to leave his trailer home. But his skills make him invaluable. He knows a hell of a lot about the internet and the darknet. Ray's in this fight because he hates minorities and anybody he perceives as trying to help them. He doesn't much care about Covid-related policies—except for vaccines, which he sees as part of a larger conspiracy against white Americans. A loopy view, in my opinion. But, hey—it puts him on my side.

Another of my confederates is a disabled guy in his mid-seventies whom the rest of us only know by his ham-radio call sign—K3LVR. We pronounce it "Klover." He's rabidly opposed to vaccines, knows a lot about them, and loves using social media and his ham radio to spread his opinions about vaccines and governmental overreach.

The final member of my squad is Dwayne, a former professional wrestler who did pretty well for himself in the WWE for half a dozen years until he got his hip and femur shattered and had to give up the ring. He walks sorta funny now, but he got a nice insurance settlement from the WWE, and he doesn't seem unhappy with his lot in life. He brings muscle to our cause, happy to get his hands dirty, no questions asked

My time in D.C. with Project Veritas had taught me everything I know about using undercover operations to discredit mainstream media organizations and progressive politicians—skills I'd honed there until my mother's poor health called me home. I hadn't planned on returning to activism after moving back to Mesa Vista.

But fate had other plans. Through a darknet connection, I found myself this past spring at a secluded estate outside Crested Butte, training with twelve others in the arts of local political disruption. The goal? Reshape school boards and other local government institutions across Colorado. Turn the tide away from liberal overreach. Take the government back from the *true* deplorables.

The local school board here in Mesa Vista is a perfect example of the problem—and the opportunity. Consider the simple math of the board's current makeup: three liberal troublemakers, two conservative allies. Amy Wilson, Paul Paxton, and Hank Levitson consistently vote against people's liberty. Rick Braswell and Abbie Parish stand with us, for freedom. But our patriots need backup. We think the easiest way to help them is to drive one of the libtards to resign, and make sure that in the coming election we secure victory for a majority slate of conservative candidates.

We've identified Amy Wilson as the weak link—a first-term board member already showing signs of stress from public confrontations. We think we can break her through a campaign of intimidation.

My phone buzzes again. Klover has picked up chatter about Wilson's 12-year-old son being harassed at school this afternoon for his mother's policies. I make a note to have Ray amplify those stories online. Pressure at home, pressure at work, pressure on her kid, pressure everywhere she turns—sooner or later, she'll break.

Now, cars are pulling into the school-board parking lot. People are hauling placards out of their trunks, two others are checking that their bullhorns are working. I see what I've been waiting for: Dwayne arrives and parks his pickup in the corner of the lot. Now that I'm certain he's here, I leave my car and head into the building to get a seat near the front. I like to be at these meetings so I know what's happening. And I enjoy causing the occasional ruckus. The board's meeting are good opportunities to push back against the mandates.

Let them call us extremists. We have a mission, and I learned long ago that history remembers results, not methods. As I take my seat, I'm already thinking of my squad's next moves. In this game of political chess, Amy Wilson has no idea she's already in check.

Chapter Three

Amy

A woman materializes out of nowhere, hurling herself in front of my car like a human roadblock. She brandishes a sign that fills my windshield—"UNMASK THE KIDS" in blood-red letters. My heart hammers against my ribs as I stomp on the brake, my tires screeching in protest as I wrench the steering wheel to avoid her. Jesus Christ—another few inches and I'd have hit her.

The education department's squat red-brick building hunkers down behind a seething mass of bodies and signs. Protesters swarm like hornets stirred from their nest, blocking every path. Someone's meaty fist pounds my rear window—once, twice—making me jump. Through my mirrors, I see nothing but a forest of signs bobbing like angry birds, hemming me in. I inch forward, scanning desperately for a parking spot, but the crowd flows with me like a toxic tide, sensing my direction. Another blow shakes my back window. Sweat trickles down my spine as I read the words painted in black or garish reds: "I CALL MY OWN SHOTS," "NO TO VACCINES FOR KIDS," "VACCINE MANDATES VIOLATE BODILY AUTONOMY."

A gap opens. I wrench the wheel hard, but the mob shifts, surging like a wave to cut me off. Another harsh thump on the back right window now, harder, more menacing. *Jesus! What the hell is wrong with these people?* Finally, I swerve to an opening, breaking free toward an empty spot near the lot's perimeter.

The instant I crack open my door, a wall of noise slams into me like a physical force. The crowd writhes and pulses, jabbing signs skyward like pitchforks at an old-time witch hunt. I witness the death of irony: a woman in an anti-abortion T-shirt throws back her head and screams, "I'm pro-choice, not anti-vax. My body, my choice." Her attempt at starting a chant with those last four words drowns in the tsunami of "Trust in God, not vaccines."

Back in 2016, when I first got elected to the school board, our meetings were as exciting as watching paint dry. Board members would debate budgets and building maintenance before a handful of spectators. There was occasional raising of voices but never of fists. No one in the audience suggested we should be hanged or shot. Those were simpler times. And Mesa Vista's changed a lot in the last few years. These days, it's like living in Lunatic City—and I say that as someone who hugs the middle of the road. To the zealots around here, a moderate like me is Bernie Sanders in a sundress.

Now, I thread my way through the mob into a hearing

room packed wall-to-wall with about a hundred people, the air thick with tension and simmering with barely suppressed violence. The Moms for Liberty contingent catches my eye, their pinched faces scanning the room like predators looking for prey. I spot the woman who assaulted Matty at school today. A nasty piece of work, that one. Their signs mingle with the 970 Alliance crowd.

I crane my neck to take in more of the crowd, a carnival of outrage and paranoia. The Three Percenters are out in force, too, their militia patches stitched proudly on their camo jackets. Their wild eyes and sneering faces seem torn from political cartoons. I feel like I've stumbled into a carnival of caricatures. If it weren't so terrifying, I might be able to laugh at these people who find government conspiracies in their breakfast cereal. Each of their faces is a different shade of crazy.

I'm still arranging papers at my seat when Hank Levitson, our chair, bangs his gavel like he's trying to drive nails. Once, twice, three times—each crack of wood sharper than the last, but still barely denting the wall of noise. Finally, after more hammering from Hank, the din settles to a low hum.

"The meeting will come to order," he shouts, shepherding us through the mundane opening rituals—approval of the agenda and past minutes, recognitions of student achievements. The crowd simmers down during the executive committee's report on the planning process for the new Mesa Vista High School; we carefully dance along the cost-versus-quality tightrope.

Then Hank glances up, clears his throat, and utters the words the audience has been waiting for: "Okay, now it's time for public comments." The energy in the room surges like someone's flipped a switch, the temperature seemingly spiking ten degrees. Hank's reminder about civility and the three-minute speaking limit feels like tossing a paper towel at a tidal wave.

The first speaker clutches the microphone like a lifeline—a sixty-something woman who claims to be a physician but delivers her remarks with all the coherence of a drunk at closing time. Eventually, her point emerges from the fog of speech: requiring masks is "essentially coercing students into a medical experiment that can cause harm." She waves phantom data about masks and social distancing increasing infection rates, earning whoops of support from the crowd that would make you think she'd just announced the cure for cancer.

Next up: a "concerned parent" who treats us to a dramatic reading of the Nuremberg Code, because apparently requiring masks is exactly like Nazi war crimes. "Covid testing and vaccines are experimental. The Nazis paved the way for what's happening now." The crowd erupts, stomping and shouting like they're at a revival meeting: "No medical tyranny!" "Wake up, America!" "Jesus is my vaccine!"

A woman named Andrea Gordon takes the mic next, a rare voice of reason, expressing support for protecting students and staff. "The medical profession has been wearing masks for over 100 years and I've never heard of any of them suffering from mask usage." The crowd turns on her like a pack of wolves, their boos driving her into retreat. If tar and feathers had been handy, she'd have been wearing them home.

Then comes the performance-art portion of our evening. A gentle giant lifts a tiny, ancient woman onto a chair at the microphone, supporting her like she's a fragile bird. She taps the mic repeatedly, her quavering voice surprisingly strong and determined: "Can you hear me? CAN YOU HEAR ME?"

Hank responds with the patience of Job: "Yes, ma'am, we can hear you."

"Well, I hope so, because I'm here to talk about something very important," she announces, twisting her head owl-like to survey her audience. "My name is Ida Jacobs, and I'm concerned about the bathroom issue. This whole—what is it?—LJPQD thing has gone too far. My friend Yolanda told me yesterday that litter boxes have been added to school bathrooms in Mesa Vista for students who think they're cats. They call themselves *Furries*."

The room splits: a third dissolving in laughter, the rest gasping in horror.

"Yes," she continues, warming to her topic. "I was just as stunned as you are. More than upset, you could say. I'm furious. There is a, uh—what's the word?—oh, an 'agenda' that is being pushed on our schools. I, for one, don't think the Mesa Vista public schools should be spending money on litter boxes for students who think they're cats."

She glares at us board members up on the dais, her face a storm cloud of indignation. "What are you people? Crazy?" Then, steadied by her human support beam, she pivots to address the crowd: "When I was young and had kids in this school system, I never would've allowed this kind of insanity. You folks shouldn't either."

The room ignites. Someone starts chanting, "No Litter Boxes! No Litter Boxes!" The chant spreads like wildfire, the crowd surging to their feet, fists pumping the air in a frenzy of collective delusion. I catch the eye of my colleague Paul across the dais—he raises one eyebrow in mock rebuke, scolding me for my pro-litterbox agenda. I can't help but laugh.

Hank waits for the hysteria to crest before speaking, his tone calm but edged with exhaustion. "Let me be as clear as I can. There is no truth whatsoever to what Ms. Jacobs has just said. There are not now, and have never been, litter boxes in the bathrooms of any Mesa Vista schools. There never will be."

"Liar! Liar!" the old woman shrieks as her guardian angel begins lowering her from her perch. The crowd picks up the cry: "Liars! Liars! Liars!"

The parade of lunacy continues. A man built like a beer keg, sausaged into a polyester golf shirt and khaki shorts, delivers a rant about vaccines before pointing at us like an avenging angel: "If you people require everyone to get the 'genocide jab,' you'll essentially be war criminals and should hang by the neck." The crowd's bloodthirsty response—"Hang, hang!"—forces Hank to cut the mic and call a 15-minute recess before things spiral completely out of control.

When we reconvene, the crowd has thinned but concentrated, like a reduced crazy-sauce. One specimen near the front sports a crown fashioned from gleaming brass bullets, each one glinting in the fluorescent light. Another man—tall, thin, with a prophet's beard—shoulders a massive wooden cross, at least six feet high, as if he's auditioning for a modern-day passion play. His sandals slap against the wood floor as he strides to the microphone and strikes a pose, the cross resting on the crook of his shoulder. Hank, apparently resigned to our descent into full carnival territory, gives him the nod to speak.

"This here pandemic," the cross-bearer intones with televangelist fervor, "is God telling humanity to change the way we're living."

Cries of *Amen* ricochet around the room.

"I'm telling you folks: we are living through what the Holy Bible calls 'the end times.'" The *Amens* evolve into *Hallelujahs* as arms wave skyward like wheat in an apocalyptic wind. I brace myself, half-expecting someone to rend their clothes or start speaking in tongues.

Pointing at us up on the dais with his free hand, he thunders, "And I am here to tell you that all your tests and masks and vaccinations are mere illusions of control over death. There is nothing any of us can do to make our days on earth one second longer than the Lord Jesus Christ wants them to be."

More *Hallelujahs*.

"We have to REPENT. We must seek God's forgiveness for the sins of quarantining, masking, developing vaccines—all efforts to avoid God's gift of death."

The bullet-crowned prophet joins in: "Amen, brother. Vaccines are Satan's Syrup. They're the Mark of the Beast."

The floodgates burst, each claim more absurd than the last, a wave of paranoia and fury crashing over the room. "Satan's allies want to put microchips inside us." "They want to try to control our minds." The cacophony swells: "Fauci is the devil's deputy." "They hate Christians and want to wipe us all out." "Vaccines make you sterile." "Masks cause Covid."

I press my forehead into my palms, uncertain whether my splitting headache comes from the noise or the sheer idiocy of it all.

Hank finally bangs his gavel—once, then twice, then gives

up. "This meeting is adjourned," he declares, his voice straining to cut through the din.

The announcement fuels fresh outrage from those able to hear it. "Censorship!" someone screams. "They're silencing us!"

Hank hurries past me, heading toward his office like a fugitive. I hear him mutter a reply, "Oh, you got your points across."

A Mesa Vista PD officer stays behind, ensuring the crowd disperses, and shepherding each board member safely to their car. As I walk across the lot at his side, the air still thick with residual anger, something catches my eye—a hulking figure heading toward a white truck on the fringe. Something about him pricks at my memory—the lumbering gait, the way his shoulders roll as he walks.

And then it clicks. I've seen him before. Not just once, but several times over the past couple weeks. In fact, come to think about it, he seems to be almost everywhere I go.

Chapter Four

Amy

I tried to sound normal when I called Will after the board meeting to see if he wanted to stop by the house for a late dinner on his way home from work. But having been together more than two years means he can read the tremors in my voice like Braille. He offered to leave the hospital immediately. I insisted I was fine. But he knows when I'm trying to sound braver than I feel, so he said he'd come right after his last patient.

Now the kitchen is quiet except for the soft scrape of my fork against ceramic as I push my salmon around my plate in aimless patterns. Across the table, Will's dinner sits equally untouched. The overhead light carves deeper shadows under his eyes—another fourteen-hour shift written on his face—but his concerned gaze stays steady on mine.

My phone lies face-down between us. In the hour since I

got home, five new emails arrived. Each one more detailed than the last, decorated with photos that turn my stomach: me outside the hospital last Tuesday, at Morrison's Grocery on Thursday, walking into the pharmacy yesterday. The message is clear. They're watching. Always watching.

They've moved beyond noise now. Beyond vandalism. This is methodical. A campaign designed to break me piece by piece —targeting my son, my home, my sense of safety. These aren't random acts anymore. This is terrorism, calculated and precise.

"You've barely touched your food," he says quietly. His voice has that careful tone I've heard him use with anxious patients.

"Not hungry." I push my plate away and run my hands through my hair—a nervous gesture Will says I'm doing more often lately, along with pushing at the bridge of my eyeglasses. The constant tension has worked its way into my every muscle, every movement.

He stands and moves behind my chair, resting his hands on my shoulders. The warmth of his touch seeps through my thin blouse as he begins to work at the knots of tension. "How was the meeting?"

A shudder runs through me, and his hands still for a moment before resuming their gentle pressure. "Will, these people are crazy. They've lost all sense of balance."

"I wish you'd let me pay for a security detail to accompany you at board meetings." His fingers find a particularly tight spot, and I wince. "It would make me feel so much better—and provide you with some protection."

"I've told you ... there's an MV cop at every meeting. It's fine. If I had my own muscle protecting me, it would only esca-late things. These people want us to look like the aggressors.

They're just waiting for an excuse." I sigh, glancing toward the stairs where the faint sound of Matt's white-noise machine hums. "And I have to think about Matt and Dad. I can't do anything that might make the situation more volatile."

"Let me stay here tonight," he says suddenly, his hands stilling on my shoulders. "I just need to know you're safe. And I want you to feel secure."

I twist to look up at him and see the worry etched around his eyes. "Will, Matt's already asleep upstairs, and Dad's probably still up reading. It's not ... we couldn't ..."

"I know, I know." The ache in his voice cuts through me like a blade. "It's not about that. I'll sleep on the couch if you like."

"Oh, what the hell," I say, surprising myself. "No ... not on the couch. Stay with me tonight. Matt knows you sleep over sometimes, and Dad ..." I manage a small smile. "Dad actually asked me last week why I'm being so old-fashioned about it."

Will pulls me closer, pressing a kiss to my forehead. His chest is warm against my back, and I can feel his heart beating steady and strong. "You're sure?"

"I'm sure." I take his hand, leading him toward the stairs. His fingers intertwine with mine, familiar and comforting. We pass Dad's room, where a strip of light shows under the door—he's probably deep in one of his public-health history books, lost in accounts of past epidemics while a contemporary one rages around us. I pause there for a moment, hear the the soft rustle of a page turning. Reassured that he's safe, I take Will to my room.

He's asleep almost before his head hits the pillow, one arm still reached out toward my side of the bed. Poor guy. His days at the hospital are so long, so demanding. I crawl in next to him and turn on my side so I can watch him sleep, his face relaxed, probably for the first time today. In the quiet darkness, memories float up unbidden of how we met, clear as photographs.

I'D BALANCED my coffee and salad as I scanned the crowded hospital cafeteria. St. Mary's was always busy at lunch, but that day it seemed like every doctor, nurse, and staff member had decided to eat at exactly 12:30. The cacophony of voices and clattering trays echoed off the institutional walls. I'd spotted one empty chair at a table already occupied by someone in wrinkled scrubs bent over a medical journal, his curly dark hair shiny under the cafeteria's ceiling lights.

"Mind if I join you?"

The doctor looked up, and I found myself looking into kind brown eyes, warm despite the obvious exhaustion in them. He quickly moved his papers aside, creating a space for my tray. "Please. Though I should warn you I'm not great company when I'm cramming for M&M rounds."

"Better than no company. Or eating this standing up." I set down my tray, grateful to be off my feet after a morning of patient sessions. "I'm Amy Wilson, by the way. OT. ... And I'll now be quiet so you can work."

He gave me a closer look. "Ah, I'm glad to meet you. I'm Will Robinson, the new hospitalist in internal medicine." He closed his journal, and I noticed his hands—strong but gentle-looking, the kind of hands you'd want taking care of you if you were sick. "This is fortuitous to meet you," he said, tapping the side of his head with an index finger. "I have a mental note to seek you out. I saw this morning that you've been assigned to a patient of mine, Harriet Sandoval, who's going to need extensive OT. A complex case—started with pneumonia, developed ARDS, spent three weeks in ICU. She's got a long road ahead."

I nodded, already thinking through the likely challenges. "Significant deconditioning, I imagine? How's her cognitive status?"

We spent the next twenty minutes discussing the Sandoval case, our lunches half-forgotten. The noise of the cafeteria faded into background as we talked. I was impressed by Will's thorough grasp of his patient's needs and his genuine concern for her recovery. Too many doctors treated PT and OT as afterthoughts, but Will clearly appreciated the importance of comprehensive rehabilitation planning.

"I'll stop by this afternoon to evaluate her," I'd said, gathering my things. "Thanks for the heads up on the case."

"Thank you for letting me hijack your lunch break with shop talk." His smile was warm, genuine, transforming his tired face. "Maybe I can make it up to you with coffee sometime?"

I'd hesitated for just a moment. Dating someone on the hospital staff could get complicated. But there was something about Will—his focus, his intelligence, the way he really listened when I spoke ...

"I'd like that."

Coffee led to dinner at Vincenzo's, where we discovered a shared love of hiking and Thai food. Over pasta primavera and a nice Montepulciano, Will told me about growing up in Seattle, where his parents still lived, and his decision to do his residency in Colorado because he loved the Rocky Mountains. I shared stories about my work with patients, my recent election to the school board, my hopes of expanding the OT department's outpatient programs. He asked thoughtful questions about Matt and Dad, showing genuine interest in understanding my whole life, not just the parts that were convenient.

We found we worked well together professionally—Will said his patients consistently had better outcomes when I was involved in their care. But it was outside the hospital where our relationship truly flourished. What started as occasional dinners became regular dates. I found myself looking forward to our Sunday morning hikes, where we could decompress from the week and just enjoy each other's company, the mountain air sharp and clean in our lungs.

Six months after that first shared lunch table, we were cooking dinner together at Will's apartment when he suddenly said, "You know, I think this is the first I've felt really settled anywhere in a long time."

I looked up from the vegetables I was chopping, the knife pausing mid-cut. "What do you mean?"

"Everywhere I've lived since going off to college has always felt temporary somehow. Like I was just passing through." He'd stirred the sauce he was making, choosing his words carefully. The kitchen was filled with the smell of garlic and herbs, and something else—possibility, maybe. Hope. "But lately ... I don't know. *This* feels like home. *You* feel like home."

Now, watching him sleep beside me, I realize that even having him here next to me, my house doesn't feel safe. So, it doesn't feel like home.

Chapter Five

Tom

The bag from Best Buy sits on the passenger seat next to me as I navigate my car through Mesa Vista's late-afternoon traffic. My brother Jack had insisted that the SimpliSafe security system offers "the ideal balance of quality and value." For a thousand bucks, it had better offer some peace of mind. Honestly, I just want something—anything—that might help protect my daughter and grandson. The thought of them being terrorized makes my hands clench the steering wheel until my arthritic knuckles ache.

When I pull up to Marley's Bar and Grille, I spot Jack already waiting outside, his powerful frame casting a long shadow in the slanted sunlight. At sixty-eight, my younger brother still looks like he could bench-press a Volkswagen. He helps me wrestle the walker from the trunk, pretending not to notice when I wince at a fresh stab of pain.

Inside Marley's, Jack pauses to inspect a potted fern near the entrance, bending his broad shoulders to peer at the fronds he's fondling. "The real McCoy." he announces, pushing out his lower lip in satisfaction. The plant's authenticity seems to surprise him, given Marley's decidedly humble appearance. The underwhelming place looks like a converted five-and-dime, though they've done what they could by adding pleasant lighting. Otherwise, no pretense or aspirations. I like that about it.

We go to Marley's in part because they have a great patio, and these days we're only willing to go out to eat at places that offer outdoor dining. The trouble is that Marley's patio might as well be in Wyoming, given the obstacle course of tables and chairs between it and the front entrance.

The hostess grabs two menus and signals for us to follow her. For the hundredth time, I long for some kind of hovercraft to float me above the maze of jutting elbows and chair legs. Instead, I begin the familiar, awkward dance with my walker, every step a negotiation with the laws of collision and gravity.

When we finally settle at our table and remove our masks, Jack grins at me. "Need a breather, old timer?"

"Keep it up, young buck. I've still got enough strength to whack you with this walker."

A striking server approaches—light brown hair cascading to her shoulders, cream silk blouse, tasteful yellow-gold jewelry. I watch Jack's eyes light up with mischief.

"Can I get you gentlemen something to drink?"

"Oh, you're here to take our order?" Jack feigns disappointment. "I was hoping you were coming over to say you want to adopt us."

A shaft of sunlight coming through the patio's pergola

makes her hair gleam. She narrows her eyes and fixes him with an arctic stare. Then she looks at me, lifting the edges of her mouth ever so slightly. I ask for a Laphroaig, straight up. Jack, properly chastened, mumbles that he'll have the same scotch, but on rocks.

"You're not supposed to joke like that with women anymore," I say after she leaves.

"I always hope they'll cut me some slack because of my advanced years. This salt-and-pepper hair—"

"Just makes you look a bit more distinguished. Doesn't hide the fact you're a dirty old man because your mouth always gives you away."

Our drinks arrive via a different server, and I fill Jack in on the latest vandalism at Amy's house. With each detail, I watch his expression darken.

"Poor Amy," he says. "I was still playing with my toes when I was her age. This kind of thing would've made me wet myself."

"Yeah, well, I'm not too comfortable with it either." I shift in my chair, trying to find a position that doesn't hurt. "I don't move very fast these days. Feel like a sitting duck. God forbid one of their malicious stunts were to accidentally set a fire."

"You want to stay at my place?"

"Thanks, but no. I need to be there for her and Matty."

He gives me that look I know too well, the one that says he's about to ask about my health. "The pain's worse, isn't it?" he asks.

"Nah. It's fine."

He rolls his eyes.

"Alright, yes. It's not good. PPS sucks."

"Sorry, bud. It's just not fair."

"We've all got our crosses to bear."

"Don't give me that. Most of us have crosses made of tissue paper or balsa. Yours is black ironwood."

I wave him off with our grandfather's favorite old dismissal. "Aw, gwan wid ya."

Jack stirs the ice in his glass with his index finger. "You gonna let me help with this harassment problem?"

I study him across the table—my retired-cop brother with too much time on his hands and enough residual muscle to make trouble. I know it's not an empty offer. The cloak of retirement hasn't settled easily on him. He's always itching for things to do. His latest time waster is buying broken appliances just so he can take them apart and see if he can fix them.

"Frank Duffy says this sort of thing usually dies out quickly. People vent their anger and frustration, then move on," I say.

Jack snorts. "Translation: Duffy's understaffed and can't help. Besides, half the cops in this town are wannabe brownshirts. I'm not sure you want to get those punk fascists involved. They'd probably think what's happening to Amy is funny—or worse, get ideas. That's why you should let me help out."

"What would you do?"

"Same as them. Poke around. Talk to people. Keep my eyes open."

From a nearby table, a loud voice cuts through the patio chatter. A bald man with a ragged beard is holding court, his face flushed with righteous fervor. "We don't need masks or vaccines—Jesus Christ is all we need," he says to his table mates. "The elites want science to replace God."

A woman with unsettling gray eyes chimes in. "Like that Wilson woman. Little dictator on her throne, handing down her commandments. 'Thou shalt wear masks. No in-person classes until I say so. Submit to the needle or else.'" She mimics a prissy voice that bears no resemblance to Amy's measured tones. The table erupts in knowing laughter.

Jack catches my eye, his mouth quirking in amusement. "Your daughter's the Antichrist now? That makes you Satan himself." He raises his water glass in mock salute. "How about showing some demonic power and turning this into Laphroaig?"

But I'm not laughing. In the late afternoon light, watching these people foam at the mouth about my daughter, I realize I can't afford to say no to Jack's offer of help. I lean forward.

"Tomorrow after lunch," I say. "Help me install that security system. And then we can talk about what else we might do."

His face lights up like a kid at Christmas. "I'm free all day."

"Has to be after noon. I've got that polio survivors' group in the morning."

"I thought you hated the very idea of support groups. You refused to try that grief one I steered you to after Laura died."

I shrug. "Maybe it's time to learn how other people cope."

Our Reubens arrive, and we eat in companionable silence, each of us pretending not to hear the continued ranting from the nearby table. But I notice Jack taking mental notes, studying faces, doing what old cops do.

Mesa Vista spreads out beyond the patio, beautiful but somehow fearsome—a town where the shadow of the Grand Mesa meets the shadow of something darker, something that burns hatred into front lawns and frightens twelve-year-old boys as they leave the school building.

I take another bite of my sandwich and start planning what,

if anything, to tell Amy about the conversation we just over-heard. It's dicey. Sometimes knowledge is power. But other times it's just another weight to carry, and her burden is already too heavy.

———

I'LL FILL you in on the polio that changed my life when I was seven. The virus is invisible to the naked eye—5,000 times smaller than the width of a human hair. I try to picture it sometimes: this microscopic invader that slipped past my parents' desperate precautions and rewrote my future. First came the fever, the bone-deep aches, the stiff neck that my mother noticed when I couldn't turn my head at dinner. Then, in a matter of hours, everything changed for me—and for all the other kids who caught the virus. Some of them needed iron lungs just to breathe. Some never walked again. Some didn't survive at all.

I was one of the last casualties of America's polio era—struck down mere months before Salk's vaccine would have saved me. By then, the U.S. had endured forty years of epidemics that left a trail of dead and disabled children in their wake. The first major outbreak hit in 1916, emerging from an immigrant neighborhood in Brooklyn they called "Pigtown." That summer, as the virus rampaged across 26 states, six thousand children—most under five—never saw autumn.

The worst year was 1952. There were 57,879 cases in the U.S. alone, with 600,000 worldwide. Parents lived in terror of warm weather. They banned their children from public pools, church gatherings, summer festivals. Some mothers wouldn't let their kids eat peaches, convinced the fuzzy skin harbored the virus. My brother and I thought our parents were being ridiculous with all their restrictions. "Polio weather," we called it with eyerolls, too young to understand their fear. But the virus found me anyway.

As I grew from boyhood to adolescence to early adulthood, I watched as the polio vaccine reduced the disease's scourge. I marveled as other vaccines came along for other diseases such as diphtheria, tetanus, measles, rubella—one by one, humanity's ancient enemies fell to science. I saw how research revolutionized everything from cancer treatment to heart-disease prevention. These public-health achievements led me to want to help bring the benefits of such advances to the public, to be a part of that revolution.

For thirty years, that's exactly what I did. I rose through the ranks of Colorado's Department of Public Health and Environment, eventually serving eight years as executive director. Before that, I spent two decades in Disease Control and Public Health Response, preparing the state for health emergencies. We worked to protect people in ways they often took for granted: vaccinating communities, tracking outbreaks, improving school nutrition, setting workplace health standards. It wasn't glamorous work, but it saved lives.

Now I watch in horror as people reject the science that saved millions of other kids from polio and other diseases. We're approaching a million Americans dead from Covid, with more falling every day.

The Covid vaccines that will be available even to young people in a few months represent a triumph of modern medicine, yet conspiracy theories spread faster than the virus itself.

For years, vaccines were as normal as brushing teeth—accepted, valued, unquestioned by most Americans. Now, a significant portion of the population views them with suspicion or outright hostility. The change wasn't sudden; it eroded over decades. DPT vaccines faced scrutiny in the '70s and '80s over supposed neurological complications. The MMR vaccine fell victim to Wakefield's fraudulent autism claims in the late '90s.

Now, millions of people believe absolutely crazy things—not only about vaccines but about viruses themselves. The latest? That 5G mobile-phone technology causes Covid. I laughed out loud yesterday when I heard that one on the radio, remembering similar nonsense that spread in 2003 about 3G causing SARS, or in 2009 when some people blamed 4G for Swine Flu. Who actually believes this stuff? It defies both common sense and scientific evidence to think that viruses can travel on radio waves.

Some nights I sit in my study, surrounded by decades of public health research, and wonder how we got here. How did we go from parents desperate for the polio vaccine to parents protesting about their kids getting a Covid vaccine? The virus that infected me was invisible, but at least the enemy was clear. Now I'm not so sure anymore.

Chapter Six

Tom

My walker's rubber feet squeak against the linoleum as I venture into the foyer of Grace Methodist's fellowship hall. I pause in the doorway, my gaze settling on the calendar perched on an easel just inside. The month's schedule unfolds like a litany of human pain: Alcoholics Anonymous, Sexual Abuse Survivors, Gambling Recovery, Eating Disorders Support, Cancer Support, Infertility Group. And now, us—the polio survivors. What illustrious company we keep.

The room is typical of church meeting halls—sterile and unwelcoming, with a couple dozen stackable chairs, a few large folding tables, and an overall vibe that destroys all joy.

Six people are already arranged in a wide circle to maintain social distance, their mobility aids forming a constellation around them—three sleek scooters, two wheelchairs (one with the quiet hum of a motor), and a single wooden cane. Mine will be the only walker in the bunch. Half the masked faces turn to me with welcoming eyes, while the others stare into middle distance, lost in their own worlds. Everyone's at least sixty-five—no surprise there, since Salk's vaccine wiped polio off the American map after '55.

I ease myself into an empty chair, wincing at the familiar ache. What the hell am I doing here? I've avoided support groups my whole life. They always seemed like pity parties to me. But here I sit, now questioning my judgment about having come.

Right at ten, a woman in a fuchsia pantsuit that could stop traffic removes her mask and speaks up. "Welcome, everybody. I'm Peggy, your group coordinator." Her smile tries for a thousand watts but barely reaches sixty. Plucked eyebrows arch over eyes caked with too much shadow. She's got the soft, comfortable look of someone who enjoys her desserts without guilt.

She launches into her introduction. "I hope you all had a good summer. It's nice to have the group meet again after a hiatus. Three of us are returnees from last year," she says. "Glad to have you back, David and Minnie. The rest of you are new, and we're so glad you've decided to join us. I'll give everyone a chance to introduce themselves in a moment. But first, I want to call your attention to an absence. Our dear friend Wanda Porter died over the summer." Every cliché in the book comes pouring out: "Wanda didn't sweat the small stuff ... saw the glass as half full ... lived for the journey, not the destination ..." Christ. I have to bite my tongue to keep from groaning. I hope poor Wanda's life wasn't as trite and hackneyed as this tribute. "We'll miss her, but her spirit lives on in the group." Peggy nods emphatically, as if to say, *By God, we will* not *forget dear Wanda.*

The fellow named David mutters "Hear, hear," and Peggy peers to the heavens with the gravity of a priest consecrating the host.

Then, with a change in vocal tone that suggests all memories of Wanda are now disappearing into the empyrean domain and her name will ne'er be spoken again, Peggy slaps her knees and says, "Okay, let's introduce ourselves." She shares her story first—polio at nine, lost use of her left arm, then got blindsided by post-polio syndrome in the '80s. "It hit me harder than the original virus," she says, and there's real pain beneath her cheerleader persona. "I need the support this group offers, so I'm glad each of you is here."

She puts her mask back on, turns to the woman on her left and indicates we'll go clockwise around the circle, introducing ourselves. Sally, with Coke-bottle glasses and nervous hands, talks about how post-polio feels like betrayal after decades of progress.

"For years, I just tried to get on with life and work each day toward improvement. And that's what I did. And it was okay. But this post-polio stuff ... there's no getting better with this, no building toward improvement. It's hard." A rueful look overtakes her as she seems to go someplace else in her head, then return. "Oh well, you folks don't need to listen to all that. You already know it."

I'm next, and I say pretty much the same thing Sally did, but then add, "Watching how society's handling Covid ... it's fascinating, isn't it? So different from the response to polio in the '50s. I don't know whether you all ever talk about that. I hope so."

"We do, Tom. And we look forward to hearing your thoughts," Peggy says. "Thank you."

David barely speaks, but his 101st Airborne cap says plenty —probably office support staff at Fort Campbell, given his polio history. The hat looks permanently attached to his head, like a soldier's second skin.

Steve rolls forward slightly in his high-end motorized wheelchair, his Oxford shirt crisp despite the late-summer heat. His voice carries the rich authority of a radio announcer as he describes a lifetime of silence about his condition. "I joined this group because I'm one of those people who has gone his whole life not talking about polio or its effects on me. When I was a kid, my family changed the subject every time I mentioned polio. Like I'd committed some shameful crime by getting sick. So I learned to behave as if my physical challenges and emotional traumas didn't exist. I never talked about it." He pauses and looks down at his lap. "Well, I'm no genius, but I'm just smart enough to know a lifetime of such behavior hasn't been good for me. I hope this will be a place where I can learn to talk about how this has affected my life."

Then Sofia speaks, and the room shifts. She's elegant, with silver-streaked dark hair swept into a perfect French twist, but it's her words that command attention. She speaks eloquently for about five minutes, dissecting our shared history with surgical precision: the 1950s mandate to fight, never complain, never show weakness. "Fight! Fight! Fight! was the polio theme song," she says, her indeterminate accent adding weight to each word. "No crying, no self-pity. You fought, you fell, you climbed, you stretched. And you buried every scrap of rage and grief deep inside."

I find myself stunned by Sofia's cogent summation of our collective situation. The hear-a-pin-drop silence in the room suggests that everyone else is equally struck by her words.

Then the woman next to Sofia clears her throat. I almost laugh out loud when she says in a high, squeaky voice that her name is Minnie. She's tiny, with a sharp, pointy nose, close-set eyes, and ears that stick out like jug handles. But like Sofia, she surprises me, in this case with her intensity. She describes being force-fed *The Little Engine That Could* as a child, with its repeated refrain: 'I think I can, I think I can." She stops, and her eyes narrow. "I deplore people who believe it's okay to ban or burn books, but I would happily make an exception for that one," she declares, earning genuine laughs.

"What a lie we were fed—the notion that determination could conquer all. I hate the psychic damage that lie caused. It wasn't true that I could do anything I set my mind to. God, I hated being told to try. I had tried and tried and tried. Until I was thirty, I believed that if I just tried harder, I would get better. What nonsense it was. The cultural expectations Sofia spoke of, along with the try-harder mantra, left me a mess psychologically." Now Minnie takes a pause, then adds, "I'm trying my hardest to deal with it. And that's why I'm returning for a second year of these group meetings."

I'm still processing this outpouring of raw honesty when Earl, the last of us, speaks up. He's a mountain of a man wedged into a scooter, his green checkered shirt straining against suspenders in patriotic red, white, and blue. After considerable throat-clearing, he says, " I suspect my story is a little different from the rest of yours. Most of you probably don't know how you caught the virus. That's the typical case. Like Sally here, most of you were probably just going about your business as kids, and then suddenly, out of the blue, got whacked by this horrible virus. You have no idea how it happened. But, I'm a rare instance of someone who knows *exactly* how he caught polio. In my case, it was from the Salk vaccine itself." The bitterness in his voice could etch glass. He peers around at us as if daring anyone to challenge him.

"There were only about two hundred of us in the whole country who got polio that way, most out here in the West." He lets out a snort that conveys both frustration and indignation. "Anyway, I'm in the same boat as the rest of you now, but how I got onboard is a little different. To be honest, I'm pretty bitter about it. And it makes me mighty sympathetic to all the folks out there now who say they'll stay far away from the Covid vaccine when it's available to them."

He stops and looks directly at me, I guess because of my earlier remark about society's response to Covid. He says, "I don't think the government should be pushing people to get it if they don't want to. Damn vaccines are never as safe as the companies and the government say." He crosses his arms and looks around the circle with a scowl.

I can't let that comment pass unanswered. "Actually, vaccines are incredibly safe and effective. The data show—"

"You don't know that. We don't know anything about this vaccine they're coming out with. Don't know what's going to happen to vaccinated people a year from now, three years from now—"

Peggy interrupts him. "Let's please not get into that now.

40

We have lots to talk about today, and we can return to this topic in future meetings." I give Earl a conciliatory nod. He offers an icy glower in return and I catalog him under "hopeless asshole"—until my grandmother's voice echoes in my head: "Presume goodwill." A little plaque saying that also hung in her kitchen for years. Maybe Grandma had a point. But damn, she never had to presume that about this guy.

By the time I get out to the parking lot after the meeting's end, Earl somehow had wrangled his scooter into his silver, side-entry wheelchair van and is already heading out the drive. The political stickers on his rear bumper extinguish whatever short-lived empathy I'd felt toward him.

Chapter Seven

Jack

The town spreads out below me as I leave my place and head to Amy's house to help my brother install that new security system. Fifty thousand souls make this high desert paradise their home. Most folks moved here to escape something—Denver's traffic, California's prices, the east coast's attitude. But some brought their demons with them, and now those demons are burning messages into my niece's lawn. Do I think we'll catch the vandals? About as likely as catching Sinatra in Sumatra. But that doesn't mean we don't try.

My thoughts turn sunnier when I see puffy clouds above Grand Mesa. The scene still takes my breath away, though I've lived in Mesa Vista over a year. It always reminds me of that Georgia O'Keeffe painting of Cerro Pedernal, the spectacular and unusual mesa in New Mexico said to be her favorite. The gods smile on this place.

I came here after retiring from police work in Denver and Boulder because my brother Tom had moved out here a few years back. He's my favorite person in the world. A kind soul wrapped in a shell toughened by decades of pain, somehow maintaining an air of good cheer that puts the rest of us to shame. Mom used to say he had quite the temper as a kid. Not surprising, given the bum deal life handed him. The remarkable thing is how he transformed that anger into something else entirely.

Me? I'm what you might call a professional grouch—and proud of it. Not the kind of asshole who kicks dogs or scams old ladies. No, but I don't sugar-coat things, don't play nice when nice isn't called for. Not a people pleaser, I guess. Can't explain it, really. Had a good life, no real hardships. Just born with a mouth that runs faster than my brain and a personality that rubs some folks the wrong way. Made me a perfect fit for police work. Most cops are assholes—it's practically in the job description.

I pull into Amy's driveway, the gravel crunching under my tires. It's a handsome house—white siding, navy-blue shutters, with a tidy yard, partly grass, partly sand and stone and drought-resistant plants. I thought my mowing days had ended when I turned in my Boulder PD badge and moved out here. But Amy's too busy to take care of her lawn, and Tom obviously can't do it. I'll yield the task to Matty in a year or so, but for now I take care of the small plot of green for them. The straw-colored letters burned into it are a personal affront to me. It really pisses me off. Whoever did this should have messed with some other caretaker.

Tom's not home from that polio support group meeting

yet. I make sure not to take his usual parking space nearer the front door. As I get out of the car, I'm slapped with the dry heat. At least it's not like the humid soup you get in many parts of the country. That's one thing I love about Mesa Vista—perfect climate, far as I'm concerned. Milder winters than Denver, summer days that cool off the second the sun drops, and mountains nearby if you need to escape the heat. Plus, my pension stretches a lot further here than it would've on the front range. Denver or Boulder these days? Expensive as San Francisco, without the compensation of good cioppino.

Inside, I grab a beer from the fridge and settle into Tom's favorite chair. I'm not usually here alone, and the house feels empty. Reminds me of being in my own place, where I'm always by myself. Wouldn't mind having someone to share it with—some soft, giggly gal who laughs at my jokes and doesn't mind my rough edges. But for now, I've got what matters: cable TV, internet, a reliable car, and family nearby. Tom, Amy, and Matt are all the family I need. Never had kids myself, so they're it for me. Which is why this harassment of Amy has my blood boiling.

My phone buzzes—a text from Tom: *Meeting's over. Home in 10 or 15.* I send a thumbs up. I finish my beer and start making mental notes about good spots around Amy's house to locate these security cameras. Twenty-five years on the force taught me one thing: assholes get careless. Sooner or later, they slip up. And when they do, they'll learn that this other asshole's been watching and waiting. Nobody messes with my family.

THE DINING ROOM table looks like an electronics store exploded across it. I've laid out every component of the security system in precise rows: motion sensors, window contacts, door triggers. Looks like enough to protect the Pentagon. Tom shuffles in from his polio support group meeting and eyes the array of gadgets skeptically.

"Christ," he mutters, leaning on his walker. "Maybe I went overboard. It's not like we're securing Fort Knox here."

"You did good," I assure him, sorting through the components. "Just the basics—window and door sensors, motion detectors, glass-break alerts. Two cameras inside, four out. Video doorbell. Nothing fancy, but it'll give us eyes and ears where we need them." I hold up one of the outdoor cameras, its sleek black housing catching the afternoon light. "These'll take the longest to position—there's an art to finding angles that maximize coverage without screaming 'surveillance' to the whole neighborhood."

By the time we finish configuring everything to Amy's WiFi and running our final tests, the sun is dipping toward the mountains. The flagstone patio out back offers a perfect spot to decompress. The rock still hold the day's warmth as we settle in with cold beers. "So," I ask, "how was group therapy with your fellow gimps?" Brothers can get away with that kind of crack.

He takes a thoughtful pull from his bottle. "About what you'd expect. Circle of old cripples comparing orthopedic shoes." His smile fades into something more serious. "But some of them ... damn. Really insightful about their experiences. Might stick with it, see where it goes."

"Good people?"

"Mostly. Could see myself being friends with a couple of

them. Though there was this one guy, a complete asshole, who—"

The back door bangs open, cutting him off. Amy storms out to the patio like a thundercloud, Matt trailing behind her with wide eyes.

"Goddamnit, I'm getting tired of this shit." Her voice cracks like a whip. Then she spots me and dials it back, moderating her volume but not her intensity. "Oh ... hi, Jack. Sorry."

I lift my beer in greeting, trying to project calm. "Hey, Amy. What's happened now?"

She hurls her purse at an empty chair with enough force to make it rock, then she collapses into another. Her glasses bounce on her face, and her dark hair settles around her shoulders like angry wings. Her hands are shaking. "Went to pick up Matt at school. Had to run inside to drop off some paperwork. Came back to find someone keyed the car—both sides. Deep scratches, all the way across." She runs her fingers through her hair, displacing its usual perfect arrangement. "It's not just the damage that bothers me. It's ... it's like they're following me. Watching me. Waiting for chances to ..." She trails off, glancing at Matt.

My brother leans forward. "You sure it happened at the school?"

"Pretty sure. I didn't notice anything when I left home or parked, but ..." She shrugs, deflating slightly. "I suppose the gouges could've been there before."

"Doesn't really matter when," I say. "What matters is someone's targeting you, and escalating." I don't say what we're all thinking: *what's next?*

"Yeah." The word comes out of her, heavy with exhaustion and something darker.

My old detective instincts kick in. "Any security cameras in the area?"

"Not down by the athletic field, where I parked—trying to get my stupid step count up for the day." She laughs without humor." Anyone else around who might have seen something?"

"Nobody down that far."

I pull out my notebook and pen—force of habit that earns a snort from Tom. "Where's your deerstalker hat and cape, Sherlock?"

I flip him off without looking up. To Amy, I say, "That woman who confronted you and Matt yesterday—you got a name?"

"Becky Dubrovsky, I think." Amy's fingers drum against the arm of her chair, a nervous tick.

My pen scratches across the paper. "Previous run-ins with her?"

Amy's voice hardens. "Just seen her yelling at board meetings, like we're trying to harm her child. She's got a kid at Grand Mesa Middle School."

"Anyone else who might have this kind of grudge?"

Amy pushes back a strand of hair, and I catch a slight tremor in her fingers. "Oh god, Jack, I don't know. I can't wrap my head around people getting this angry over trying to keep kids safe." She pauses, then adds quietly, "Though ... there is Danny."

Tom and I exchange glances. "Your ex?" I prompt, pen hovering.

"Yeah." Her jaw tightens. "Three years since the divorce and he still sends these rage-filled emails about how I destroyed his life, left him broke, what a terrible mother I am." She looks at Matt, who's drifted to the far end of the patio, pretending not to listen. "And he's part of this group of teachers at the high school who've been fighting the Covid policies tooth and nail."

"You still have those emails?"

"Every last one. Never know when you might need evidence, right?" She tries to smile but it doesn't reach her eyes.

I write DANNY — HIGH SCHOOL in my notebook, underlining it twice. "Smart thinking. Might want to take a look at those later." I flip my notebook closed, trying to project more confidence than I feel. "Two leads is better than none."

Amy nods, but her eyes drift to Matt again. "I can handle them coming after me," she says softly. "But involving my son, targeting me in places where he'll see it ... that's different."

I follow her gaze. Matt's crouched down, absently petting Annabelle who's wandered out to join us. His shoulders are tight, and I wonder how much of this is sinking into his twelve-year-old psyche. Amy must be thinking the same thing because her expression shifts from anger to a mother's fierce determination.

"I won't let them drive me off the board," she says, steel in her voice. "But I need to know who's behind this. I need it to stop."

"We'll figure it out," I promise, already planning my next moves. "Now you've got cameras watching your property, alarms on every entry point, and a crusty ex-cop of an uncle who's pissed off."

Amy manages a real smile this time, small but genuine. "Thanks, Jack. You too, Dad." The late afternoon sun casts long shadows across the patio as she stands, squaring her shoulders. "Matt, honey? Let's go see what we can scrounge up for dinner."

As they head inside, Tom turns to me. "You really think we can catch these people?"

I take a long pull from my beer, considering. "Maybe. But first we need to figure out if we're dealing with an angry mob or someone with a personal vendetta." I tap my notebook. "The news about Danny burns my ass. That little shit."

Chapter Eight

Matt

I'm scrolling through TikTok for the millionth time today when my phone buzzes. It's a DM from some rando: *Tell your mom to stop killing our freedom.* I block them, my hands shaking. That's the third one this week. They're getting creative with their dummy accounts.

Mom tries to act normal, but I catch her jumping at every loud noise, looking through the blinds a dozen times a day. She used to laugh at horror movies, now she triple-checks the locks before bed. I get it though—really get it. Back in fourth grade, Theo Martinez and his crew made my life hell for three months straight. But at least I could see their stupid faces, know exactly who to avoid in the hallways. These shadow people messing with my mom? We don't know who they are. That's next-level scary.

Sometimes I catch her watching me when she thinks I'm

not looking. There's this guilt in her eyes that makes my chest hurt. Last night, I heard her crying in the little room she uses as her home office, talking to someone on the phone about maybe stepping down "for Matt's sake." That made me feel even worse. Because, yeah, part of me wants her to quit, but another part remembers how she used to tell me bedtime stories about standing up to bullies, about doing what's right even when it's hard. Quitting would be going against what she believes in. I'd feel bad if she did that.

Thank god for Pops being here. He's like this zen master, all calm and wise, telling stories about the old days that somehow make everything feel less terrible. He had polio, so he can't chase down bad guys, but just having him in the house makes it feel safer, you know? Like those weighted blankets they advertise for anxiety, except it's a person. Last week, when I was having a total meltdown about all this shit, Pops wheeled into my room with hot chocolate and these ancient comic books from when he was a kid. We spent a couple hours reading them together, and for a little while, I forgot about everything else.

And then there's Uncle Jack. Picture the Rock, but with dad jokes. Seriously, the guy's built like a tank but spends half his time coming up with these terrible puns that somehow still make me laugh. Hard to believe he used to be a cop—TV cops are all brooding and serious, but Jack's more like a stand-up comedian who accidentally got issued a badge.

I haven't told Mom, but this whole mess is spilling over into school. Yesterday, Kyle Liebens "accidentally" slammed his lunch tray into my back, slopping milk all over my new hoodie. "That's for your mom forcing us to wear face diapers," he whispered. *Real original, Kyle.* The thing is, Kyle used to be kind of my friend. Not close or anything, but we'd partner up in science sometimes, trade Pokémon cards. Now he looks at me like I'm infected or something. Like my mom's crazy ideas might be contagious.

The worst part is, I don't even know what to think anymore. Mom, Pops, and Jack are all about masks and vaccines, talking about science and public health like it's obvious. But half the town acts like Mom's trying to steal their souls or something. My Instagram feed is a war zone of people fighting about it. I'm just a kid—how am I supposed to know who's right?

Sometimes I sit in on their conversations, listening to Mom quote statistics and studies, watching Pops nod along with this proud look on his face. Jack will chime in with stories from his cop days about protecting people, about responsibility to the community. They all sound so sure, so confident. Meanwhile, I'm just trying to figure out why this had to happen to us, to our family. Why couldn't someone else's mom be the hero?

What I *do* know is that every time I hear a noise at night, my stomach turns to ice. Every time my phone pings, I'm afraid to look. Every time I walk down the school hallway, I brace for impact. I've started having these dreams where I'm running through an empty school, trying to find Mom, but all the hallways lead back to the same place, and there are shadows moving behind all the windows.

I wish Mom would just quit the school board. Like, I get standing up for what you believe in and all that, but is it worth ... *this*? Maybe that makes me a coward. Maybe I should be proud of her for not backing down. But mostly, I just want to sleep through the night without wondering if someone's out there, planning to hurt us. Then again, would I even be able to sleep, knowing my mom gave up on something she believes in because of me? Pops says courage isn't about not being scared—it's about doing what's right even when you're terrified. I haven't the faintest idea what's right. Maybe Mom does, but lots of people don't seem to think so.

Chapter Nine

Jack

The coffee maker gurgles and spits in Amy's kitchen while I flip open my laptop at the breakfast table. Tom settles in beside me, his walker scraping against the tile floor. Time for some old-fashioned detective work, starting with our prime suspect, Becky Dubrovsky. Anyone brazen enough to accost Amy and Matt outside the school deserves the top spot on our list.

"Ever been on Facebook?" I ask my brother as the laptop connects to Amy's wifi.

"No, thank god."

"Smart man. It's a cesspool of rage and misinformation, punctuated by endless vacation photos, humblebrags, and dancing-puppy videos. But for what we need"—I tap the keyboard with flourish—"it's perfect."

"Are you ... what's the word? A member?"

"User. And as of last week, guilty as charged. Welcome me to Hillary's basket of deplorables."

I turn the screen so Tom can watch as I navigate to Mesa Vista's chapter of Moms for Liberty. Their logo appears next to the group description: "Private Group, 91 members. Moms for Liberty is dedicated to fighting for the survival of America by unifying, educating, and empowering parents to defend their parental rights at all levels of government."

Tom squints at the screen. "I don't really understand what I'm looking at."

"Facebook's like a million little clubs under one roof. Whatever you're into—crafting, motorcycles, home brewing, conspiracy theories—there's a group for it. Most are open to anyone, but some, like our liberty-loving moms here, are exclusive. Had to get special approval from a group administrator to join."

"And you did? Just like that?"

"Well, I may have embellished the truth. Told them I'm a concerned grandpa with kids at Chatfield Elementary and Grand Mesa Middle School, furious about the school board's Covid policies."

"They let men into a moms' group?"

"Check the fine print: 'We're not just Moms. We are Moms, Dads, Grands, Aunts, Uncles, Friends.' In other words, they'll take anyone who boosts their numbers and drinks their Kool-Aid."

I show him the photo Becky Dubrovsky has loaded in. Smiling, beatific.

"Looks pretty benign to me," he says.

"I guess she has another side to her. ... Anyway, I discovered through her Facebook page that she works at IHOP here in town. Let's go have breakfast there. Maybe we'll be lucky and she'll be working this morning."

Seeing all the photos of women with blue Moms for Liberty T-shirts reminds me of my purchase. I reach into a bag by my chair and pull out two blue T-shirts emblazoned with "Grandpas for Liberty." I toss one to Tom.

His face darkens as he holds the shirt like it's radioactive. "Jesus, Jack."

"What's wrong?"

"Putting on a T-shirt is torture for me," he snaps. "Why do you think I wear button-ups?"

"Your shoulders?"

"Yes, my damn shoulders." The vehemence in his voice makes me flinch. He takes a breath, visibly trying to calm himself.

I messed up. I should've known better. Decades of weak legs means he's relied on his arms for everything—getting up, sitting down, basic daily functions. Now his shoulder joints are shot. Arthritis, bursitis, tendinitis—the whole bundle.

"I'm sorry, I wasn't thinking," I say, diving back into the bag. "Here, forget the shirt. Just wear this." With a flourish, I produce a bright-red MAGA cap.

"Absolutely not." His voice could freeze hell.

"C'mon, it makes even more of a statement than—"

"I said no, Jack. Drop it."

I raise my palms in surrender. "Just trying to make us look legit."

"You always go overboard."

The accusation stings like a slap. "I don't *always* do

anything. But fine, forget it." I snatch my keys from the table.
"Let's go."

We drive in brittle silence along Route 6, Mesa Vista's boulevard of broken dreams. If Dante had designed a modern circle of hell, it would look like this: a plastic canyon of decay stretching to the horizon. Dollar stores with burnt-out signs huddle next to vape shops with barred windows. Gas stations and fast-food joints alternate with liquor stores and pawn shops in an endless loop of desperation. Pizza parlors, nail salons, and discount-tire stores compete for space with establishments hawking everything from storm doors to sex toys. The sidewalks collect cigarette butts and crushed energy drink cans, while vacant lots sprout weeds through cracked asphalt.

The rest of Mesa Vista isn't like this. There are tree-lined streets in the old neighborhoods, where Victorian houses stand proud behind well-tended gardens. Family-owned restaurants where three generations work the kitchen. Art galleries, tucked into renovated warehouses, the live music spilling from pub doorways on summer evenings. But here on this main drag, watching another plastic sign flicker and die above a payday loan store, I feel something in me withering. Even the morning's coffee turns to acid in my stomach, and we haven't even reached IHOP yet.

I steal a glance at Tom, rigid with displeasure in the passenger seat, and wonder if I've already torpedoed this investigation before it's properly begun. Some detective I am—can't even launch a simple undercover operation without pissing off my own brother. Maybe he's right about me going overboard. Always have, probably always will.

Chapter Ten

Tom

The IHOP squats between Buffalo Wild Wings and Olive Garden like the last tooth in a neglected mouth. A "Soulful Cajun" food truck idles across the street, completing Mesa Vista's answer to the *Rue des Martyrs*. The parking lot is a battlefield where frost has won the war, leaving the pavement scarred and cracked, bordered by a chainlink fence that looks like it's been losing a decades-long fight with rust.

While Jack wrestles my walker from his Toyota's trunk, I watch an elderly man with a wispy goatee shuffling past. Matching his pace is an ancient dog, connected by a leash that's more electrical tape than nylon at this point. The dog assumes the position near a scraggly weed, and the man studies its contribution to the landscape before continuing on, leaving their gift to the community. Welcome to fine dining in Mesa Vista.

The double glass doors pose their usual challenge—try

managing a walker through those sometime—but we finally make it inside. A hostess whose skin has the texture of crumpled tissue paper appears with menus, leading us to a table on the tiny patio, giving us a prime view of Route 6's endless parade of decay. "Your server Becky will be with you in a moment."

Through the open patio door, I spot Becky at the servers' station, deep in the pages of *National Enquirer.* The hostess's words snap her out of what I'm sure was a riveting exposé. She tucks her literature between a coffee maker and toaster oven, her face suggesting we've committed a grave sin by interrupting her scholarly pursuits.

"Coffee for you fellas?" She looms over our table, her body poured into black stretchy pants that hide absolutely nothing— every dimple, every roll, every anatomical detail rendered in high-definition spandex. Her red uniform shirt strains against the task of containing her, a black name tag clinging precariously above the swell of her chest.

"That would be great," Jack drawls, his eyes wandering north to the tag, "uh, Miss Becky."

As she fills our cups, her eyes catch Jack's shirt. "Grandpas for Liberty, eh? I'm a Mom for Liberty."

"Really?" Jack's feigned surprise could win him an Oscar.

"Yup. One of the charter members of our Mesa Vista group."

"Well, ain't that something. He raises his mug in my direction. "We're in mighty fine company, Tom. Another patriot." I marvel at this sudden transformation of my Denver-born brother into a Texas good ol' boy. His performance is so convincing that I decide to keep quiet—no sense risking a slip that might break whatever spell he's casting.

"You fellas know what you want or should I give you a minute?"

"Aw, hell, Becky. I think we know what we want. I'll take a short stack of buttermilk pancakes and a side of link sausages. My little buddy here will have—"

I cut him off. "Eggs over medium, crisp bacon, and whole-wheat toast, please." She heads off toward the kitchen, and I turn to my brother. "Where you from, pardner?"

He grins. "According to the Facebook profile I created, I'm fresh out of Texas. Figured I needed some backstory. And since I created it, I thought I'd better live it."

"Well, let's hope you can keep it up."

"Pretty sure ol' Becky ain't exactly Professor Higgins when it comes to dialect studies. I could probably talk like Daffy Duck and she'd buy it."

Becky returns, coffee pot swinging like a pendulum. "Top that off for ya?"

"I'd rassle the devil himself for more of that coal oil," Jack declares, holding up his mug. The idiocy of this almost makes me guffaw.

She tops it off and parks the pot on a neighboring table, then crosses her arms and surveys Jack like he's a prized bull. "Nice of you to lend your support to Moms for Liberty."

"Hell, honey, there ain't nothin' 'nice' about it." Jack's voice drops an octave, serious as a heart attack. "This here country's hitched its wagon to a falling star. We're goin' down the crapper under this Biden fella, and we's all obliged to do what we can to fight against those who stand in the way of our freedoms—there in Washington, DC, like them patriots did on January 6th, and right here in Mesa Vista, too."

Becky's head bobs like one of those dashboard dogs.

Jack, sensing blood in the water, presses on. "Why, you take this local school board, for instance. Three of the five are libtard wackos. That Amy Wilson? Well, I think she's the devil incarnate. If she had her way, we'd all be wearing astronaut suits around town to 'protect others,' and we'd be hooked up to IVs 24/7 so the government could pour chemicals into our veins whenever it wants."

I hide my smile behind my coffee cup. My brother might have missed his calling—clearly, he should've been on stage.

"You are exactly, one-hundred percent correct, mister," Becky breathes, looking at Jack like he's the Second Coming. "That woman is just plain evil."

Jack and I exchange glances at the word 'evil.'

She's building steam now, her voice rising. "So are those other two on that board. I swear, we're gonna have to do whatever it takes to get them off of there. Whatever it takes."

The cook's bell saves us momentarily as Becky fetches our food. But she's back in a flash, pulling up a chair uninvited. "You don't mind if I set a spell, do ya? I don't have any other tables."

Jack removes his MAGA cap with the flourish of a Southern gentleman. "Why, honey, nothin' would please us more." He studies her face like he's trying to place it. "Say, do you have a kid at Grand Mesa Middle School?"

"Yes, I do. My son Simon is in the seventh grade there."

Jack snaps his fingers, then slaps the table. "I thought I'd seen you before. 'Course, a pretty lady like you is hard to forget. I remember seeing you outside the school a week or so ago. You was angry, yellin' at some woman in a car. You had a Moms for

Liberty T-shirt on, and you was really givin' that woman hell. I couldn't see who it was, but she won't soon be forgettin' the tongue lashin' you gave her."

Becky leans her upper body forward and beams with pride. "Yes. That was me. And that woman in the car was Amy Wilson."

"No."

"Yes, sir, it was."

"You took the fight straight to the devil herself?"

"I did."

"Well, Miss Becky, I am right proud of you. Not everybody has the guts to confront these people directly. Some folk talk the talk, but they won't walk the walk. You know what I mean? Then there are folk like you who aren't afraid to walk right up to the beast."

Now, Becky beams. "Oh, that wasn't a big deal. Just gave her a piece of my mind, that's all."

"Don't you understate what that's worth, my pretty friend. Why, that's golden." Here, he pauses, and points his fork at his pancakes. "These here are just the finest flapjacks around. Mmm, mmm." He takes another bite and then shoots a look up at Becky like he's just seen the risen Lord. "Oh, my. I just thought of something. I heard that somebody cut down a young tree at that Wilson woman's house and burned 'EVIL' into her lawn with chemicals." That look of his—unalloyed admiration. "I'm now guessin' that might have been you, lovely lady. Not many other folks around here would have the gumption to do that. I salute you, Miss Becky. You're a patriot."

"I wish I could take credit for that," she giggles, setting off a chain reaction of jiggles. "But I can't."

"Well, my gosh." Jack's voice drips with manufactured awe. "If it wasn't you, who could it have been? I've only been in this town for a while, but you're the first person I've met with true courage."

The blush that spreads across Becky's face could heat a small house. "Aw, I'm not that courageous. And, honestly, I don't believe in damaging another person's property, no matter how angry you are at 'em. I have a sister who fired a pellet gun at every window in her boyfriend's house when she found out he was cheating on her. I told her I thought that's just wrong. I draw the line at that kind of thing."

"So, you wouldn't do that, eh?"

"Nope."

Now, I'm not a great lie detector, but I have no trouble saying Becky's being truthful. I'm starting to think she's not our culprit. Jack sees an opportunity to probe in another direction.

"Do you know who did it?"

She shakes her head. "I don't."

Jack gives her a conspiratorial look. "Well, I'm a good-ol' country boy with few scruples. Any idea who I might connect with around here if I wanted to cause some ... trouble ... for heavy-handed officials like that Wilson woman?"

Becky actually looks up and points her index finger under her chin, as if this pose is the time-proven way to summon a name. "I can't say for sure, but maybe a fella named Marty Stauffer. He often shows up at meetings of local public boards and makes a ruckus. He likes to shout and hurl insults. I don't know if he's into vandalism, but might be."

A young couple gets seated at the table next to us. Becky

gets up to serve them. "Well, I wish you both well. Maybe I'll see you at a Moms for Liberty meeting. What are your names, fellas?"

Jack offers his hand for a shake. "I'm Jack, Miss Becky. And this here is my brother Tom. It's a real pleasure to meet you. We'll make a point of stopping into IHOP again, now that we know we have a pretty friend here. Why, you're pretty enough to make a cowboy forget his horse, Miss Becky."

"Aw. And you're a flirt, Jack. Do be sure to come back." She places the check on the table before heading off to get the coffee pot.

Outside in the parking lot, I turn to Jack. "Jesus! After how she treated Matt and Amy, you shouldn't have left her such a big tip."

"We want her on our side. She's got loose lips. ... But, you know what? As nasty as she was to Amy, I don't think she's our vandal."

"Nope. Me neither."

Jack starts the car, his Texas drawl finally dropping away. "But now we've got a new name to check out. Marty Stauffer." He pulls onto Route 6, leaving Becky and her temple of pancakes behind. "Something tells me he might be more promising."

Chapter Eleven

Amy

The Valley View neighborhood is all sprawling lots and pre-war charm. Agnes Moore's house rises from its manicured lawn like a faded photograph—light yellow clapboard with forest-green shutters, dormers poking through the hip roof like curious eyes. The brick walk leads to a front door flanked by sidelights—the very picture of serenity except for the three security chains I hear rattling behind the door after I ring the bell.

The door opens two inches, releasing a gust of air that hits me like week-old kitty litter mixed with forgotten bath towels. The faint sound of a television buzzes from inside—something old and shrill, like a game show from the '70s.

I step back instinctively as one rheumy eye peers through the gap. "Yes? What is it?" Her voice wheezes like air escaping a punctured tire.

"Mrs. Moore? I'm Amy Wilson, an occupational therapist. I have an appointment with you this morning."

She shifts, presenting her other eye, like a lizard checking a predator from multiple angles. "Are you from the government?"

"No, I'm a healthcare worker. Your doctor arranged for me to come see you."

"I'm not sick."

"No, but he says you've fallen twice in the past month. He wants me to help you stay safe and independent in your home."

"Damn meddlers," she mutters, but the chains slide free. The full assault of her odor hits me as I enter—something between sewer gas and stagnant water in a vase of dead flowers. I fight the urge to gag. My mask feels useless against it. I follow her walker's path across multiple grimy throw rugs, noting the dark stain on her skirt that I refuse to contemplate. A cat skitters past my feet, a mangy tabby with patches of fur missing. Its accusing yellow eyes glance at me as if I'm part of this problem.

The woman settles into an overstuffed chair like a bird folding its wings, pulls a blanket across her lap, and crosses her arms in silent challenge. Her skull-like face turns to me, deep-set eyes burning. "Tell me again what this is about."

The smell is manageable from twelve feet away. I explain the doctor's concerns, and she gives me her story: 84 years old, widowed a decade ago, son twenty minutes away in Loma, daughter in New Jersey begging her to move east or offering to pay for Agnes to move into a retirement community in Mesa Vista. "Not gonna do that," she says. "I plan to remain in my own home as I grow older. And nobody's gonna talk me out of that."

"Agnes, I'm not here to persuade you to do anything. I'm here to help you stay where you want to be—safely."

She stares through me, then: "I'm glad they didn't send no black person out here to help me. I wouldn't like that at all."

The casual racism hits like a slap. I force myself to focus on the task. "I'm going to help you find solutions that work for your needs and budget." Dear god, I need air. "Today is just an introduction, to give you things to think about before next week."

A nod breaks her granite facade, followed by a coughing fit that sends her reaching for an empty water glass. I take it to the kitchen, expecting squalor but finding surprising orderliness. The smell, I realize, is purely human in origin.

I take the water back to her and say, "I want you to think about what you're having trouble with. Could be anything. Fixing meals, opening jars, turning doorknobs, climbing stairs, driving to the store." I pause and consider what I should be saying instead: *bathing, changing your clothes.*

I look around the densely appointed living room. "I'd also like you to think about trimming the number of objects in each room to reduce your risk of tripping or falling—unnecessary throw rugs, chairs, electrical cords, things like that."

I gesture toward the blanket on her lap. "I bet you love that. Looks cozy. But it's big and could easily snag your foot when you stand, toppling you over. Consider a much smaller lap blanket."

She seems a bit miffed by that comment and looks at me like she's just caught me trying to steal her jewelry. But I don't care. That damn blanket is a genuine hazard. I reach into my tote bag and pull out some tip sheets to help jog her thinking. "We'll make this work for you, so you can continue to live independently. Okay?"

She nods grudgingly.

I stand and give her my business card. "Call me if you have any questions. Now, you stay there. No need to get up. I'll let myself out and I'll see you next week."

WHEN I'M FINALLY BACK OUTSIDE, I tear off my mask and gulp fresh air. I sniff my shirt sleeve to see if the miasma has permeated my clothing. Seems okay. I'm meeting Will for lunch and really don't want to bring Agnes's essence with me.

Driving to Bin 707, I consider how common these situations are with elderly clients. Sometimes it's depression—when every day's the same, why bother getting clean? Sometimes it's fear—bathrooms become danger zones of slick surfaces and hard edges, each shower a gamble with gravity. Sometimes it's pure stubbornness—the last grasp at control in a world that's slipping away. Caregivers and family members can nag all they want, but the more you pester them about something, the more they tend to resist. If left to work through it on their own, often they change their own behavior.

Exiting Agnes's neighborhood, I see a woman walking with a boy about Matty's age, and I think about how it's not just old people who respond poorly to nagging. Last year, I was having a hard time getting Matty to do his homework. I was at wits end about it. I'd harangue him and nag him endlessly. Finally, his teacher suggested I stop doing that. "Get off his back," she said. So, I did. And, amazingly, after a couple weeks, it worked. He started doing his homework on his own, with no badgering from me.

Yeah, I know there's a lesson in all this. And it's not lost on me. I get it. People generally don't like to be told what to do. They don't want to be told to wear masks, stay six feet apart, get vaccinated. Even if it's for their own good and the good of others. In fact, many will just double-down on their resistance. But what am I supposed to do as a public official? Just say, *Aw, to hell with it? Public health and safety be damned. Let everybody do what they want.* No, and we all know that the people who resist public-health measures aren't going to magically change their minds on the matter if we leave them alone. The whole thing makes my head ache. I can't wait to get a drink.

I swing my car into Bin 707's parking lot off 5th Street. Like a precision skater, Will's Kia Nero pulls in right next to me. A shaft of light pierces his sunroof and illuminates his dark hair, its textured spikes reminding me of curved meringue peaks on a pie. When he steps out of the car, my heart does that familiar little skip. We hug, his arms wrapping around me with the perfect pressure that comes from hundreds of embraces, and I breathe in the subtle cedar of his cologne.

We head directly to the patio with its cheerful turquoise chairs. Trees line the edges and plants hang on the railings. There's no roof. The effect is of dining in a private treehouse in a lush garden, though we're no more than twenty feet away from a poorly paved parking lot. After being at Agnes's house, this feels like the Garden of Eden.

Kelly, our favorite server, arrives at our table in less than a couple minutes. She knows our habits so well she's already bearing two frozen margaritas—one with salt for Will, one without for me. It's become our Thursday ritual whenever his rounds at St. Mary's align with my client schedule.

"Menu?" Kelly knows better. Our lunch orders never vary —seared salmon BLT for me, pork katsu sando for Will. When we first started dating, we'd spent weeks trying everything on the menu until we found our perfect matches. Now it's just tradition.

"Just the usual," I say, earning her theatrical eye-roll.

"You guys are in a rut." She's the kind of server whose affection for her customers is expressed through feigned disdain: the greater the apparent scorn, the deeper her fondness.

Will winks at me, then says to her, "Hey, smart ass, please ask Tony to put a dollop of that plum tapenade on the side for me." He polishes his knuckles on his shirt. "Getting out of the rut. Breaking out of the mold."

Kelly peers over her sunglasses. "'Smart ass, eh? We'll see what you get on the side. I might hock a loogie into your ta-pe-NAD." She sashays away as we clink glasses, his fingers brushing mine in that deliberate way that still makes me smile after all this time.

I tell him about Agnes: "She's racist and she stinks."

"Ah, that's redundant." He squeezes my hand, his impossibly long, dark-skinned fingers elegant against mine. "Sounds like a challenge. You always get at least one difficult client."

"Statistical probability. The world's full of assholes ... like my vandals."

Will grimaces, his eyes suddenly full of concern. "How are your dad and Matt handling it?"

"Dad's solid as a rock and Matt's quiet as one."

When our food arrives, I immediately set aside half of my salmon sandwich. "For Annabelle."

Will watches me with fond exasperation. "Live a little. Eat *all* of your sandwich. Have salt with your margarita. Have a root-beer float for dessert. Eat pizza in bed."

"*This* is the advice I get from a physician?" I reach over to pinch his cheek, loving how his serious doctor persona melts away when we're together. "Must be a high fatality rate among your patients."

"Nah. People thrive under my excellent care." He grins, carefully navigating his sandwich's dual threats of katsu sauce and tapenade. It's like watching a high-wire act, until the inevitable splat of reddish-brown on his blue shirt.

"Hey there, piggy. Oink, oink," I tease.

He laughs. "Yep. Adding the tapenade might have been an unforced error."

"Good thing you have that starched white coat at the hospital to hide your mess."

Looking at Will's sauce-stained shirt and bright eyes, I feel the morning's darkness lifting. Sometimes the best method of blocking persistent thoughts of life's assholes—my unknown harassers and the Agnes Moores of the world—is just this: good food and someone who can make you laugh.

Chapter Twelve

Tom

The ceiling fan hums overhead, lethargically stirring the air in the church-hall meeting room, as we endure another outsider's presentation to the post-polio support group. Today's speaker, a wispy man from the Area Agency on Aging who could be Wally Cox's twin, drones on about disability resources. His voice barely carries to where I sit, gripping my walker, fighting the urge to wheel myself out of here. Everything he's saying is in the glossy pamphlet wilting in my lap. If I'm going to drag myself to these meetings, I want to hear from the survivors themselves, not this modern-day Mr. Peepers.

Peggy finally rises, her jewelry catching the harsh light as she thanks him. Her perfectly manicured hand smooths her blouse —a nervous habit I've noticed. "As mentioned last time, I asked everyone to prepare to share about their hobbies today. Hobbies aren't just pastimes—they keep our minds sharp, encourage movement, foster connections. They're vital for our emotional and physical wellbeing." She pauses, scanning the room with the practiced eye of a veteran support group leader. "Who'd like to start?"

Minnie's hand creeps up like she's expecting it might get bitten off. Her red mobility scooter, festooned with a collection of cheerful stickers, matches her perpetually flushed cheeks.

"Go ahead, Minnie," Peggy encourages.

Minnie's hand flutters to her throat—another nervous gesture in a room full of them. "Oh goodness, I'm just so excited to share this." Her whole body rocks with genuine enthusiasm, making her scooter squeak slightly. "My passion is calligraphy. You know what that is, right?" We nod, doing our part.

She describes learning it from her father at the family dining room table. Her voice grows stronger as she speaks. "Some of you might assume calligraphy is obsolete." She slowly looks around the circle as if to identify who among us might be guilty of such a thought. "Oh, it's certainly not. It's still very popular. What I love about it is it helps my brain." She taps her right temple with a pale, attenuated index finger. "When I practice calligraphy, I feel myself entering a more focused state that instantly banishes my anxiety and—like Peggy said—makes me feel less depressed. Plus, there's money to be made. Why, I've made lots of money over the years, doing things like addressing wedding invitations or transcribing love poems."

She nods vigorously, as if perhaps we wouldn't believe that.

When she passes around samples of her work, I have to admit: her flowing scripts are impressive, each letter a small work of art.

The sharing continues around our circle. David, never seen without his 101st Airborne cap, practically vibrates with intensity as he describes his passion for building military models—everything from Bradley tanks to B-1 bombers, warships to anti-aircraft weapons. "I just love it. Keeps me in constant mind of my days with the Screaming Eagles. It's just so damn satisfying when I finish one of my models. If any of you want to come by my house sometime and see my arsenal, I'd be proud to show it to you."

Sofia smooths her carefully coiffed hair and says, "My hobby is genealogy. You know—figuring out family trees, lines of descent. I started out doing it with my own family tree. I was able to trace both sides of my family back more than three hundred years. Now, I mostly do the research for friends who are interested in knowing more about their own families."

She looks around the room, her eyes full of life. "Or, for fun, I just pick people out of the news—like a mayor or a county commissioner—and see what I can find out about their family history. Yesterday, for example, I spent some time delving into the ancestry of Anthony Fauci. Did you know his maternal grandfather was a noted artist? Giovanni Abys. Very interesting. With the help of Google and the internet and genealogical sites, you can find out so much about people. I tell you, it's fun. Keeps me busy. And it's less fattening than my other hobby—cooking."

Steve shows off photos of his vinyl collection, while Sally demonstrates macramé knots with trembling but determined fingers. I begin to think I might throw in the towel on this damn group. Apart from one reference to polio by the man from the aging council, the word hadn't been mentioned in the hour we'd been there. What the hell was I wasting my time for?

When it's my turn, I straighten as much as my weakened muscles allow. "Well, I admire all your productive hobbies. But I've never had one. My parents didn't either—guess it runs in the family." I pause, noting Peggy's slight frown. "But, I do a lot of reading—"

Minnie chimes in, "Reading's a hobby." She bobs her head up and down. "It certainly is."

"—and keep up with the news, take naps, spend time with my daughter and grandson. Add in some TV, and my days are full. Haven't found time to take up pole dancing or beekeeping." The words come out sharper than intended, and I clamp my mouth shut before more sarcasm can escape.

"Well, thank you, Tom," Peggy says. "*À chacun ses goûts*, I guess." She giggles. "I should have added that I also dabble in French." Another giggle. "*Un petit passe-temps.*" She beams with self-satisfaction. "And last, but not least, Earl."

This guy's face is a thundercloud and his voice oozes ill temper when he says, "Those are mere *hobbies* you all are talking about. Mine's a service. I run a ham-radio station and maintain a substantial presence on social media. I keep my audience informed about politics and about the people in government who are trying to take away our freedoms. It's good to stay informed—and to inform others." He shoots a pointed look at me—I guess because I just proclaimed myself a consumer of news.

He continues. "People need help knowing *what* to think. Like about face masks or these vaccines they're developing. I help people see what's wrong with public officials and their misguided policies. We've ceded too much control to government. People need to know how to challenge officials. I give them ideas about what to do. I'm a modern-day Thomas Paine, spreading common sense. The airwaves and the internet are my parchment." He sits back, arms crossed. The look on his face reads, *I guess I just topped all you losers.*

Peggy says, "Well, that's certainly interesting, Earl. I'm sure there are many people out there grateful for your help in knowing what to think." I can't tell if she's being earnest or sarcastic. I hope the latter.

The real conversation finally begins when Peggy steers us toward discussing post-polio syndrome's onset. "Tell us how it started for you, how you noticed it. As always, I want everyone to feel free to talk—or not—as you like."

David says, "In my case, I first noticed my new weakness when I was in the garden. My wife and I had always enjoyed gardening together. And I'd have no trouble getting down to do planting or weeding, but it gradually became so difficult for me to get back up that I had to stop." He allows a wry smile to cross his face. "It's always bothered me that the garden's appearance hasn't suffered from the loss of my ministrations." Several of us laugh in appreciation of his self-deprecatory humor.

We all sit quietly, waiting for someone else to speak. It reminds me of a Quaker meeting I once attended. It was of the unprogrammed kind, where, after someone has been moved to speak, there's a silence of several minutes for everyone to allow that person's message to sink in. To me, that's an excruciatingly long time to sit quietly with a group of people.

Now, thank god, Steve speaks. "Well, you know, I think it's pretty common for us polio survivors to be in denial when we notice the onset of post-polio syndrome. Sure, maybe we tire more easily, or we can't walk as far as we once could, or our muscles seem weaker, or perhaps a leg collapses occasionally, or our breathing is more labored. But none of us wants to admit that the new problems might be permanent or that they represent a new stage in our relationship with impairment. I'd go through these periods where I'd drop into total denial. After all, the medical people had told us that we weren't going to get worse—that one of the few good things about polio was that our condition was stable. So, what kind of sick joke was this?"

A long, poignant silence is our collective response to Steve's reflection. Peggy looks at her watch, then speaks. "Well, I think we have time to hear from one more person, if anyone else feels like talking." Minnie and Earl are both shaking their heads. And I'm not going to talk, at least not today. But Sofia raises her hand, signaling that she'll speak. Again, she looks elegant. A hip-length gray cashmere sweater, her hair pulled back, twisted higher on her head this time than last. She's wearing thin horn-rimmed glasses that accentuate the intelligence of the eyes behind them.

"My post-polio symptoms emerged over a number of years, but I steadfastly resisted the implication that these new problems required any major changes in my life or in my way of dealing with polio's legacies. The changes began when I was in my late thirties. At first, it was merely a matter of fatigue. ... I found it increasingly difficult to stand for more than a few minutes, even with these." Here, she knocks on the braces underneath her wool pants.

"But the real problem all along had been falls. When I was a young girl learning to walk with crutches and long leg braces, I learned to fall safely so as not to hurt myself when the inevitable happened. Equally important, of course, was learning how to raise myself to a standing position once again. As long as I could pick myself up and stand on my own two feet—brace-bound and crutch-propped though I was—a fall was an opportunity to show my ability to overcome physical challenges. The polio mantra, as I said last time we met, was, 'Do it by yourself, no matter how hard, no matter how long it takes.'"

Minnie excitedly interjects. "Damn that 'little engine that could.' Damn it to hell." Everyone chuckles.

"Yes," Sofia smiles empathetically. "Damn it to hell. Because there comes a time when the little engine simply *can't* do it." She pauses, sighs, and presses her flat palms down against her pants. "I vividly recall the first time I simply couldn't get myself up after a fall. My left crutch had slipped and I'd fallen to the sidewalk, as I had so many times before. But when I turned over and tried to use one crutch to boost myself to my feet, I discovered I couldn't do it. A passerby had to help me up. The strange thing is that I don't think it was even a matter of strength. Rather, it had to do with a subtle, mysterious change in my own sense of balance, a permanent disturbance of my inner gyroscope."

"That must have been hard for you—to accept that help, to let go of the polio mantra," I say.

"It was. But it was even harder to accept that I might never again get to my feet on my own; to accept that a part of my life had ended; to accept that my body had decided—and decided autonomously, all on its own—that the moment had come for me to face up to my limitations."

Another long silence prevails. I assume everyone is doing what I am—thinking how hard, but how necessary, it is to accept limitations.

Chapter Thirteen

Ray

onald Trump opened my eyes. Before he came along, I didn't pay much attention to politics or what was really going on. Sure, I knew eight years of that black bastard Obama had driven this country into a ditch. But I had my own problems to deal with, you know? No room in my life to dwell on the nation's issues—except for the blacks, of course.

Trump tells the truth. He's the first politician who understands our pain, who's willing to fight for the white man. Nobody else is looking out for us.

I'll never forget Hillary Clinton sneering at people like me, calling us "deplorables." She's the real deplorable, her and all the coastal elites—the Jews, the bankers, the technocrats like Bill Gates. They're the ones targeting real Americans, trying to take our country away.

I know their type. Met plenty of them at UC Boulder,

where I busted my ass to put myself through college and earn a computer science degree. The professors loved talking about "diversity in tech" and "creating inclusive spaces." What about including guys like me? I was working night shifts at a gas station to pay tuition while these smug little shits discussed their gap years in Europe and dipped into their trust funds to fund their ski trips and cocaine habits.

I was good. Damn good. Could code circles around most of my classmates. Landed a sweet job right out of school at a Denver startup, pulling down ninety grand a year. Had my own apartment in LoDo, was finally starting to build something. Then 2008 hit. Company was starting to go under. "Last hired, first fired," they said, but I noticed who they kept: two Indian guys and a black woman from Howard University. "Diverse perspectives are valuable in challenging times," HR told us. Valuable. Right.

After that, it was one shit job after another. Six months here, eight months there. Always the same story: I'd do great work, then someone would find my online posts or overhear me talking politics. Suddenly I'm "not a culture fit" or I'm "creating a hostile environment." Meanwhile, every company's falling over themselves to meet their diversity quotas or to hire foreign workers on H1-B visas.

What I love about Trump is that he gets it. He knows we're being invaded by immigrants, that the ones truly left behind in this country aren't the so-called minorities. It's white guys like me. We're the ones abandoned by a system that promised us more. I work hard, pay my taxes, follow the rules, but am I getting ahead? Hell no. I'm stuck in a crappy trailer twenty miles outside Mesa Vista while the Mexicans and blacks—the takers—seem to be doing just fine. It's not right.

Trump matters because it's not easy to find people who tell the truth like he does. Other politicians sure don't. The mainstream media? Mouthpieces for liberal elites. Fox News is okay, but even they're too cautious sometimes. Mealy-mouthed. The real warriors hang out on social media like Parler or on the darknet. There's a whole underground world out there, people willing to say what needs to be said, what others won't.

It was through the darknet that I connected with Marty. Smart as hell, that guy. He's got a vision: rebuild this country from the ground up. Forget Washington. The real power lies in school boards and town councils, and he's convinced me and a couple of others that we can take control here in Mesa Vista. I know how to cover our digital tracks—VPNs, encrypted channels, the works. Skills from my old life that still come in handy.

Our squad is small, but effective. Marty's the brains, a master at political strategy and agitation. Then there's Klover, a ham-radio operator who's like an encyclopedia about vaccines. He's the kind of guy who sees patterns where others don't, connecting dots most of us wouldn't even notice. Dwayne, our muscle, is a former wrestler with a chip on his shoulder and a knack for dirty work. And me? I help Marty keep an eye on the big picture, making sure we're all rowing in the same direction. I also handle our tech security—something I learned fast after getting doxxed at my last real job. Three years of building their precious database systems, then suddenly I'm not hireable because some snowflake found my Parler account. Tell me that's fair.

Marty is laser-focused at the moment on radicalizing the

anti-vax crowd. He says the more distrust we can sow, the better. Less compliance means more force required to impose mandates, which only fuels the fire. And he's right. People are scared, and scared people are easy to manipulate.

The other day, Marty messaged us on our private Signal channel: "Push the anti-vaccine propaganda. The fewer people take the jab, the more pressure builds. That'll make it easier for us to radicalize the patriots who already feel cornered."

Klover chimed in: "Let's not call it 'propaganda.' That implies what we're saying is misleading. Call it what it is: information. The truth is terrifying enough to do the work for us." That's Klover for you—always precise.

And he's right: the truth about vaccines is horrifying. They're being rushed through production, with no real understanding of the long-term effects. Who knows what kind of damage they could cause? Dwayne thinks they're tools for microchipping the population, a way for corporations and the government to track us and vacuum up our personal data. I know enough about data mining from my tech days to tell you they want our info. Every line of code I wrote for those startups was about gathering information, building profiles, tracking behavior. But Dwayne's microchipping notion? Seems crazy. He definitely has some screws loose. But hell, I don't know. Nothing would surprise me these days about the government and big companies.

Me? I see the bigger context. Vaccines are just another step in the "Great Replacement," the systematic erasure of the white race. It's not an accident that here in the U.S., minorities are set to outnumber whites in a few decades. That kind of demographic shift doesn't just happen—it's engineered. I watched it happen in Denver's North Park Hill neighborhood where I grew up, watched it happen in tech, watched it happen everywhere. Vaccines are part of the plan. The drugs will contain antigens that will sterilize white women. The shots given to white men will pump them full of carcinogens that will kill them. They want to wipe us out. That's why we have to stop the school board. If they and the public-health agency mandate vaccines, it'll be catastrophic for the white community.

The liberals pushing vaccines are the same people whining about "structural racism" and "white privilege." They promote this "critical race theory" bullshit. They get teachers to tell kids that whites are inherently racist, oppressors by nature. Just like those diversity trainings they made us sit through at every tech job, where they'd tell us to "examine our unconscious bias," while hiring managers passed over qualified white candidates. They push ethnic-studies curricula, LGBTQ clubs in schools—all of which just moves this country down the crapper at a faster speed.

I'm sick of it.

This is a white country. Whites built it, whites made it great. Kids shouldn't be taught that being white is something to be ashamed of. I learned to code on my own, spent nights teaching myself Python and Java while working that gas station job. Nobody handed me anything. But now? Now I'm living in a trailer park, doing cash-only IT jobs for local businesses too small to care about background checks, watching diversity hires with half my skills pull in triple my old salary.

It's all bullshit. And somebody has to fight back. I'm proud to be doing it.

Our little squad of true believers is having one of our meetings by video. Ever since we started, I've insisted we use Signal for these meetings. I'm paranoid about security in ways that would seem excessive if the stakes weren't so high. But I know better. I learned my lesson. I know firsthand how they can track you, how they build their digital profiles. How your life can unravel as a consequence of what they find. So, for our team, there's no Zoom, no Teams, nothing that could leave a digital trail.

Now, Signal's encrypted video window splits into four squares, each of our faces bathed in the blue glow of screens.

Dwayne's massive frame crowds his portion of the screen, his cauliflower ear and bent nose testament to years on the wrestling mat. He's practically vibrating with barely contained energy, like always. The man's a loaded spring, ready to snap into violence at the slightest provocation. Sometimes I wonder if those countless matches rewired something in his brain, left him always hunting for the next fight.

"We need to step it up with Wilson," he growls, leaning into his camera. "The tree was nothing. Keying the car? That's amateur hour. Even burning 'EVIL' into her lawn hasn't gotten her running to the press like we wanted."

Klover's voice crackles through, tight with the fury that seems to consume him these days. I've never understood the source of his rage—what made a disabled man so passionate about fighting mask mandates and vaccines. But his intensity feeds our cause, even if he can't join the physical aspects of our campaign. "Dwayne's right," he says. "We're not making enough noise. The bitch needs to feel the pressure."

I lean back in my chair, mentally reviewing our escalating acts of harassment. The sapling was indeed too subtle—could've been any neighborhood punk. Keying her car myself had been more personal, a small thrill in catching her vehicle unattended near the school. Just like the old days in North Park Hill, watching those first families' cars get vandalized. Opportunity knocks, but it won't do your dishes—you've got to seize the moment.

Dwayne's been following Wilson, watching her routine. His face lights up as he describes a confrontation he witnessed last week—some Moms for Liberty woman getting in Wilson's face outside her kid's school. Marty jokes about recruiting her, but I can see Dwayne's wheels turning toward something more direct.

"Let's confront her ourselves, directly," he suggests, predictable as sunrise. "Catch her in a parking lot, make sure she understands—"

"And give her a clear view of your distinctive mug?" Marty cuts in. "That's assault in Colorado, and you're already pushing it with the stalking. We need to be smarter. We have to be strategic about these things."

Klover clears his throat. "What about her house? That white siding is like a blank canvas. We could paint something ... memorable." His quiet voice carries unexpected weight. "Her name in a red cancel circle. Simple. Clear message."

The idea clicks. We all agree it's a good proposal. Dwayne promises to handle it "before you can say knife"—one of his weird expressions that always make me wonder about his past. And worry about the future.

"While we're planning," Marty says, "I think it's time to expand our scope beyond Amy Wilson. Diana Tarrant at the Health Department is another person who needs to learn she's not untouchable. In some ways, she's the real force behind these oppressive policies. So, we start in on her, too."

"Let's crack her like an egg," I add, watching Dwayne's face split into a predatory grin.

Klover nods, his glasses reflecting his screen's glow. "We can use the same playbook. No need to reinvent the wheel when we've got a working strategy."

As our meeting winds down, I feel that familiar surge of purpose. We're fighting for freedom, one act of intimidation at a time. The faces in my screen share the same dark satisfaction—soldiers in an invisible war most people don't even know is being fought. I check our VPN connection one last time, a habit from my coding days. They may have pushed me out of their precious tech world, but they can't take away what I know. What I can do.

This little group of ours is great. We're going to succeed. Time and pressure. That's all it takes to break anyone.

Chapter Fourteen

Jack

Tom's face contorts in dismay. "You *trespassed*?"

"I had a little look around," I say, enjoying his discomfort.

"You entered someone's property without consent. That's trespassing."

"If you put it that way ..."

"How else would you put it?"

"I. Had. A. Little. Look. Around." I savor each word. "But I repeat myself."

"We're trying to catch malefactors, not become ones ourselves."

"Oh, naive brother." I lean back, amused. "If only you knew how thin the line is between criminals and cops. Malefactors all. Besides, I'm a ghost—in and out, no trace."

He sighs, shoulders slumping. "Fine. What did you find?"

I describe Danny's dump—a decaying wood-frame house with its corrugated metal garage. No saws. No gas cans. No weed killer. Nothing in the trash. I found nothing that could have torched Amy's lawn or felled her tree.

"Doesn't mean he didn't do it," Tom points out.

"No. Just means he didn't leave evidence lying around." I check my watch. "He should be home from work now. Think I'll pay him a visit."

Tom's face darkens. "I'll sit this one out."

I flex my biceps theatrically. "Probably better. No witnesses needed if things get ... physical."

"Jesus, Jack. Don't rough him up."

"He'll fold at a hard look," I promise, already heading for the door.

THE SUN BLEEDS orange across the horizon when I get to Danny's isolated corner of town. The houses here are scattered like dice thrown by a careless hand. Dogs bark in the distance when I shut the car door, and wood smoke hangs heavy in the cooling air.

Danny answers the doorbell in sweatpants and a T-shirt that's seen better days. He's smaller than I remember—maybe 5'8", 150 pounds when soaking wet. Thin hair falls over his ears, and that pathetic mustache droops beneath small, dark eyes set deep under a jutting brow. The years since Amy haven't been kind.

"I'm selling *Architectural Digest* subscriptions," I announce with mock cheer. "Judging from your attire, I gather you're the proprietor of this elegant property. I'm hoping you might be interested."

He tries for intimidating. "Take a hike." A one-eyed Barbie would scare me more.

The door starts to close. My foot blocks it, then my shoulder follows through. He stumbles back as I enter his space.

"What the hell? Who—"

"I want to have a little chat, Danny. Don't you remember me?"

He shakes his head.

That hurts my feelings. I'm a sensitive guy. "Amy's uncle," I say. "The wedding?"

Recognition flickers across his vacant face. "Uh, okay. What do you want?"

"My niece has been having trouble with hooligans," I continue. "Your name came up. Something about abusive messages?"

"What kind of trouble?"

"Vandalism. But I suspect you already know that."

"Look, I don't know anything about it." He tries to usher me back out the door, but has no luck.

"I'm betting you *do* know something."

He backs away. Seems to consider what to say. "Listen, a lot of people hate Amy," he spits suddenly. "They don't like her ordering teachers and students to wear masks and all that shit. She drives around town in that fancy Volvo, eats at ritzy restaurants with that doctor boyfriend of hers. Who does she think she is, the Queen of England? Half the town would cheer if someone strung up that bit—"

My forearm finds his throat before he finishes the word,

slamming him into cheap wallboard that crackles in protest. "Try calling her that again," I growl, "and I'll break your thumbs." I press harder. "What do you know?"

His eyes bulge. When I ease up, he gasps: "Nothing. I swear."

I release him, watch him gulp air. "If I find out different, our next chat won't be so friendly." At the door, I turn back. "And no more messages to Amy. Clear?"

Silence.

I grab him, twisting his arm until he yelps.

"Are we clear?" I demand again.

"Yeah. Clear."

I fling him against the wall and leave Chez Danny. Glamorous as it is, I hope not to return.

LATER, drinking scotch with Tom, I fill him in on my enchanting conversation with his former son-in-law. "What a little weasel he is. How did you stand him all those years?"

"Fortunately, I seldom had to see him. But I'll tell ya, I was never so happy as when Amy told me she was divorcing him."

"I can understand that." Then I replay Danny's bitter words about Amy's Volvo. "He said it with palpable envy. No wonder. I saw the decrepit junker he drives. I think the disparity makes him crazy. Enough to make him want to key Amy's car. He envies her that car, her obviously higher economic order." I take another gulp of scotch. "I'll bet you a bottle of this he's the one who keyed it."

"How would you prove it?"

"Might be blue paint in the grooves of one of his keys. Most people don't carry screwdrivers around. They use what's handy. ... Damn. Wish I'd demanded to see them."

Tom tops off my scotch. "Next time."

"It won't go well for him if I have to go back there again."

Chapter Fifteen

Amy

The aisles of the Sprouts Market blur as I hunt for Dad's birthday dinner ingredients. It's not Whole Foods, but it'll do. My mind drifts to tonight's guests: Jack and Matt, of course, and Will, who said he'd have to arrive fashionably late because of late rounds at the hospital.

I'm most excited that Hannah will be here, too. Her voice echoes in my mind from our phone call last week. "Wild horses couldn't keep me away." We're a four-hour drive from Denver, but she didn't hesitate. "Do I get to sleep in the same bed with your dad?" she'd teased. I knew from her tone that her eyes were twinkling. And I knew she was joking. Well, probably joking.

"I guess that's up to you two."

"Not solely my decision?"

"Probably not."

"Damn." A long pause. "Well, let's see if this ol' gal still has it. What do you think? A red teddy? camisole and tap pants?"

This cracked me up. "Whatever happens, Hannah, I know he'll be absolutely delighted to have you here. He loves you to the moon and back." I sincerely doubt my dad has slept with a woman in the eight years since Mom died. But if he were going to do so, I'd hope it would be with Hannah.

"Yeah? Let the old codger show it."

As I reach for a bag of Santitas chips to go along with the salsa and guac already in my cart, the memory of that phone conversation makes me laugh again. This would be a fun few days with her around—a nice respite, I hope, from fear and worry.

I pick Matt up at school on my way home from the market.

"Good day?" I ask, trying to take in his mood.

"Sucked."

"How so?"

He hesitates, as if trying to decide what to reveal. "I got a C on Tuesday's math test."

I reach over and rub his shoulder, look at that sweet face. "I know it's bad parenting to say this, but not since my own math classes have I ever had to calculate the area of a cylinder or solve a quadratic equation. So, I think you're just fine, bud. You can add, subtract, multiply, and divide. Beyond that, don't worry too much about it. You'll learn what you need to know, when you need it. And the internet offers solutions to any problem you might come across."

He smiles. "Sheesh. *This*, from a school-board member? Maybe I should alert the media to your thinking."

"Good idea. I don't have enough problems."

I pull into the driveway. We carry the groceries into the house, and I start in on the evening's meal, Dad's favorite: caesar salad, beef bourguignon, and key lime pie for dessert. Usually, I'd make the bourguignon in the slow cooker, but I hadn't got my act together early enough today to do that. Fortunately, I have just enough time to follow Julia Child's stovetop directions. But it'll be tight. I work assiduously, frying the bacon, sautéing the carrots and diced onions, adding the minced garlic, pearled onions, wine, and tomato paste.

The doorbell chimes just as I'm sliding the bourguignon into the oven. Hannah stands there, silver-blonde hair perfect despite the drive, holding a wrapped package that threatens to slip from her grip. "Christ, let me put this down before my arms give out." She lowers it, and the box thuds the last few inches. "Not breakable, thank god."

Her hug is fierce, genuine. That smile hasn't changed—still full of mischief, still hinting at adventures waiting to happen, like she's saying, *You know what would be fun to do?*

"Damn, it's good to see you," I say. "You don't look a day older than the last time I saw you. How do you do that?"

She laughs. "Sweetie, there's nothing here but artifice. Everything's pushed up, pulled in, tucked around, pressed down, wrangled here and there. If I sneeze, all hell's gonna break loose."

I laugh and take a closer look. At sixty-five, she's mastered the art of aging gracefully. Expert makeup enhances rather than masks, and the laugh lines around her eyes tell stories of a life well-lived. She's been my dad's closest friend since their public health department days, and something in their dynamic has always made me wonder if there could be more.

"Welcome, dear lady," I say.

"Thank you. It's so good to be here." She gives me another tight hug, the sort of hug that says, *I really mean this. It's good to be with you.* "Where's the birthday boy?"

As if summoned, Dad appears with his walker, silver hair swept back, brown eyes bright and full of intelligence. A new gray cashmere cardigan over a pale blue shirt—he's dressed for company. For Hannah. He rolls on until he reaches us, pushes his walker aside, then pulls Hannah into a tight hug that speaks volumes, and I suddenly find the kitchen counter needs my immediate attention.

Will arrives an hour later. We're all out on the patio, where Jack is losing another round of fetch with Annabelle, my Great Pyrenees-Border Collie mix who never learned the "return" part of the game. I introduce Will to Hannah, then he hugs me and disappears inside to make himself a drink.

"This dog could be taught to bring the damn ball back, you know," Jack insists, lunging for the tennis ball Annabelle keeps just out of his reach.

"Where's the fun in that?" I counter. "Right, BellieBelle?" She comes to me and pushes her face under my forearm, slopping some of my wine onto my jeans. I put the glass down and go for the ball. She turns her head away and I miss it. Her eyes dare me to try again. I feint with my right and grab at the ball with my left. I miss again. Jack then thrusts for her, but Annabelle does a fast 180-degree spin and evades his grasp.

"You two are being outsmarted by a dog," Matt observes from his perch on the patio's low surround. "No wonder you can't catch the vandal."

"Vandal?" Hannah's voice sharpens, instantly alert.

Jack grabs Matt in a headlock and says, "Okay, smart guy. If you think you could do a better job, we'll deputize you onto our investigative squad." Jack gives him a noogie.

"Yeah, Matt. Maybe some of your mathematical skills would come in handy in sussing out our perp."

Matt gives me a wounded look. "Low blow."

"It was. Sorry, bud."

Hannah looks around, as if pleading for *someone* to answer her. "Vandal? Perp?"

When Dad explains the recent property damage and other harassment, her face hardens. "Have you filed police reports? Set up cameras?"

Will moves closer, his hand finding the small of my back. "We're taking precautions," he assures her, but I can feel the tension in his touch.

As if empathizing with Dad, Annabelle comes over and rests her head in his lap. She looks up at him, her eyes outlined in black. Her broad white shoulders push against his legs and her well-furred, fox-like tail sweeps back and forth with sweet affability. But then she hears a squirrel moving along the fence. She spins around, spots it, and tears after it. Half way down the yard, the squirrel does a quick about-face and runs back the other way. Belle's momentum carries her a few yards forward before she's able to pull off a course correction. Now advantaged, the squirrel makes it safely to the neighbor's tree that overhangs our fence. The wily rodent chatters noisily down at poor Belle, amplifying the dog's frustration and humiliation.

Matt, feeling sorry for Belle, asks her if she'd like a treat, and Belle bounds toward the door. We all take the opportunity to move the party inside.

"Oh, my god, that smells so good," Hannah says, reacting to the wafting aroma of the bourguignon.

I smile at her. "If you need to freshen up before dinner, now's a good time. This should be ready in about ten minutes." I busy myself adding the mushrooms for the final few minutes of cooking time. I cheat with the mashed potatoes, microwaving store-bought mashed rather than making my own.

THE EVENING FLOWS, wine and conversation mingling with the savory aromas of the meal. Hannah regales us with tales from the health department trenches, her stories revealing the steel beneath her charm. She and Dad trade inside jokes and meaningful glances until Jack starts needling them both about their "bureaucratic glory days."

Unfortunately, the discussion then turns to national politics. I wish it hadn't, because Jack's more conservative than my dad on lots of matters, and things often get heated. Fortunately, on this occasion, the brothers bicker, but manage not to have a full-out row—maybe because of Hannah's calming presence or my well-timed presentation of the key-lime pie. In any case, comity prevails.

I clear the table with help from Jack, Matt, and Will. Hannah and my dad head to the living room. When Annabelle hears the neighbor's dog barking, eighty pounds of excited fur rockets through the room, clipping Dad's legs. The crack of his head against the coffee table stops every heart in the room. Blood streams from above his ear, turning the evening sideways.

Will snaps into doctor mode, at Dad's side in an instant—examining, comforting, staunching the bleeding. He decides we should go to the ER. "We'll take him there ourselves. No sense waiting for an ambulance."

Jack asks Matty if he wants to come with us. Matt shakes his head. Jack tells him to stay inside, that one of us will come back soon. He arms the security system, and Hannah, barely containing her worry, helps me get dad into the car. Will calls the ER on our way there, so they take him right in when we arrive. The ER doc decides to admit him and keep him overnight, so they can monitor him for signs of a concussion or a cranial hematoma. That seems wise to all of us.

Jack and I say goodbye to Dad and leave the room so he and Hannah can say goodnight without us around. When she eventually joins us in the waiting room, she's smiling. She says, "That guy is just remarkable. He refuses to let things get him down. He kept making jokes about falls being par for the course for an old cripple. I pointed out that any one of us could have had a nasty fall if Annabelle had clipped us. He said, 'Yeah, but Belle is especially fond of taking me down. She knows she can do it. I suspect she was frustrated at not getting that squirrel, so decided to go for an easier target. *Topple the crip.* That's Belle's motto.'"

As we walk to the car, I feel for Hannah. She must be worried about Dad—and disappointed not to have the evening with him that she'd been looking forward to. I put my arm around her shoulder. "I'm sorry you got cheated out of time with him tonight. Would you be willing to consider staying on longer than you planned?"

She brightens. "Of course. If you hadn't suggested it, I'd have had to ask. Thank you."

My phone vibrates against my hip. Matty's name flashes on

the screen, and my stomach drops before I even read the message: *"The alarm system's buzzing. I think there's somebody in our yard!"*

Jack's already moving fast, car keys jingling in his hand. Will's on the phone with police dispatch, his voice tight with controlled urgency. Hannah's fingers find mine in the back seat, squeezing hard enough to hurt, but I barely notice. All I can think about is Matt, alone in that house, waiting for whatever's coming.

The speedometer climbs as Jack weaves through traffic. Each red light feels like an eternity. Jack ignores the last two. My mind races faster than the car—replaying every threat, every act of vandalism, every warning sign I ignored. What kind of mother leaves her child alone when someone's actively terrorizing their family? The question burns in my throat like bile.

They knew we'd left the house. They were watching, waiting for their chance. And I handed it to them, gift-wrapped with a bow.

Please, I think, watching the familiar streets blur past. *Please let him be okay.* Because if anything happens to Matt, I'll never forgive myself. And I'll make damn sure the people responsible pay dearly for targeting my child.

Chapter Sixteen

Jack

Seven minutes with the accelerator floored, and we're still too late. No fleeing vehicle to intercept, no shadowy figure to chase down. I'd been prepared to throw the car into a slide to block the road if a vehicle was exiting Amy's cul-de-sac. No such luck. The quiet, empty street mocks my racing pulse.

Matt opens the door before we reach the porch, and Amy engulfs him in a fierce hug. She's crying as she says, "I'm sorry we left you alone, Matty. So, so sorry. I don't know what we were thinking. Are you okay?"

"Yeah. Fine." His voice wavers slightly, betraying the bravado. Will places a steadying hand on Matt's shoulder.

"Did you see anyone?" I press.

"The alarm startled me. I checked the locks, turned on the outside lights." Matt's hands twist together. "Didn't see anything."

I grab a flashlight from Amy's mud room and step into the darkness. The night air carries the chirping of crickets in the bushes and layers of scent: fresh-cut grass from next door, then—sharp and chemical—wet paint.

The garage door hits me like a punch to the gut. A massive red circle, "WILSON" scrawled inside, bisected by a violent slash. Careful job, not some rushed graffiti. Our vandal took his time with this ominous cancel symbol. I take a photo and go back inside.

Amy's reaction mirrors my own disgust. "God DAMN it!" Her scream tears through the careful quiet we've maintained. Hannah wraps her in a hug, Annabelle wedging herself between them like a furry mediator.

"Bellie didn't bark?" I ask Matt.

"Slept through it. Only moved when the alarm sounded."

Amy's laptop reveals what we need. The security footage shows a large figure in dark clothes, including watch cap and gloves, moving with purpose. Not Danny—too big.

But Amy recognizes something about that gait, a telltale asymmetry. "Yes! That stride—I've seen him. After school board meetings, around town. He's been everywhere lately."

A chill runs through me. "Look, Amy, I don't want to scare you even more. But if you've seen him in multiple places, it means he's stalking you." Will moves closer to Amy, his protective instinct evident. I say, "I want you to be extra careful. Always park near other people. Keep your eyes open. Be aware of who's around you. If you see him again, be cautious, but try to find out what he's driving."

"White pickup truck, I think."

"Okay. If you see it again, try to get a license plate number."

She's made Hannah and herself some chamomile tea. "It's just as well Dad's not here. He'd really be upset by this."

I nod, and pour myself a glass of Johnny Walker Red.

She watches me, gets up, dumps her tea into the sink and pours herself a glass of scotch, too. She holds it up and says, "Hannah, this is a better choice than tea, don't you think? One for you, too?"

"Christ, yes."

The amber liquid burns, a poor antidote to worry. Will insists on staying the night, taking the couch. Smart man.

"We'll find him," I promise Amy at the door. "These people always make mistakes."

"What makes you so sure?"

"Because they're not as clever as they think they are." And neither am I, if I let this go on much longer.

Chapter Seventeen

Amy

The kitchen still carries the smell of the hickory-smoked bacon I fixed for Hannah and me after getting Matty off to school. Hannah cradles her coffee mug in both hands, her silver rings catching the morning light. We settle into the living room, where she opens the digital *New York Times* on her iPad, the blue light reflecting off her reading glasses. I make the necessary calls, canceling most of my appointments except for one late in the afternoon. By then, we'll either have Dad home from the hospital or know he's in for another night at St. Mary's.

Cindy, a cordial person who answers my call to the nurse's station, speaks with the cheeriness typical of medical staff delivering good news to worried families. Dad's doing fine, she tells me, and the doctor's inclined to send him home. "Check back around eleven," she adds, "and I'll have better timing on the discharge."

Hannah's been watching me over the rim of her coffee cup. When I hang up, she says, "Sounds like he's coming home." I nod, and relief softens her features. "Good. He'll be more comfortable here, and we'll keep a close eye on him." She takes a thoughtful sip, then continues, her voice dropping. "To be honest, I wasn't prepared for how much weaker he seems since I saw him last. This post-polio stuff is just ravaging that poor body of his."

My throat tightens. "It's horrible. Some days, I don't know how he goes on. In fact, I'm sure there are days he doesn't want to go on." The words slip out before I can stop them, and I see Hannah flinch. I backpedal, trying to soften the edge of what I've just shared. "But your arrival yesterday showed just how much he can rally. He hasn't been so chipper in months. You're just the tonic he needs."

Her smile is tinged with sadness. "You're sweet to say that, Amy. I love the old goat, and I'm sorry to see him suffering."

Jack's distinctive knock at the door—three sharp raps that sound more like a warning than a greeting—precedes his entrance. He bursts in like a walking hardware store, armed with a bucket, new sponges, white vinegar, and lemon juice. His faded dungarees and threadbare blue chambray shirt, complete with elbow holes and a splash of dried green paint, make him look like he's about to tackle a full-weekend project."Captain Clean, reporting for duty, ma'am," he announces with his usual mix of humor and determination.

"Aw, Jack, you don't have to do this."

He hoists his cleaning supplies like trophies. "Well, I read that there's a better chance of getting it all off if you deal with it in the first twenty-four hours, before it takes hold. Going to try the eco-friendly approach first." He waggles the vinegar and lemon juice. "If that doesn't work, I'll bring out heavier weaponry."

"Thank you," I manage, the simple words carrying the weight of everything I can't express.

"Hear anything about Tom?"

"Looks like they're letting him come home, probably early afternoon."

"Good. If I get right to work, I can probably be done before he gets here."

Hannah and I watch him disappear into the garage, hear the mechanical groan of the door rising and falling. "You're lucky to have Jack here in town," Hannah says, her tone carrying a hint of envy for the ready support I have at hand.

"Don't I know it. He raises Tom's spirits. And especially now, with all this crap happening, I feel slightly less vulnerable with Jack around." The admission costs me something—I've always prided myself on being self-sufficient.

Hannah removes her reading glasses, folding them deliberately. "Amy, why do you want to stay on the school board? I understand not wanting to give in to intimidation, but really, is it worth it?"

I let the question hang in the air, heavy with implications. "I'm struggling with this. And, hell, I'm starting to wonder if I shouldn't just pack it in." My fingers trace the warm ceramic of my coffee mug. "But I don't want to let these assholes drive me from the board. I've liked the work—up until all this started. And I really believe we've been making the smartest, most rational decisions for the community during this pandemic, even if there are a lot of people who feel otherwise." The words come faster now, heated with conviction. "I don't know, Hannah. *Somebody*'s gotta do it. And maybe I sound arrogant saying it, but I think I'm as capable and reasonable as anybody else. But it's obvious many in the community don't like our decisions. I'm up for re-election next year, and they can replace me then if they choose to."

"True." Her voice takes on the measured tone of someone who's navigated similar waters. "But you know as well as I that turnout for elections like school board or county supervisor is horrid. The advantage goes to whichever side is more organized, and that's usually whoever's angrier. And we know who that is right now." She leans forward, elbows on knees. "What I'm saying is, it sounds as if you're not likely to win re-election in any case. Why not just let the air out of their balloon? Announce you're not running for re-election and defuse the situation? Buy yourself some peace and safety right now?"

The suggestion lands like a life preserver thrown to a stubborn swimmer. "Yeah, maybe you're right. I'll think about it."

She smiles, the expression warming her eyes. "I'm not trying to talk you out of public service. Lord knows I believe in it. I spent my life at it. But, as Kenny Rogers advised, 'you gotta know when to fold 'em.'"

I laugh, grateful for the lightening of mood. "Not my favorite singer, but good advice, nonetheless."

Rising, she stretches with casual grace. "Well, if you don't mind, I'm going to go take a shower. I didn't get to try to seduce your dad last night, but hope springs eternal, and it's a new day."

Four hours later, we're bringing Dad home. The hospital had shaved his hairline above the gash, making the six stitches look like black insects against his pale skin. The bruising has spread like watercolors, but he insists it doesn't hurt much—probably because the familiar aches in his joints and muscles speak louder. When we tell him about the previous night's vandalism, his face darkens with a fury I rarely see.

Jack has worked his magic on the garage door by the time we pull in. The red cancel symbol is mostly gone, leaving only a phantom outline that he's confident will vanish with some specialized cleaner from Ace Hardware. "But we'll see," he says, moving to help Dad from the car. He wraps Dad in a gentle bear hug. "Glad you're home, bro. Hard to keep a tough man down."

Dad's laugh carries a trace of his old vigor. "Maybe so. But not hard to knock him down in the first place. Just ask Annabelle." The joke lands differently now that we've seen his vulnerability up close, but we smile anyway, protecting his dignity like the precious thing it is.

Chapter Eighteen

Tom

The house settles into mid-afternoon quiet after Amy leaves for her work appointment. Hannah's arranged me in the big easy chair like I'm a fragile antique; she props pillows behind my back until I'm properly anchored. She sits on the sofa beside me, close enough that I can smell her familiar lavender perfume. It hasn't changed in all these years.

We've been trading stories about old times—mutual friends, favorite projects, shared triumphs and disasters. Her laughter fills the room like sunshine. But I sense her steering us toward harder truths.

"Obviously, getting clipped by Annabelle isn't a regular occurrence," she says, her eyes crinkling with concern, "but has falling become a problem for you?" Her voice carries that gentle, probing tone I remember from our days working together.

She'd use it on staff members she suspected of withholding information.

I laugh, though it comes out hollow. "Actually, Annabelle is a menace, a constant threat looming in the house. She doesn't regularly knock me over, but she has a few times, so I'm wary of her—she's big enough that just brushing against me can topple me." My fingers drum against the chair's worn arm. "But the bigger risk factors are what PPS has saddled me with: greater weakness, poor balance, bad reflexes, worsening arthritis." Each word feels like admitting defeat.

"I can see that those things would make you more prone to falling." Her eyes watch my restless fingers.

"Not only more prone to falling, but not as good at falling safely." The words taste bitter. "I mean, less capable at folding my body as I'm going down, to protect myself, minimize the damage. The consequences of a fall for me are likely to be more severe than for someone who never had polio." My voice drops. "I worry about breaking a wrist or an arm or—god forbid—a leg."

Hannah's grimace mirrors my own fear. She clasps her hands together. "Yeah, that would be horrific ... You mentioned greater weakness. Is that mostly in your legs?"

"No." The word comes out sharper than I intend. "It's generalized weakening of the muscles. I hate it. " Heat rises in my face. "I feel like my body is constantly flashing signs to the world in bright neon: *This guy's body is weak.* Things like needing the walker or sometimes the mobility chair. Or not being able to do the outdoor grilling anymore because my shoulders hurt too much to lift the heavy lid of the gas grill."

My voice rises with frustration. "That's a tiny thing, I know

—by itself, unimportant. But it overlaps with other little things to suddenly have meaning. It's not easy to accept that now I have a hard time lifting a casserole dish to wash it, or raising a stack of clean plates to an upper cupboard." The words tumble out now, breaking free of long constraint. "Frankly, that's tough to take, psychologically or emotionally. It makes me feel like a wimp. There's this disturbing element of humiliation to my weakness that I hadn't experienced before. It's hard."

Hannah reaches across the space between us, her warm fingers wrapping around my hand. "Nobody thinks you're a wimp, Tom. In fact, everyone admires your spirit." Her thumb traces circles on my skin. "But I'm sorry about how it makes you feel. I'm sure it's incredibly challenging—and exhausting."

The word 'exhausting' hits home like an arrow finding its target and unlocks something further in me. The constant muscular fatigue is a nightmare. But worse is the mental exhaustion from being slightly depressed, the exhaustion from being constantly vigilant. I tell her about the latter.

"What do you mean, mental vigilance?" Her head tilts, professional curiosity mixing with personal concern.

I stare at our still-joined hands, searching for words. "Whenever I have to go anywhere or do anything outside the house, I find myself totally preoccupied in advance. Worrying about whether I can get there, how far away I'll have to park, will there be stairs I can't climb, will the walking surface be smooth and clear of things that could easily trip me, will there be chairs that aren't too low and that have firm arms at a height that will let me push myself up from sitting." Each concern builds on the last, a tower of anxiety. "The list goes on and on."

My free hand gestures at invisible obstacles. "And it's not

just the physical environment, but the human element, too. How many people will I have to talk to? How long will I have to stand to talk with them? If the only chair that's good for me is off by itself, will people think I'm being antisocial if I sit in it?" The words taste like defeat, and my voice roughens. "I find all of it absolutely exhausting. It makes it hard for me to want to do anything, go anywhere, be with people. So it's not just mentally draining; it's also isolating."

Hannah rises with a fluid grace I envy, moving behind my chair. She leans over, running her hands down my chest, and rests her chin on my head. Her breath stirs my hair. "How awful. I knew things had gotten worse for you. But I see now how little of it I'd even imagined." Her lips press against my crown, a benediction. Then she moves around and kneels beside me, her eyes, shining with unshed tears, level with mine. "And I bet you don't talk about it with Amy and Jack, so they don't know any of that."

"Oh, they know about the weakness. And they know that I worry about going places and don't like being in a group of people." I swallow hard. "But they don't know the extent of my feelings about all that, no."

"Thank you for sharing it with me. I wish there were something I could do, but I know there isn't." Her voice carries decades of friendship and understanding.

"Just having you here helps. Thanks for coming. It means a lot to me." The words feel inadequate for the comfort her presence brings.

"Well, how about if I stay longer? Amy suggested that I do so, but I want to make sure it's okay with you."

"Are you kidding? That would be wonderful." For the first time today, my smile feels genuine.

"I'm going to make a drink." She stands, smoothing her slacks. Her smile turns conspiratorial. "Do you suppose you can have scotch even though you're taking a pain killer?"

"Try to stop me." The old defiance feels good, even if it's just over a drink.

Chapter Nineteen

Jack

The smell of nail-polish remover seeps through the thin walls of Marty Stauffer's insurance office on Route 6, a shabby storefront wedged between a nail salon and dry cleaner. When I enter, he rises from behind an old metal desk, hand extended. "Marty Stauffer. What can I do for ya, friend?"

He's trying for the polished insurance salesman look, but misses by a country mile. A lacework of broken veins maps his cheeks like red rivers on a topographic map, and his widow's peak retreats as if having given up the battle. The Western getup —boots, dark jeans, and a plaid shirt topped with a hand-tooled leather belt—looks silly on a man pushing paper in a one-man insurance shop. Marty's as authentic as a three-dollar bill.

"Name's Jack Franklin. Here to talk about property vandalism." I watch for a flinch, a tell, anything. His face stays blank as an unwritten policy.

He waves me to a chair. "Got a homeowner's policy already, Mr. Franklin?"

"I do."

"Well, most policies cover vandalism damage. But I'd be happy to review your coverage, see what else we might do for you."

"Not concerned about my property, Marty. Nobody's messing with mine."

"Then whose property are we talking about?"

"My niece's."

His pen hovers. "Where's her home located?"

"Paradise Hills."

"Nice area," he says, scribbling.

"It is."

"What's your niece's name?"

"Amy Wilson."

The pen freezes. His face tightens like he's swallowed something bitter. "The woman from the school board?"

"You know of her?"

"Everybody knows of her."

"Know anyone who'd want to damage her property?"

A smirk plays at his lips—the kind that makes my trigger finger itch. "I imagine lots of people would," he says.

I plant my hands on his desk, leaning in. "How about you, Marty?"

"How about me what?"

"Don't get smart. Did you vandalize my niece's property?"

Fear flickers behind his eyes. "I certainly did not."

"You know anything about who did? Hear anything?"

"No." He tries meeting my gaze but his eyes skitter away like water on hot metal.

Through the grimy window, I spot two cars in the angled parking spaces. The faded blue VW Jetta I'd noticed earlier is plastered with stickers—Trump, guns, and anti-abortion. "That your VW, Marty?"

"Yeah. Why?"

"Like to have a look in the trunk."

His laugh sounds forced. "What makes you think I'd let you do that?"

"Just a hunch, Marty." I let my windbreaker fall open, revealing the Glock 43 at my belt. "I'm a former cop. Know how to handle this if needed. Keep those hands where I can see them. Let's check your car."

His eyes dart around like trapped animals before he rises and heads outside. At the car, he pops the trunk and steps back. I motion him sideways, keeping him in view. The trunk's clean except for a white placard declaring "No Masks! No Vax!" Underneath, just a spare tire. No saws, no chemicals, no red paint. Nothing to connect him to the vandalism at Amy's house.

"Let me look inside the car."

He glares, but complies when I pat the Glock. The passenger compartment's equally clean—just a crushed pack of Marlboros on the seat. I know his apartment on North 12th has no garage. Unless he's got a storage unit somewhere, this rolling tetanus box of a car would be where evidence would hide.

"I don't know what you're after," he says as I close the door. "And I don't know when this vandalism took place. But I've been in Texas for the past six weeks. Just got back day before yesterday. So, I haven't been in town. Didn't damage your niece's property, and don't know who did."

"Why Texas?"

"My mother was in the hospital. Died last Wednesday." He pulls up an obituary for Miriam Stauffer on his phone.

"Covid?"

A nod.

"She vaccinated?"

A head shake.

"That change your mind about vaccines?"

"Not at all."

"Well, Marty, that proves you're stupid enough to be a vandal. If I find evidence linking you to this, our next chat won't be so friendly."

I give him a cheerful honk as I drive away, watching his rigid figure shrink in my mirror. Nothing conclusive, but I don't think I'm finished with Marty. Not by a long shot.

Chapter Twenty

Amy

The fluorescent lights of the public meeting room cast harsh shadows across the sea of hostile faces before me. The board finished its usual business thirty minutes ago, and Hank Levitson, our chair, opened the floor to public comments. Since then, we've endured a parade of citizens whose anger seems to pulse in the stale air.

A tiny woman approaches the microphone. Her white hair is neatly coiffed, and she wears a powder-blue blazer with a pearl brooch. For a moment, my shoulders relax. Finally, I think, someone reasonable. But her gentle appearance proves a mask for malice. Her finger jabs toward us on the dais like a weapon. "You people have allowed the schools in this District to indoctrinate students with ways of thinking that are contrary to Christian and patriotic beliefs." Her voice quivers with righteous fury. "Force-feeding your ideologies about race and gender. Glorifying homosexuality."

She turns to the crowd, drawing strength from their rumbling approval. "The schools are shaming students into believing they're homophobic or racist for having normal American opinions or beliefs. They're interfering with parents' responsibility to raise their children in the fear and admonition of the Lord, according to the Bible." Her fist shoots skyward, transforming her from grandmotherly figure to revolutionary leader. Turning back to face us, she cries, "You ought to be ashamed of yourselves for bringing this division to our midst." The crowd bristles with energy, electrified by this chameleon who morphed from Andy Griffith's Aunt Bee to Joan of Arc in two minutes flat.

The following speakers hammer the same themes with increasing fervor. A man clutching a Bible points to us and commands the crowd to "dump hot coals on their heads" for our "evil decisions." A young mother, a baby squirming on her hip, declares, "Our schools should focus on reading, writing, and arithmetic. All this diversity and equity crap has nothin' to do with them basics." Her voice rises over her child's fussing. "It's your job to get our schools back to the basics. You don't have the right to indoctrinate our kids the way you're doin'." The crowd's roar drowns out the baby's cries.

A woman identifying herself as a local police officer launches into a tirade about an English assignment featuring *The Hate U Give*, a book about a Black teenage girl who witnesses a white police officer fatally shoot her Black friend. "That essay assignment was inappropriate and one-sided. This board needs to unmask our kids and stop dividing us with all this critical race theory crap." The word "crap" echoes through the room like a chorus.

Hank finally gavels the meeting closed, though the audience vibrates with unspent fury. We'd planned to wait in the board office until the crowd dispersed—Paul, Hank, and I had arranged to get drinks afterward. But thirty minutes later, the parking lot still teems with protesters, and an MV cop helps us wade through them to our cars. Women wave Trump flags that snap in the evening wind. Signs bob in the darkness: "My Body, My Choice" and "Masks = Child Abuse." Two children, urged on by hovering parents, shriek into megaphones: "Don't touch me, pedophiles." The absurdity of it would be funny if it weren't so chilling. Adults chant "Shame on you," as we make our escape.

The Goat and Clover Tavern feels like sanctuary. We claim a high-top in the bar area, where Paul vents his frustration. "The crazy thing is, critical race theory isn't taught anywhere in the District 51 system. Nowhere. Not a single classroom. But you'd never be able to convince those people of that."

"Right," Hank says, rotating his beer glass. "They think anything about race—like the essay assignment the cop mentioned—is CRT. They haven't the faintest idea what it is, so they're scared. They think their kids are being taught to hate themselves."

My mind drifts to the woman at the previous meeting who'd ranted about litter boxes for "Furries" in school bathrooms. A giggle escapes me, then another, until I'm grabbing fistfuls of cocktail napkins to wipe tears from my eyes. Paul and Hank watch, bemused, until I squeak out "Furries." and they collapse into laughter too.

"Oh, god," I gasp. "I'm about to pee myself. I need a litter box." Our howls draw stares from nearby tables.

When we recover, Paul straightens his glasses. "I researched that after that night's meeting. The same rumor's infected school boards in Maine, Iowa, Michigan, Pennsylvania—all over the country. Extremists take a kernel of truth and twist it into something diabolical."

"There's actually truth to it?" Hank asks, eyebrows raised.

"Only that there's a subculture who craft animal alter-egos. A 'Furry' might draw themselves as a cartoon tiger or dress as a dragon at conventions. It's decades old and pretty harmless compared to other American subcultures."

"So this nonsense about school systems accommodating them is happening because—?" I prompt.

"Because it fits their campaign to discredit public education. If you convince people we're giving special treatment to students who 'identify as cats,' you've succeeded in turning them against us. You've got them hooked."

Hank flags down our server. "Another round, please."

Paul chuckles into his empty glass. "In Texas, a Moms for Liberty candidate for school board claimed schools were lowering cafeteria tables so Furries could eat without utensils—like dogs eating from bowls."

"Oh, good Lord," I wheeze.

"And in Iowa, some blog claimed Furries were excused from homework because the kids said they couldn't grip pens with their paws."

Laughing, Hank clutches his stomach. He finally says, "Jesus Christ. Pure idiocy."

Fresh drinks arrive as the laughter fades. Paul's expression darkens. "Here's the serious part. This isn't organic. It's orchestrated by groups with deep pockets and long arms. Teams of national influencers stirring up local politics."

Hank studies his beer. "Yeah, and their harassment is driving school board members across the country to quit."

I weigh whether to tell them about the harassment I've been getting. Hell, I've kept it to myself too long. Maybe it's the alcohol loosening my tongue, or maybe it's weeks of holding the fear and frustration inside. But I take a deep breath and begin, "So, guys, I have something to tell you ..."

We stay at that high-top long into the night, our glasses propagating condensation rings on the wood as I share my story.

Chapter Twenty-One

Jack

As I describe my encounter with Marty Stauffer. Tom's expression darkens with each word, his reaction even more severe than when I told him about my chat with Danny Wilson.

"I let my windbreaker hang open so he could see my weapon," I say, watching my brother's face. "I think that shook him up."

"You flashed your Glock at him?" Tom's coffee mug hits the table harder than necessary.

"I didn't say I flashed it. I said I let him see I had it." I keep my voice steady, reasonable. "There's a difference."

"So, in your view, you weren't threatening him?" Tom's jaw tightens.

"Absolutely not. I didn't say I was going to harm him."

"Jesus Christ. You guys ..." He pushes back from the table, wood scraping against tile.

"We guys?"

"You cops. No wonder people call you pigs."

The word stings more coming from my own brother. "Hey. Not nice. How is one supposed to deal with people like Marty Stauffer?"

"What do you mean, 'people like Marty Stauffer'?" Tom leans forward, both palms flat on the table. "You said yourself that you found no evidence that he's involved in this intimidation campaign against Amy."

"True." I trace the rim of my mug, choosing my words. "But it was letting him see I had a gun that persuaded him to show me the inside of his car."

"So, you agree you threatened him."

"No, I do not."

Tom rubs his palm down his face and looks across the kitchen table at Hannah, who's been watching our verbal tennis match with poorly concealed amusement. "Do you want to weigh in on this?"

She laughs, the sound cutting through the tension. "No. I'm enjoying your whole conversation immensely. I don't want to interrupt."

I look at Tom, studying the familiar stubborn set of his shoulders. "So, what else do you want to know?"

"Why do you trust what he told you?"

"I didn't say I trust it. I said he gave me no reason to believe he's responsible for the vandalism."

Amy walks into the kitchen, her heels clicking against the floor as she bustles about preparing to leave for work. The

124

normalcy of her morning routine feels almost surreal against our heated discussion.

Tom sighs, deflating slightly. "Okay. Where does this leave us?"

"It leaves us at square one." The admission tastes bitter. "We have no idea who is doing this shit. And that's embarrassing. Pathetic." I gesture toward Amy, guilt gnawing at me. "I told Amy that the people behind this aren't geniuses. But at this point, they're still outsmarting us."

"Do you want to summarize what we know so far?" he asks.

"Not particularly." My answer comes out sharper than intended.

"Okay, then I will." Tom straightens and starts ticking points off on his fingers. "We *know* nothing. We *think* Danny Wilson is not involved. We *think* Becky Dubrovsky is an activist, a protester, but not a vandal. We *think* Marty Stauffer is not involved because he claims to have been in Texas for the past six weeks."

"You're on a roll, bro." I slouch deeper into my chair.

"We don't *know* who the hulking dark figure on the security tape is. The person who vandalized the garage and seems to be stalking Amy. We don't even know what to *think* about him, other than that he's a scary asshole."

"True." The single word holds all my frustration.

"Gee. No wonder the world still doesn't know who killed JonBenét Ramsey. You cops are incompetent."

The jab hits harder than it should. "Again, I say, 'Not nice. And that's a particularly low blow. No fair.'" I look over at Hannah, seeking an ally in this fraternal crossfire.

She smirks, eyes dancing. "That's clearly a foul."

"Thanks, ref. Good call." I manage a weak smile.

"I calls 'em as I sees 'em." She grins, clearly enjoying her role as umpire.

Tom scowls, then his posture softens as he bows his head and shoulders toward me. "Okay. Apologies to my fraternal Hercule Poirot. But this is your line of work, not mine. Could you tell us where we go from here?"

How the hell do I know? The thought must show on my face, but I can't admit complete defeat. "I guess we ought to ramp up our inspection of social-media sites. That seems like the obvious next move." I force a lighter tone. "And, just so you know, I've been spreading my social-media wings, big bro. Little Jacky here is now on Instagram. I have aspirations to become an influencer. Maybe do some Insta-marketing for Speedo."

Hannah snorts, nearly choking on her coffee. "Good lord. What a horrifying thought."

Amy grabs her keys, shaking her head. "I agree. And I'm outta here. See y'all later."

Tom calls, "Wait. How was the board meeting last night?"

"I'll tell you tonight. I'm late. Gotta go. Bye, all."

The front door closes behind her with a decisive click.

Ever mature, I stick out my tongue at Hannah, trying to maintain the moment of levity.

"Okay," Tom says, his earlier anger replaced by familiar exasperation, "after Speedo pours its treasury into your bank account, what else do you hope to do on Instagram?"

"Find people who talk smack about Amy. I'm also on Facebook, Twitter, and TikTok, where I hope to do the same."

Tom grimaces. "And?"

The lightness fades from my voice as I shake my head. "I'm

sorry to say, from what I've seen so far, she's certainly not a popular gal in town. But we already knew that."

"So, you're coming up with lots of suspects?" Hannah asks, her tone gentler now.

"Not yet. No." I stare into my coffee, watching the surface ripple with reflected morning light. "But my instincts tell me these are fertile fields to plow. And I'm tuning up my tractor."

Chapter Twenty-Two

Tom

Steam rises from the bowl of green beans as Amy brings them around the table to me. She knows I can't reach across for them—my arms, if extended straight out, don't have the strength anymore to hold the bowl, and the attempt would send daggers through my shoulders. She scoops some onto my plate, the beans glistening with butter. "More?"

"No. That's enough. Thanks, sweetie."

The conversation flows around the dinner table, warm and familiar as the aroma of Amy's pasta bolognese. We'd started with Hannah's crudités platter while Amy shared stories about last night's chaotic school board meeting. Now Jack steers us back to the topic of public behavior, but with a darker edge.

"It's not just at public meetings," he says, gesturing with his fork. "*The Sentinel* reported that at Mesa Center, some guy pushed an elderly usher to the floor for asking him to keep his mask on. Another got called a Nazi for the same thing. People have lost their freakin' minds."

Hannah nods, swirling her wine. "At Sprouts on Sunday, I watched an older woman blow her top over—get this—the *shape* of one of the breads. Demanded the baker be fired. I couldn't believe what I was seeing."

I'm secretly grateful for my increasingly homebound life. Sounds like a jungle out there. "Seems like civility is dead. Rampant boorish behavior is becoming normalized the longer Covid has its finger pressed on our collective buttons."

Hannah pats my hand—a well-intentioned gesture that makes me feel like a praised house pet.

"Apparently, airplane flights are the worst," Jack adds. "Last week, some goofball on Delta mooned the flight attendant after she asked him to to wear a mask."

Matty laughs mid-sip, milk spraying across his pasta. His reaction sets me off, too. Seems my seventies have rewired my brain to that of a twelve-year-old.

Hannah raises her wine glass in a toast, the ruby liquid catching the light. "Amy, this is delicious. Thanks for going to all this trouble."

Jack, cheeks full, points to his plate with dancing eyebrows. "Mmmmm, mmmmm." A thumbs-up punctuates his enthusiasm.

The conversation stirs memories I've been pondering. "It wasn't like this during the polio epidemic of the '50s. People united then. Now, some think Covid doesn't even exist. Think it's a hoax."

Amy rises for more butter for the French bread, Annabelle

materializing instantly. That dog could hear a refrigerator door opening from three miles away.

Hannah leans forward. "People don't trust government anymore. At any level. Trust has been declining since the '60s, but now we're at rock bottom."

I drag a piece of bread through the rich sauce. "It's not just distrust of government. Lots of people don't trust science either."

Matt looks up from his plate. "Why are people anti-science?"

"Good question," I say, looking into his earnest eyes. "Some resist what they can't understand. Scientific talk sounds like mumbo-jumbo. And some religious folks fear science threatens their faith."

A drop of bolognese sauce betrays me, landing on my shirt. My attempt at cleanup with a water-dampened napkin fails miserably. Everyone's watching as my dabbing at the spot simply makes things worse.

Hannah, perhaps to shift attention away from me, redirects the conversation. "What we need now is what we had in the '50s —non-partisan truth-tellers outside government."

"Like the March of Dimes," I say, catching Matty's puzzled look at the phrase. I imagine he's picturing a long parade of ten-cent coins. "It's an organization," I tell him. "Originally called the National Foundation for Infantile Paralysis. They funded the race for a polio vaccine through donations—one dime at a time."

Jack joins in explaining all this to Matt. "And when it was announced in the spring of 1955 that a safe and effective vaccine had been developed, people went wild with joy. I'm tellin' ya, Matty, it was like the end of a war. There was a huge national celebration. People really got on the bandwagon to get vaccinated. All around the country. Unfortunately, it came a year too late for your granddad."

Matty's hand finds my arm. "Sorry, Pops."

I smile. "It's okay, kiddo. Made me tough as nails."

His eyes, framed by those girl-magnet lashes, seek mine. "What was the worst part of it?"

The table falls quiet. "Oh, gosh, I don't know, Matty. I suppose, at first, it was the isolation. My parents couldn't enter my hospital room—had to stand outside in masks and robes. No one explained anything. It was scary to be alone, lying flat on my back and not knowing what was happening."

I pause, memories flooding back. "Then came the treatments. ... The worst was what they called hot packs. They'd wrap my leg in scalding hot towels. They smelled horrible. Actually I think they were made of wool army blankets. A nurse on our ward would reach into a tub of boiling water with a stick and run a steaming wool blanket through a wringer before wrapping it around my leg—too hot for her to touch but apparently fine for my seven-year-old leg."

Matty's eyes widen. "How long were you there?"

"Months. After I finally got home, I had physical therapy for a long time. A nurse would come and massage my leg and exercise it, trying to keep the muscles active. When she stopped coming, my own grandfather—we called him Pops, too— would come almost every day and do the same thing. He'd stretch me out on a towel on the living-room carpet and get to work on my leg, massaging it and bending it." I'd been talking a long time. "Good lord. I'm sorry. I've turned this into a pity party. Let's talk about something else."

"*Aw, pshaw,*" Jack says, employing another of our grandfather's favorite phrases. "You've never been self-pitying. At least not out loud. But who knows what thoughts rumble around unspoken in that head of yours?"

I lighten the mood. "Mostly I think about which superhero I'm like."

Hannah's smile brightens. "And? Who would that be? Captain Marvel?"

"Used to be Superman—polio was my Kryptonite. Now I'm more like Spider-Man, clinging to walls to avoid falling."

Annabelle nudges my arm with her snout, seeking handouts. "And here's Underdog. Best known for knocking down old cripples."

Matty bursts into the Underdog theme song, surprising us all: "*When criminals in this world appear / And break the laws that they should fear* ..." The familiar tune and words awaken old memories, and soon we're all laughing, shouting "Underdog," the earlier heaviness dissolving into warmth and connection.

Jack's voice is thick with amazement. "How can you possibly know that theme song, Matt? That show was decades ago."

Matt gives his uncle a pitying look, sad at his ignorance. "Well, you see, old timer, there's this thing called the internet, where—"

Jack lunges for Matty and snaps him into a headlock.

"Boys, boys. Settle down." Amy says, and pats Annabelle's head. "As for UnderBelle here, maybe she should spend less time searching for calories and more time catching criminals."

Matt, apparently loving all this superhero talk, looks up at Jack with wide eyes. "Which superhero are you, Uncle Jack?"

"Little buddy, I am Captain America. Honest, up-front, loyal, noble, dependable. And the best-looking avenger, for sure." He turns his face from side to side and tilts it up so we can better appreciate his profile. "I have no super powers, but I don't need 'em. I've taken down countless bad guys without 'em."

I put my head in my hands. "Jesus Christ."

"Hey, yeah, that's a good comparison, too, Tom. Like Christ, I'm an all-around good guy."

Chapter Twenty-Three

Marty

As I pull up Signal for a squad call, all I can think about is that Jack Franklin—Amy Wilson's uncle. I'd never before been confronted by someone packing heat. That guy wasn't playing around. The cold look in his eyes told me he'd use that Glock without hesitation.

When he'd dropped her name, my stomach lurched. No way this was coincidence. Someone had slipped up, left a trail. Probably that mouth-breather Dwayne. Thank god I had my aunt's obituary PDF on my phone. I don't know if he'd have believed my Texas story without it. It was a calculated gamble that Jack Franklin hadn't seen me around town, but what choice did I have? And I didn't know what he was looking for in my trunk. But my heart was racing anyway, and I'm sure as hell glad he didn't find anything that set him off.

The Signal chat pings as the others join. Ray's first reaction to Franklin showing up at my office mirrors mine—blame Dwayne.

"Look, I don't think so," Dwayne protests, his voice thick with defensiveness. "I was careful the night I painted her garage. Dark clothes, mask, truck parked well away from the house. Yeah, they'd added security cameras since last time I was there, but nobody could've ID'd me. And even if they did, how would they connect me to Marty?"

Ray eventually concedes the point, but the damage is done. We're rattled.

Klover's voice cuts through the tension. "Time to dig deeper on Amy Wilson's family. We didn't know about this uncle. That concerns me. Former cop, you say, Marty? We need to know if that's true or just intimidation. We need full background, family connections, other potential threats."

"How we gonna find all that out?" Dwayne asks, demonstrating his usual insight.

"I know someone familiar with genealogy. I'll ask her to give me some pointers. Shouldn't be difficult to find out more about Wilson's family."

"Good. Get on it fast, if you can, Klover," I order, trying to steady my voice.

"Roger that."

"Next steps?" I ask the group. The silence stretches.

Ray clears his throat. "I say we call Child Services. Anonymous abuse claim. I've done it before—causes endless grief."

"Use a burner phone," I warn.

"Obviously."

Klover jumps in. "We haven't even done the basics yet. Let's dox her."

"Docks?" Dwayne asks, and I have to mute myself to hide my gasp of frustration. We recruited this moron for his brawn and his inability to think through consequences, but Jesus Christ ...

Klover explains doxxing with saint-like patience. "Publishing personal data online. Contact info, address, everything. Gets more people involved in the harassment. Some'll order unwanted deliveries, emergency services; others might escalate to threats, vandalism. At minimum, she'll drown in angry messages. Best case, she'll fear for her safety."

Dwayne's voice is hesitant. "Oh. But I wouldn't know how—"

"Nobody's asking you to handle it, Dwayne," I cut in before he can finish displaying his incompetence. "Klover?"

"I'll take care of it."

Ray pipes up again. "Dwayne and I were thinking a GPS tracker on her car. Track her movements, help us plan better."

"Cost?"

Ray replies, "About three hundred, including subscription. I'll coordinate with Klover on the best model."

"OK. What else we got? Any other news or ideas?" I ask.

Ray hems and haws a bit, then drops the bomb—Amy Wilson is his mother's new occupational therapist. The coincidence sends ice through my veins.

"Jesus Christ, what are the odds?" My voice sounds hollow even to me.

"Too weird," Klover agrees. "With Franklin showing up ... you think they're onto us?"

Ray dismisses the concern. "Don't see how. The two things *have* to be unconnected. ... But I'll get rid of her—"

"Wait." An idea forms. "Keep her. Your mother could be our eyes and ears. She could talk to Wilson. Find out what she's thinking."

"Mom's not sharp enough anymore to pull that off."

Klover catches my drift. "But *you* could be there, Ray. Perfectly natural for a son to visit during an OT visit. You could talk to her, gather intel."

"I'll consider it."

Dwayne's barks a laugh. His thoughts are stuck a minute or two back. "I like that idea," he says. "Smother Wilson with pizza deliveries. I'm gonna order pizzas from five different—"

I end the call before he can finish. My hands have stopped shaking, but the fear has been replaced by something worse— the nagging sense that we're no longer as invisible as we thought.

Chapter Twenty-Four

Hannah

Watching Tom navigate this crisis with Amy, I see the same quiet strength that first drew me to him decades ago. He carries his worry like he carries everything else—with dignity, without complaint. The polio that shaped his childhood, the post-polio syndrome stealing his strength, Laura's death—none of it has ever broken him. He's never once asked "Why me?" It's one of countless things I love about him, though it wasn't what first caught my eye. That was the whole package: the sharp mind, the devastating charm, the way his eyes crinkle when he laughs, creating constellations of fine lines that speak of wisdom earned through both joy and sorrow.

Twenty years ago, I walked into his public policy course for MA students at the University of Denver, and my world shifted. There he stood at the podium, the respected head of Disease Control and Public Health Response for the state, breaking down complex community conflicts over schools, public health, airports, parks—making them fascinating. His brilliance showed as he took us through case studies he'd written, teasing out nuances most of us missed entirely. But what captivated me most was how he wove real human stories through the dry policy frameworks, bringing statistics to life with compassion and understanding.

And he was great with students. He had this way of leaning forward slightly when students spoke, as if their thoughts were precious gifts he couldn't wait to unwrap.

I wasn't subtle about my attraction. Some might say I flirted shamelessly, lingering after class with questions that probably fooled no one. He noticed—how could he not?—but maintained his professional distance. He was married, ethical. That didn't stop my heart from racing whenever he called on me in class, or my pen from pausing mid-note when he'd roll up his sleeves during particularly animated discussions.

Two years later, I heard he was going to be giving the keynote address at the National Association of County and City Health Officials convention in Denver. I wasn't even a member yet in those days, but I went. The grand ballroom of the Brown Palace Hotel was packed, and I sat there mesmerized as he commanded the room with the same effortless grace I remembered from his lectures. After his speech, I waited with the crowd of admirers until I could catch his eye, watching him navigate questions and conversations with the same genuine interest he had showed his students.

"Hannah." His smile was genuine, warming me through like summer sunshine. "I didn't know you're a NACCHO member."

"I'm not." I let my smile turn playful, feeling like that eager graduate student again. "I heard you were speaking. I came to see you."

"That's kind of you. How are you?"

"Good. I'm wondering if you have time to catch up. Are you free for a drink? Dinner?"

Something flickered across his face—regret? A hint of temptation quickly mastered? "I can't. My wife and I are taking our daughter out for her 21st birthday."

I covered my disappointment with teasing. "Just how every young woman wants to celebrate—dinner with her parents."

His laugh eased the moment, though it didn't quite reach his eyes. "She's going out after. But lunch tomorrow?"

That lunch was so fortuitous for me. I'd just finished my MPH, having switched from public housing to public health. Over chicken Caesar salads and iced tea, Tom told me about an opening in his division, encouraged me to apply. His enthusiasm for the work was contagious—he painted a vision of what we could accomplish that made my previous career plans seem pale in comparison.

Over the next fifteen years, I eventually became his deputy, and we grew close—cherished friends and colleagues, nothing more. But there were moments, fleeting and precious, when our eyes would meet across a conference table or our hands would brush reaching for the same document, and electricity would crackle between us.

I remember when Laura died. Twenty-seven years of happy marriage, ended in thirty seconds when she collapsed from a brain aneurysm while crossing their living room. The trauma would have crushed most people, but Tom carried on. At work, he remained razor-sharp, though sometimes I caught him staring into space, twisting his wedding ring. I wanted so badly to comfort him, but I kept my distance, respecting his grief. Still, I made sure there was always fresh coffee in his office, that someone brought him lunch when he forgot to eat, that the administrative staff knew to reschedule meetings when he needed space.

There were many times in the years since then that I hoped—and a few occasions when I was certain—that Tom and I would find ourselves together. I lost count of our dinners, work trips, drinks after stressful days. Sometimes I'd cook for him, filling my apartment with the aroma of herb-roasted chicken or homemade pasta sauce. Sometimes he'd cook for me, surprising me with his skill at Thai curries and Mediterranean dishes.

I tried every subtle trick I knew to shift us from friendship to something more. But the timing was never right, or I misread signals, or he simply wasn't interested. I'll never know—it's one of many things left unspoken between us, though lately, during this visit, some of those unspoken things have begun to find their voice.

Then he moved here to Mesa Vista to live with Amy and Matty. The news shattered me like a crystal glass dropped on tile. This brilliant, beautiful man who'd become the center of my world was leaving Denver. He'd retired, and I'd been dreaming of retiring too—imagining us exploring the world together, growing old side by side. But he left, and I didn't know if I'd entered his thoughts at all as he'd made that decision. I buried myself in work to cope with the heartache. Now, at sixty-five, I still live in Denver, still work at the state's health department, and still carry this torch for a man who lives a four-hour drive away.

But being here with him and his family these past couple weeks has been transformative for us both. The crisis Amy's facing has stripped away our careful facades, our comfortable routines of deflection and denial. Tom and I have had plenty of time to talk—really open up to each other—about our feelings and about what each of us wants. Sometimes late at night, after Amy and Matt have gone to bed, we sit on the back patio and let the words flow as freely as the wine. There's something about the darkness that makes honesty easier, that makes hope feel less risky. Turns out, we both now want to find out what our relationship could become, what it could grow into if we gave it a chance. The realization feels like dawn breaking after a very long night.

I told him yesterday that I've extended this impromptu vacation about as long as I can, but will stretch it a few more days, then head back to Denver. When I asked if it would be okay if I drove out here for weekends with him, arriving Thursday evenings and leaving Monday mornings, his face lit up with such joy that my heart nearly burst. He answered me with a smile and a kiss that blew holes through the toes of my socks. If that's all I were ever to get from my twenty-year wait, it would have been worth every moment.

Now, I'm late waking up. I hearTom call goodbye to Amy and Matt. I don't need to look at the clock to know that the two of them have lingered in the kitchen as long as they could without being late getting Matt to school. The morning routine in this house has its own rhythm, as familiar to me now as my own heartbeat.

I brush my teeth and run my fingers through my hair, then head downstairs. Tom's at the kitchen table, reading the *Sentinel*. He looks up and smiles, and my breath catches just like it did twenty years ago in that classroom. Annabelle does him one better, hurrying over to me and nuzzling her nose in my crotch.

"Hey, hey, Annabelle. Come here," Tom calls, embarrassed at the dog's curiosity.

"She's okay. She's just saying good morning, aren't you, BellieBelle?" I ruffle the thick fur on Annabelle's neck. Her magnificent tail wags with pure joy, and I can't help but share in her unabashed happiness. "We alone?"

"Yup. Just us."

I smile and move to him, opening my robe and pressing his face to my bare skin. The morning sun streams through the kitchen window, warming us both.

Chapter Twenty-Five

Tom

After days of threatening, the clouds have finally let loose, releasing the first real rain in weeks. Through the patio door, I watch sheets of water blur the landscape while debating whether to skip this morning's PPS support group. Leaving Hannah alone seems ungracious, but she waves off my concern.

"Go, go. It'll be good for you. I have plenty to keep me busy." Her voice carries both warmth and firmness. "But I'm driving you. I can drop you off right up close to the door. Otherwise, you're going to get soaked crossing that parking lot."

"I'll be fine."

"Of course you'll be *fine*. That's not the point. I'm taking you."

By quarter to ten, we're navigating through the downpour toward Grace Methodist. The wipers struggle to keep pace, and oncoming headlights refract into ghostly halos through the rain.

"My theory," I tell Hannah as we climb into the higher reaches of town, "is that the hills around here form a natural funnel, steering storms right over us."

"Any evidence for that?"

I grin. "None whatsoever. But I hold tight to it."

Water cascades down the steep streets, carrying twigs and early-fallen leaves like tiny rafts until they jam in storm drains, creating pond-sized puddles that swallow the sidewalks. Hannah maneuvers under the church hall's portico, getting me as close to the door as possible.

Inside, the meeting room reeks of wet wool and anxiety. Everybody looks a little frayed. Our usual circle is thinner today —the weather keeping one or two away.

Steve clears his throat. "Peggy can't be here today, so she asked me to moderate our session in her absence. If I remember correctly, we were talking about how each of us has been coping with PPS. Tom, we haven't heard from you at all on this, so why don't you start us off, if you would."

I gesture to my head wound, still sporting a row of stitches and still discolored. "Suppose I should address the obvious first. Yes, it was a fall, but not just from weakness and imbalance this time. My daughter's seventy-pound dog clipped me, sent me into a table. Which brings me to my topic—falling, something I do more frequently now, something that haunts my thoughts. I suspect everyone here, especially those with lower-extremity weakness, understands this particular fear. Sofia spoke eloquently of the problem at our last meeting."

A thought occurs to me. "Let me conduct a little survey.

How many of you have fallen this month?" All but one raise hands. "More falls this year than last?" Every hand goes up. "It's scary, isn't it? And we all know that breaking a wrist, arm, or femur would be far worse than this head wound I got. So yeah, we all worry about that."

My voice catches slightly. "Then there's the growing weakness. You'd think I'd have adjusted gradually. Back when I was working, feeling myself struggle more each day with the long walk down the hallway from the elevator to my office—*that* I could accept. But now? Having trouble lifting a pot off the stove hits differently. Cuts deeper."

Minnie leans forward. "Absolutely, Tom. When it starts affecting the most basic daily tasks is when it really wounds your spirit."

I fall silent, wrestling with whether to share more. The humiliation of weakness, the exhausting mental calculations PPS demands. I could tell Hannah about all that, but here? Even among others who'd understand, it feels too raw.

Steve picks up on my hesitation. "Want to continue, Tom?"

I decide to offer one more thing. "Pain is constant or variable for all of us. Excessive activity triggers it, sure. But here's what's curious: I'm just as likely to get pain from inactivity or non-movement—in other words, from holding still. Holding any position too long becomes its own torture."

The group comes alive. Minnie says, "Exactly. When I'm doing my calligraphy, if I keep my head and shoulders at a particular angle for too long, the pain is horrible." Dave talks about the aches he gets sitting at his model-building table. Steve shares tips about changing positions as often as possible to "shift the load to a different group of muscles or tendons."

Their eagerness suggests this particular aspect of PPS isn't one they've discussed before, making me glad I brought it up. The conversation shifts to breathing and swallowing difficulties —complications I pray I never face.

When we break early, nobody rushes out. People stay and chat, sharing symptoms and stories. Laughter mingles with groans of sympathy and recognition. This, I realize, is the group's real purpose—this connection, this understanding.

Other conversations, unrelated to our health, also emerge. Steve and David discuss military models while Earl chats animatedly with Sofia about her genealogical work. In response to a question from me, Minnie elaborates on her calligraphy struggles.

The rain finally eases as Hannah picks me up, suggesting lunch at a restaurant she'd read about this morning. Because it's new and unfamiliar to me, my mind immediately starts its usual cycle of worrying about walker access, steps, seating height. I weigh being "brave" against my new mantra: *It's okay to say no.*

The morning has left me drained but feeling lighter, foolish for having dismissed support groups all these years. Sometimes emotional release comes disguised as simple conversation. Maybe old crips can learn new tricks, after all.

"No," I tell Hannah. "I'd rather go home. We've got plenty of food there."

She smiles, understanding everything I haven't said. "Great."

Chapter Twenty-Six

Amy

Autumn sunlight hits my windshield at the exact angle to spotlight the coffee rings on my dashboard. Today, I'd stretched breakfast with Hannah to its breaking point, hoarding these last moments before she heads back to Denver. Now I'm late to Agnes Moore's, where eighty-four years of accumulated bitterness await.

Agnes yanks open her front door before I reach it. Her thin frame radiates disapproval like heat from asphalt. "You're late."

Miserable old vulture.

I check my watch, pasting on my professional therapist smile. "Six minutes, Agnes. My deepest apologies for this grievous breach of protocol." The sarcasm slides off her like water on waxed linoleum. Part of me wishes it would stick, lodge somewhere between those beady eyes that are constantly measuring the world for fault. "How are you feeling today?"

"Okay, I guess." She turns away, already tallying this morning's sins against me.

Agnes wobbles toward the kitchen, her too-tall cane doing more harm than help. *Note to self: proper cane fitting, ASAP.* Her gait is essentially a series of controlled falls, each one barely caught in time.

She settles into a kitchen chair with the air of someone cradling world-changing gossip. "My Raymond researched you." Her thin chest puffs with pride. "He's very good with the internets. Found out *all* about you."

"Did he now? Must've been quite the investigation." I imagine Raymond, hunched over his keyboard, following breadcrumb trails of hate.

"He discovered you're that Wilson woman. From the school board."

I smack my forehead. "No! And here I thought I'd kept that so well hidden. What's his next case—finding out if water's wet?"

The sarcasm bounces off her like rubber bullets. "Oh, Raymond's very thorough." She leans forward, cupping her hand beside her mouth like a schoolyard conspirator. "You should see what he's dug up about that Kamala Harris woman."

"I can only imagine. And I bet the very first thing he ever noticed about her was the color of her skin?"

Agnes's eyes light up. "Why, yes! Isn't it terrible? A black woman as Vice President. I keep asking Raymond, 'What's this world coming to?'"

"I ask myself that same question every single day, Agnes." I slap my thighs, the crack of palm against flesh cutting through the toxic fog of her kitchen. "Well, we should get started."

I spend the next hour cataloging hazards masquerading as a home. Exterior stairs that belong in a liability lawsuit need replacing with ramps. The microwave—her "most favorite gadget"—should be lowered to a floor stand from its precarious perch in a raised cabinet. Small throw rugs on hardwood and tile: death traps. The deep-pile carpet in the living room: perfect for snagging feet that drag. I add a medical alert system with a wearable device, a smart-home setup for automated lighting and medication reminders, and an electric lifting chair to help her stand.

"I'll leave you a complete list, Agnes. And, if you like, I'd be happy to email it to Raymond." The words taste metallic. "All this will cost money, of course. But it ultimately will be cheaper than moving to an assisted-living facility. And you'll be able to stay here in your home, which is what you want."

"Oh, you can give it to Raymond in person." Her watery eyes gleam. "He insists on being here for your next visit. You'll need to schedule it in advance." She leans forward, pupils contracting to pinpoints. "Tell me something. Are you truly as wicked as they say?"

The question hits like a slap. "Excuse me?"

"I hear you're the one suffocating children with masks."

And we're done. I don't even know how to reply to this. As usual, I opt for dark humor. "Agnes, if you lived with school kids, you'd understand the urge to suffocate them. ... See you next time." I'm out the door before she can respond.

As I drive away, I think about my next visit there and having to meet her son. *Perfect. Now the bigots are organizing my appointment calendar.* My blood pressure doesn't start dropping until Valley View disappears in my rearview.

My cell phone's ring shatters the moment of calm.

"Is this Amy Wilson?"

"Yes."

"I'm Trudy Brown from the Mesa County Department of Human Services." The woman's professional tone sends ice down my spine. "We've received an anonymous tip on our hotline alleging that your son Matthew is the object of physical abuse in the home."

The world tilts sideways, and my carefully recovered calm evaporates like morning dew. "Oh my god! Are you serious? Who would say such a thing? Why would anyone say that about me? That's absurd."

"Mrs. Wilson, it's our responsibility to investigate all such claims, even those filed anonymously." Her voice remains steady, practiced. "I'm calling to let you know that Matthew will be picked up at the end of school today by one of our protective-service officers. She'll interview him and take him home after that. We've already contacted the school to let them know an officer will be getting him. We, of course, have not said why. We'll need to talk with you, too—and any other adults in the home."

Years of social-work experience kick in. I know better than to rage, better than to let the fury and fear pouring through me show in my voice. I force myself to breathe, to quiet the thunder in my head. "Well, I think I know what this is about. I'm a member of the school board, and somebody is engaging in a campaign of harassment and intimidation against me. I suspect this is part of that." *Stop. You're babbling. Defensive.* "Okay, so someone will pick Matt up and then bring him home? And someone will be contacting me?"

"Yes."

"Soon?"

"Yes."

"Okay. Thank you."

I barely manage to pull the car over before the tears come. My forehead finds the steering wheel as sobs wrack my body. The pain is physical—a fist squeezing my heart, a weight crushing my lungs. My thoughts spiral in dizzying circles. With trembling fingers, I dial my dad's number, hysteria climbing up my throat as I try to make sense of this latest assault on my very being.

How much more can I take? This is beyond the pale, beyond anything I could have imagined. But surely, it won't be a problem.

Will it?

Chapter Twenty-Seven

Marty

The squad meets up in person for breakfast the first Tuesday of each month. I've never been comfortable with it—keeping contact confined to Signal seems smarter—but Klover insists these monthly meetings are good for squad morale. Today, though, Klover couldn't make it, so Ray and Dwayne and I switched to lunch instead. Their tastes usually run toward fast-food chains. The thought of those places makes my skin crawl. I'm not rich, but I'd rather choke than eat at any of them. The desperation seeps into the food.

I suggested Bin 707, my favorite place in Mesa Vista. When Ray and Dwayne whined about the expense, I offered to pay. The truth is, I don't care about their fancy menu items. What draws me is the exceptionally attractive patio, where we're now seated under canvas umbrellas, screened from casual observers by trees and carefully arranged planters.

Our server appears—a gorgeous young woman named Kelly. Not my cup of tea, but I watch Ray and Dwayne's expressions brighten. Their eyes follow her movements like hungry dogs tracking a steak. They order draft beers while I get a vodka tonic. We each ask for a Binburger, with nachos to start.

Dwayne leans forward, his bulk making the metal chair creak. "I got the GPS tracker. And it's already on her car." He pulls out his smartphone, stubby fingers navigating to an app. "See? It shows me in real time where her car is."

"Have you learned anything else useful from it yet?"

"Not really. Just got it on yesterday morning." A grin spreads across his face. "Followed her to a shopping center. Slapped it on the inside of the front bumper while she was in a store."

I nod approvingly. "Good. It's bound to be useful over time. We can fine-tune our harassment. And if we find patterns in her movements, we could share that information with the women at Moms for Liberty. They could stage little mini demonstrations against her at the hospital, or wherever else she goes regularly."

Dwayne's face scrunches in concentration. "Any progress on the, uh, what do ya call it—doxxing?"

I nod. "Klover has been very effective at getting Wilson's personal information out there." I pause as Kelly approaches with our drinks and nachos, steam rising from the melted cheese.

As she turns away, I see Dwayne watching her. Then his voice carries clearly across the patio: "I'd like a big bite of that ass."

Kelly pivots, green eyes flashing. "You want ketchup with that?"

Dwayne and Ray laugh, but fury rises in my throat. How many times have I warned Dwayne about drawing attention to ourselves? We don't want anyone remembering us. I fix him with a glare that could melt steel.

Dwayne raises his hands, palms out. "Sorry, sorry."

"She's the one you should apologize to, not me." His return look suggests he'd sooner bathe in battery acid.

After a tense silence, I continue, lowering my voice. "Anyway, Klover's using his radio and various darknet forums to post Wilson's personal information. We may not know the full effect, but it's bound to lead to a big increase in the number of abusive voicemails and emails. Might even spark some pop-up protests at her house. Klover's asking people to report back on how they use the information, but who knows if they will." I notice Kelly hovering near a servers' station, her posture rigid as she watches our table—too alert to us for my taste.

Dwayne attacks the nachos like he's racing the apocalypse, cheese stringing from his chin. Ray and I exchange glances—a mix of disgust and fascination. I laugh, drawing Dwayne's attention briefly before he dives back in. It must take serious fuel to maintain that kind of mass.

The conversation drifts to the school board. I'm the only one who made the last public meeting. "It's interesting. Covid-related controversies seem to be waning."

Ray's eyebrows lift. "Really? What makes you say that?"

"For the first time in months, more discussion time went to critical race theory, equity, curriculum divisiveness, parental exclusion—topics like that—than to masks and vaccinations."

Dwayne releases a beer-fueled belch.

Ray asks, "Why you think that is?"

"Not sure. Maybe people have exhausted the mask and vaccination arguments. Or maybe those CRT debates in Virginia are influencing discourse nationwide. Either way, it doesn't matter much to us. Stoking racial flames works just as well as vaccination fears."

Ray nods so hard his jowls quiver. "Well, that's just fine with me. I personally care more about the race stuff than the Covid stuff."

No kidding. Ray's the most openly racist person I've ever met. "I know you do, Ray. I know you do." I think of Klover's vaccine obsession. "Different strokes for different folks. Right?"

Kelly brings our burgers. Ray requests ketchup, his tone dripping with false politeness.

I shift topics. "Dwayne, what's the status on Diana Tarrant?"

"All systems go." He grins, showing teeth stained with nacho cheese. "Everything with Amy Wilson has been like a rehearsal. Targeting Tarrant's easy as pie." His laugh booms across the patio. "It feels like—what's that expression?—*deja vu* all over again."

Kelly appears with the ketchup, placing one bowl carefully before me. As she moves toward Dwayne, her tray tilts. Two dipping bowls of ketchup cascade onto his neck, white t-shirt, and forearm. "Oh, what a shame. I'm so sorry to soil such an attractive shirt. Please forgive me." Her smile could cut glass.

She leaves, then returns a moment later with a few napkins. Ray, oblivious to her presence, keeps needling Dwayne. "If Amy Wilson ever finds out who you are, that'll be shit splattering on you, not ketchup." His laugh dies as he catches Kelly's sharp look.

Goddammit. I silently swear never to be seen in public with either of them again.

Through the rest of lunch, I watch Kelly circling our table like a shark—filling salt shakers, refolding napkins, topping off water glasses. We keep talking about school boards, conservative agitators, Republican senators we admire. I repeatedly hiss at Ray and Dwayne to lower their voices.

When the bill comes, I pay cash. No way am I leaving Kelly a name to remember, not with the way her attention has locked onto our conversation. I hustle them out while she's busy inside with another party, not wanting her to see our license plates. *Good lord, what a shitshow.*

Chapter Twenty-Eight

Amy

Of all the things they've done to me, this hurts the worst. This false claim of child abuse cuts deeper than any vandalism or harassment. Each previous attack shook me, but this allegation has rocked me to my core. When my hands finally stop trembling enough for me to drive safely, I pull away from the curb and head home. Thank god one of my clients cancelled their afternoon appointment. And I'm in no shape for the team meeting at St. Mary's Hospital. I call the office, my voice barely steady as I claim illness.

Dad meets me at the door, arms open. The moment he embraces me, the dam breaks. Sobs pour out in great, soulful gulps, my whole body shaking like autumn leaves in a storm. Tears and mucus streak my face, soaking the shoulder of his shirt. After what feels like forever, his arms lower—four or five minutes of holding me up must have strained his shoulders. I wipe my face with my sleeve, shame flooding through me. "Oh, Dad. I'm sorry. Come on, let's get you seated." I guide him to his chair, helping him ease down.

He looks up at me, those big brown eyes carrying all the worry his words won't express. "Sweetheart, it'll be alright. They'll quickly determine that this was a false allegation, and it'll all go away."

I know he means well, that he's doing his best to comfort me. But we both know there's a chance this won't just "go away" quickly. And the trauma of this allegation has already carved something permanent inside me.

"I'm going to take a valium and lie down, Dad." In my room, I curl up on the bed, but sleep refuses to come despite my emotional exhaustion. I can't stop thinking about the unknown person who's done this to me. How can someone be so deliberately cruel? I've always believed people are basically good, that most mean no real harm to others. But everything that's happening—especially this—is eroding that fundamental belief like acid eating through metal.

Eventually, merciful sleep claims me. When I venture out of my room later, I find Dad's note:

While you were sleeping, a Trudy Brown from the child-welfare agency came to the house. I told her you had been traumatized by the news of the claim against you and that you were getting some rest. She said that was fine and asked if she could talk with me, since she would have to interview me at some point anyway, seeing as how I live with you and Matt. I can tell you more later about our conversation. The upshot: I allayed her concerns; said you're an excellent, loving mother; and explained

I stare at the note in my lap, anxiety gnawing at my stomach. For the tenth time, I imagine Matt being picked up and interviewed by a protective-services officer. I know I've never harmed him physically, never given him any reason to suggest mistreatment. But what if he has bruises from normal kid activities that I don't know about? What if anxiety makes him appear nervous under questioning? What if the school reports behavioral issues I'm unaware of? What if he tells them we left him home alone the night we took Dad to the ER? All sorts of things could make them think the allegation has merit. Tears blur my vision again as scenarios spiral through my mind.

Desperate for distraction, I throw myself into making Matt's favorite meal—meatloaf. The rhythmic chopping of onions gives my hands something to do besides shake. I've learned that if I dice them fine enough, they cook through during baking without needing to be sautéed. Into a large bowl goes lean ground beef, the minced onions, dried bread crumbs. Then milk, egg, ketchup, and Worcestershire sauce, followed by dried parsley, garlic powder, salt, and pepper. I mix it all with my hands, the cool meat grounding me in the present moment. After spreading it in an even layer in the loaf pan, I whisk together the glaze—ketchup, brown sugar, and red-wine vinegar—and pour it over top before covering the pan and sliding it into the refrigerator.

After what feels like years, the front door opens. Matt walks in, followed by a middle-aged woman who introduces herself as Helen Miller. I rush to hug Matt, who endures the public embrace before immediately retreating to his room. I shake the woman's hand, fighting to keep my voice steady. "May I get you something to drink? Water? Tea?"

"No. Nothing. Thank you."

"Won't you please sit down?"

"No. I should be on my way." Her expression gives nothing away. "I understand from Trudy Brown that she was unable to interview you today, but did speak with your father, who also lives here. Is that correct?"

"Yes, I think she did, yes." My tongue feels thick, clumsy.

She turns to go. "Well, she'll need to speak with you, too, before this case can be resolved. I'm sure she'll try to get back to you in the next day or so."

When she's gone, I close the door and press my back against it, legs trembling. Christ. I need a drink. The gin and tonic goes down like water, and I force myself to walk, not run, to Matt's room. I knock gently. When he grants permission, I find him cross-legged on his bed, earbuds in, watching something on his iPad.

He stops the video. "What was all that about?" His voice carries an edge I've never heard before.

"I wish I knew, honey." I explain what I think has happened, as best I can through the fog of anxiety.

"Why are these people doing this to you? To us?"

"My guess is that they hope to get me to resign from the school board."

"I wish you would."

The words hit like a physical blow. "You do? Why?"

He looks at me, tears welling up and spilling onto his cheeks. "Because this just sucks, that's why."

"What does?"

"All of this!" The words explode from him. "The vandalism, the scary people showing up at school and here at the house. Now, this. That woman asked me all kinds of questions about you and Pops—how you treat me, whether either of you ever hurt me or yell at me. I didn't like it. Not one bit. And I didn't like being picked up at school like that by someone who suspects you of abuse ..."

"She–" I start to explain that she didn't "suspect" me of abuse, was just doing her job investigating an allegation. But I see the hurt in his eyes and know he wouldn't care about the distinction. I try again.

"These people who—"

Matt cuts me off, his voice cracking. "You think it's only you getting shit over your board decisions? I do, too. Kids at school harass and bully me all the time because of you and the stupid school board." Fresh tears stream down his face.

The revelation leaves me speechless, gut-punched. It never occurred to me that he might be taking flack at school because of me. What kind of mother never even considers how her choices might affect her child? Self-loathing rises like bile in my throat as I wrap my arms around him, holding him tight against my racing heart. "I'm so, so sorry, Matty. I wish you'd told me ... I wish I'd asked if you were experiencing anything like that. Please forgive me."

But how can he? My neglect is unforgivable.

Chapter Twenty-Nine

Jack

The text message Amy shows me on her phone makes my stomach tighten: *Amy, get in touch with me when you can. I recently served three men who were talking about you in a way I didn't like. I want to tell you about it.* It's from her friend Kelly Albertson, a server at Bin 707, and something in the careful wording sends a chill through me.

I don't give Amy a chance to argue about going alone. The autumn sun is high overhead as we pull into the restaurant's parking lot, and I find myself scanning the vehicles, looking for anything suspicious. Old habits die hard.

We choose a table in the corner of Bin 707's outdoor patio, positioning ourselves with clear sight lines to both the entrance and the street. As we wait for Kelly, I study the menu, my investigator's mind momentarily distracted by the realization that any restaurant that's a semi-finalist for a James Beard Award is several steps above my meatloaf-and-potatoes comfort zone.

Kelly appears with drinks: margaritas for us, condensation already beading on the glasses, and a lemonade for herself. Amy makes introductions, and Kelly sits.

She turns her face to the sun, stretching her arms up over her head. "God, the sun feels good out here today." She pulls her shoulder-length hair into a ponytail, securing it with a turquoise elastic ribbon. The gesture seems to buy her time to organize her thoughts.

"I was serving a table of three guys two days ago, right about this time," Kelly begins, her voice low despite the relative privacy of our corner. She takes a sip of lemonade, ice cubes clicking against the glass. "One of them stood out—dressed sharp, but not flashy. Neatly pressed chinos, crisp button-down shirt."

She leans forward, her elbows on the table. "The other two ... different story. Especially the big guy. Something off about him. Thuggish, you know? The kind of customer that makes you want to keep your distance."

The sun feels less warm as she continues. "They'd had a couple of drinks each, tongues getting loose. Started out with normal stuff—Covid, mask policies, Biden." Kelly's fingers trace patterns in the condensation on her glass. "But then they started talking about the school board, and I heard your name, Amy."

Amy shifts in her chair. I catch the tension in her face. Her fingers work through her hair—a nervous tell I've noticed before.

"What exactly did they say about her?" I keep my voice steady, professional.

Kelly's eyes dart between us. "They were talking about doxxing—said someone had put everything out there. Personal email, phone number, address, photos. All of it."

"Did they mention who was behind it? Where it was posted?"

"Not that I caught. But ..." She hesitates, then continues. "One of them laughed—not a nice laugh—and said something about 'incoming fire.' Then the other guy, the one who looked kind of depressed, said 'She's about to get scorched.'"

I guide Kelly through more detailed descriptions, watching her face as she recalls details about each man. The sharp dresser with his ruddy cheeks, close-cropped hair, and big silver belt buckle. The big man with his bald head and flat nose, a distinctive damaged ear. The third man—tall, skinny, long-nosed, with unkempt dark hair and a haunted look.

"The bill?" I ask, though I suspect I already know the answer. "How did they pay?"

"Cash. About one-twenty total. The sharp dresser handled it—left me twenty-five bucks." Kelly's eyes narrow slightly. "You know who they are, don't you?"

I share a look with Amy. "Not for certain. But this was really helpful." Marty Stauffer's face floats in my mind, along with the shadowy figure from our security cameras. The pieces are fitting together, but not in a way that would satisfy any judge or jury. Not yet.

As we thank Kelly and stand to leave, I notice Amy's hands trembling slightly as she gathers her purse. The threat feels closer now, more real, having been discussed in this sunny corner of an upscale restaurant's patio. I make a mental note to check all our security measures again when we get home. These men—Stauffer and his confederates, I'm almost certain—are escalating their efforts. The question is: what's their endgame?

The air seems colder now as we walk to the car, and I find myself checking all around, watching for any sign we're being followed. Sometimes paranoia is just good sense wearing a cheap suit.

Chapter Thirty

Amy

The coffee maker sputters and spits, in the last throes of its first brew of the morning, when Dad enters the kitchen, squeaky wheels heralding his arrival. I'm perusing the *Daily Sentinel*. A creature of habit when it comes to newspapers, I still prefer the tactile pleasure of newsprint to the cold glow of digital screens. So while I read the *New York Times* online, I have the *Sentinel* delivered every morning. It's probably not worth the subscription price, but it's essential to keeping me informed about the community.

A page-two article catches my eye: "PUBLIC HEALTH OFFICIAL DESCRIBES INTIMIDATION EFFORTS." The words swim before me as I read about Diana Tarrant, Deputy Director of the Mesa County Department of Health, being the target of an intensifying harassment campaign. My throat constricts as the article catalogs a series of incidents that mirror my own nightmare: her car keyed, the word "EVIL" burned into her lawn, "Vax=Bad" spray-painted on her house. She's started receiving threatening messages on her personal phone—clear signs of being doxxed. The familiar taste of copper fills my mouth as I read her words: "Whoever is behind this seems to be ramping up their efforts to menace and scare me."

My heart hammers so hard I can feel its rhythm in my fingertips. "Look at this," I gasp, turning the paper toward Dad and spreading it across the breakfast table with trembling hands. As he starts to read, his mouth draws into a thin line, and I watch his knuckles whiten around the paper's edge.

I rise to get coffee for each of us, needing movement to dispel the nervous energy coursing through me. The article has shaken loose all my carefully constructed defenses. It seems sickeningly obvious that Tarrant and I are being targeted by the same people, using the same methods. But she's suffered even worse than I have. "They" threw a stone through her son's bedroom window, striking him on the shoulder and showering him with shards of glass as he sat on the floor, playing with toy cars. And her husband broke his arm falling from a bike that someone had tampered with, removing the brake pads.

The image of her son being struck by that rock keeps flashing through my mind. My hand trembles violently as I fill our mugs, and scalding liquid slops over their rims onto my skin when I ferry the coffee to the table. "God damn it." I run my hands under cold water, but the burning sensation barely registers against the ice-cold fear gripping my chest. Trying to stop tears that flow from terror, not the burn, I whisper, "So, I'm not the only one with a crosshairs on my forehead."

Dad must hear the raw panic in my voice. He looks up and

when he sees my face—I must look as haunted as I feel—he frowns and reaches out a hand. I grab it like a lifeline and hold it for a moment. He rubs his thumb in my palm, the same way he did when I was little and scared of thunderstorms, trying to offer comfort and reassurance. But this isn't a storm that will pass by morning.

I manage to steady my voice enough to say, "Looks like we can rule out any personal animus behind all this. Like from Danny."

"Good point." He shakes his head, still holding my hand. "But I never really thought that's where all this was coming from, anyway."

"Nor did I." The words taste like ash in my mouth.

I take my seat and tap my index finger on the photo accompanying the article, trying to focus on facts instead of fear. "I've met Diana Tarrant. She and John Kirby, the public health director, came to an executive meeting of the school board in summer 2020. They discussed masks, social distancing, potential vaccines—all that. She's completely reasonable. Not a zealot or radical by any measure—at least, not that I saw. Kirby seemed more adamant about mandates than she did. I wonder why she's the one being targeted."

"My guess is it's not coincidence that you're both female." Dad's voice has taken on an edge I rarely hear. "Maybe whoever's behind this thinks they can harass and intimidate female office holders more easily than males." He pauses, as if weighing his next words. "What do you think about contacting the reporter at the *Sentinel*"—he scans for the byline—"this Brad Johnson, and telling him your story? That you're experiencing essentially the same intimidation tactics as Diana Tarrant?"

The suggestion sends a fresh wave of anxiety through me. I consider this, trying to think past the fear clouding my judgment. "I don't know. I see advantages, including increasing pressure on the police to stop this. But there are risks." My voice catches. "It might draw more harassment, encourage copycats who haven't thought of doing this kind of shit. And if I do leave the board, I'd rather the community didn't know I was driven out. ... Those are my initial thoughts." I glance at the clock on the oven. "Right now, though, I'd better get ready for work. I have an early meeting at the hospital before my first OT appointment. ... You don't mind getting Matty to school?"

"Not at all." He reaches for my hand again and gives it a squeeze. The concern in his eyes makes my chest tighten.

I stop at Matt's door and listen. Hearing nothing, I open it as quietly as I can and peer in. He's still sound asleep, peaceful and vulnerable. I tread to his bedside and gaze at this sleeping angel, a tiny stalactite of drool stretching to his pillow. The thought of a hurled stone striking him or bullies' venom wounding his psyche tears at my heart. Then I have an image of someone "accidentally" knocking Dad down in a parking lot or grocery store aisle, his walker clattering away as he falls, and the tears start all over again. I've always prided myself on being strong, on facing challenges head-on, but this is different. This isn't just about me anymore. Every shadow now holds a potential threat, not just to me, but to the two people I love most in the world.

Chapter Thirty-One

Amy

Two endless days pass before I finally get to meet with Trudy Brown from Child Services. She'd been out sick yesterday, but now she sits across from me in my living room. My hands won't stop trembling. The consequences would be unbearable if somehow, horribly and wrongly, the determination went against me.

Ms. Brown interviews me for an hour, her pen scratching across her notebook as we cover everything from discipline methods to household routines. Finally, she closes the notebook and removes her glasses, the simple gesture making my heart skip. "Ms. Wilson, as you know, our agency is required by law to investigate any allegation of child abuse or neglect. My colleague Helen Miller, who picked Matthew up at school and interviewed him, found no reason at all to believe that he is being neglected or abused in any way. She said he seems like a happy, well-adjusted, truthful boy. His reports of how you interact with him give Helen no reason for concern." She pauses, and I feel the weight of the world suspended in that silence. "Similarly, after speaking with you and your father and seeing your home, I find no reason to believe Matt is experiencing any neglect or abuse. You seem like a very good mother, and this seems to me to be a safe, loving home for Matt."

The breath I didn't realize I'd been holding rushes out, tension draining from my body like water through a broken dam. She continues speaking, but her words blur together, only fragments breaking through: "... unsubstantiated allegation ... obviously not true ..." Tears stream down my cheeks. She disappears into the kitchen, returning with a glass of water that she presses into my shaking hands.

"Unfortunately, we get lots of anonymous tips that are false," she says gently. "Some are well-intentioned—the caller actually believes a child is being harmed. But many allegations are born of malice. Often, there's a divorce or custody issue involved. It's sad. A horrible thing to do to another person. And it's a shameful waste of our agency's scarce resources. Looking into these things is time-intensive."

I grab a tissue, dabbing at my face as she continues.

"I understand that you suspect this allegation is part of a larger pattern of harassment you're enduring as a consequence of your position on the school board. Is that correct?"

I can only nod through my sniffles.

"We recently had a similar complaint lodged against another public official in town. Also totally unfounded. It's a shame there are such malevolent people out there willing to do this to others."

We talk for another ten minutes before she gathers her things. As she stands, she catches my wrist. "I'm sorry for your troubles, Ms. Wilson. I wish you only the best. And for what it's worth, I want you to know that I, for one, am a big fan of how the school board has handled everything related to Covid." Her grip tightens slightly. "Be strong. Have courage."

I walk her to her car. Heading back, I feel the anxiety and apprehension of the past days beginning to dissipate—until my eyes fall on the lawn. The word "EVIL" still shows through Jack's repair attempts, like a scar that won't fade. Reality crashes back: this isn't over. Not by a long shot. This nightmare has no end in sight.

I call Will with the news about DCS clearing me. After discussing the interview and my overwhelming relief, he says, "Let's celebrate. We haven't been out for dinner in a while. Are you free tonight?"

"Sure. Let's do it."

"How about Spoons?"

"Could we go to *Le Merise* instead? I really need a treat."

"Sounds good. I'll call for a reservation and pick you up about 7:15."

"No, you know what? We'll take my car. I need gas and won't have time to get it first thing in the morning. I'll get it on the way to your place. See you then. Love you."

An overhead patio heater bathes our table in soft light and comforting warmth. The double doors to the dining room are wide open, and the two areas feel like one continuous, welcoming space. We've skipped salads for *Le Merise's* legendary appetizers—my prosciutto-wrapped asparagus and pears arrive broiled to perfection, glistening with balsamic reduction. Will's jumbo lump crab cakes perch on crisp crostini, crowned with smoky jalapeño remoulade.

I study Will over my smoked Manhattan, letting the cocktail's warmth settle my nerves. "Why do you suppose people love the smell of smoke so much?"

A smile plays across his face. "Well, you see, young lady, the sense of smell is lodged in an ancient part of the brain called the limbic system, which houses emotion and long-term memory. At one time in history, before gas and electric stoves, all cooked food would have had an element of smoke. Our brains now think of smoke as an important dimension of food."

I've covered my face with my palms, feigning exasperation. Looking up, I say, "I'd have gotten even more dressed up if I'd known I'd be having dinner with Bill Nye the Science Guy. Thanks for the episode of mansplaining, Bill."

He laughs, eyes crinkling. "Guilty as charged. It just so happens that yesterday I read an article about how cooked food helped humans evolve because it took less time to digest, leaving more time for us to do other things, like invent fancy cocktails or serve on the school board. There were a few paragraphs about the connections between humans and smoky food. I found it interesting. I tend to remember things I find interesting."

I take another sip, savoring that ancient scent. "Your mind is underrated, you know."

"By whom?"

"By me. I don't like to think that I might have to change my estimation of you."

His laugh rumbles deep. "Well, you're not the only one who might need to do some reassessing. I may have been over-rating you all this time." He navigates a precarious heap of crab to his mouth with surprising grace.

"What? How so?"

He swallows, dabbing his mouth with his napkin. "Choosing to stay on the school board might be a sign of mental imbalance."

I wrinkle my nose. "Nice, supportive boyfriend you are."

"I do support you. I just have a strong protective instinct toward you, and I don't like seeing you putting yourself in the line of fire from all the crazies out there."

"They're the crazy ones. Not me."

"But it's crazy for you to keep doing this when you don't have to."

The familiar argument settles like lead in my stomach. "Will, can we not do this right now? Please?"

His huge brown eyes—the first thing that drew me to him —soften with concern. "Of course. I'm really not trying to irritate you, Amy. I wish only to save you from yourself."

"Will."

"Okay, okay." He mimes zipping his lips.

Silence stretches between us as we focus on our food, pretending our thoughts have moved on. I let my gaze drift around the cozy dining area, drinking in the sublime ambiance. It still amazes me that places like this exist in Mesa Vista. I feel so lucky to live here, to be with this caring man who, despite his misgivings about my service on the school board, supports me in countless ways. Lucky to have my sweet son, kind father, and protective uncle. My eyes mist with gratitude.

Then movement catches my attention—a man approaching our table with unsettling purpose. Middle-aged, smallish frame carrying too much weight, what's left of his hair cropped close. His drooping mustache twitches as he raises a glass of beer. Before I can process what's happening, amber liquid drenches my face, hair, and dress.

"Aw. Maybe you should have been wearing a MASK!" he shouts.

As I gasp from the assault, Will launches to his feet. "What the hell?"

The man drops the glass with a sharp crack and throws a wild right hook at Will's head. I watch in stunned admiration as Will blocks it with his left forearm. Another clumsy left hook follows, which Will dodges before using the man's momentum to spin him around. Will plants his foot against the attacker's rear and shoves. The man stumbles, loses his balance, and crashes between two nearby tables, splayed on the floor like a spatchcocked chicken.

Diners and servers converge around me, forming a protective wall. The hostess appears with napkins while the manager rushes over, promising to comp our meal and offering anything else we need.

"I just want to get out of here," I whisper. Will wraps an arm around me, and we make our way through the shocked dining room with what dignity we can salvage.

Footsteps crunch on pavement behind us as we cross the parking lot. I turn to see a massive man bearing down on us, barrel chest heaving. He grabs Will's shoulder, spinning him around before landing a punch to his stomach. Will stumbles but recovers, circling the man with careful steps. When he sees his opening, Will unleashes a roundhouse kick, his shin connecting with the outside of the man's knee. A howl of pain cuts through the night air as the attacker doubles over. But then he explodes upward, his right fist catching Will's jaw with devastating force. Will drops like a puppet with cut strings.

I'm already running back toward the restaurant where the manager and a server are struggling to restrain my beer-throwing attacker. "Help!" I scream, pointing to Will's motionless form.

"Run, Jerry! Let's go!" the big man shouts, already sprinting toward a white pickup. The shorter man breaks free, joining his partner in their escape. As tires squeal against asphalt, a voice carries through the night: "We'll get you, you evil bitch!" The darkness swallows their license plate.

Will manages to sit up, but it takes both me and the manager to get him on his feet and back inside. Somewhere in the distance, a siren's wail grows closer, its sound mixing with the pounding of my heart.

Chapter Thirty-Two

Jack

My brother's assholish remark the other day about the unsolved JonBenét Ramsey case wasn't random. It was a nasty jab at me. I was one of the original investigators on the case. Tom knows I ache that we weren't able to solve it—and am still in pain over the death of that cute kid. Let me tell you, seeing the body of a six-year-old girl who'd had her skull smashed in and been strangled with a garrote changes you forever. After that, few things rattled me. But this shit involving Amy? It's getting under my skin in a way I haven't felt in years.

I've spent the day piecing together what happened at *Le Merise* last night, interviewing staff and comparing notes with Mesa Vista police. Nobody on staff recognized the attackers. The timeline emerged like a photograph developing in dark room fluid. According to the restaurant's seating system, Mutt and Jeff—as I've started thinking of them—arrived moments after Amy and Will. My niece and her boyfriend had reservations; the attackers didn't. The assailants had pounded through two rounds of beer and started their third without ordering food, telling their server they were "still deciding." The server recalled both men rising simultaneously—the shorter one heading for Amy's table with his beer, the taller one slipping out the front door.

The pattern's clear: This wasn't some drunk recognizing Amy and deciding to teach her a lesson. These guys followed them there with intent. The coordination's too perfect for coincidence.

The restaurant has no security cameras—an oversight the manager promises to correct immediately. Small comfort now. One diner managed to capture cell-phone video after Amy got doused, showing the shorter attacker getting kicked down and later struggling with the manager near the front door. But it's all from behind and his left side—no clean shot of his face. At least we know his name is Jerry, thanks to his partner's shout. It's not much, but it's something. Still, finding these guys won't be easy.

There's a silver lining: The assault, combined with the vandalism and harassment, has finally gotten the full attention of the police. They've copied our security footage showing the garage vandal. Amy was too shocked last night to compare the large attacker's gait, but he did have a white pickup—matching what she's seen before. Small connections, but they add up.

The police suspect the same people harassing Amy are behind the intimidation of Diana Tarrant. "In a way, that's good," one detective told me, leaning against his desk. "The more they're doing, the greater the chance they'll make a mistake, expose themselves, get caught. All we can do is be as vigilant as possible."

When the police scanned Amy's car, they found a tracker. They removed it for Amy's safety and planned to see if, working through the manufacturer, they could find out who purchased it and installed it. I convinced them to get the identifying information from the tracker but then to reinstall it on the car. No sense tipping our hand. I've done enough surveillance work to believe I can keep an eye on Amy most of the time when she's away from home. I can watch and wait. Maybe I can spot someone tailing her or showing up where she parks.

BACK AT AMY'S house at day's end, I track down Matt. I've fumbled around on social-media sites and grasp the basics, but I know when to admit I need help. A tech-savvy 12-year-old knows more about this stuff than a retired cop any day. Within two hours of explaining what I needed, he'd transformed my understanding. He showed me the ins and outs of Twitter, Facebook, and TikTok searches, dismissing Instagram with a wave: "Useless for this purpose." He set up Google Alerts for his mother's name and the Mesa Vista school board, then added Social Mention—a monitoring tool that continuously scans blogs, news sites, and social media for designated topics. The kid's a natural.

Now, past 10 PM, I'm drowning in the initial results. I'd searched "Amy Wilson," "Mesa Vista School Board," "District 51 School Board," each paired with terms like "mask" and "vaccinations." Christ, if this is the volume for a local school board member, imagine what turns up for actually famous people.

The findings paint an ugly picture: Mostly Twitter and Facebook posts attacking Amy and two other board members. Doctored videos manipulate her words into things I know she never said. And everywhere, this K3LVR character keeps appearing—especially on Twitter and Parler—maintaining a steady stream of vitriol against the school board and Amy in particular. But trying to unmask the person behind the handle leads nowhere, like chasing shadows in the dark.

As I scroll through another wave of hateful posts, I feel the weight of that Boulder basement from years ago. Different evil, same darkness. But this time, the victim's my niece, and I'm damned if I'll let these cowards hide behind keyboards and fake names forever.

Chapter Thirty-Three

Tom

We tell ourselves stories about our own lives. Tell them often enough, and they crystallize into truth—our personal truth, backed by carefully curated memories, cultural touchstones, media impressions, and the echoing stories of those close to us. These personal truths become sticky, tenacious things, clinging to us like old wallpaper that refuses to be stripped away.

The story I've told myself about growing up in 1950s Denver might as well have sprung from an episode of *Ozzie and Harriet* or *Leave It To Beaver*. In my mind's eye, I see a cleaner, simpler version of what society would later become. I know now it was the sheltered perspective of a middle-class boy in a safe, homogeneous community, insulated from the stresses and hardships that countless other American kids faced in their neighborhoods, within their families. But back then, it was my entire world. Yes, I had polio—but life rolled on despite that, like a steady stream around an unmovable stone.

In the story I've constructed, the kind of violence Amy and Will experienced at *Le Merise* would have been unthinkable in the 1950s. Not to people of their social class, not at a nice restaurant, and certainly not over something as mundane as face masks. But am I remembering truth or mythology? The fifties and sixties were hardly the golden age my memory paints them to be, especially for Americans pushed to the margins because of their race, gender, social class, or sexual orientation. Segregation ruled—legally by race, socially by gender—and intolerance flourished like weeds in a neglected garden. Yet, would people then have attacked a public official or vandalized their property over a school face-mask policy? I don't think so, but I'm neither historian nor sociologist. Maybe nostalgia has tinted my memories in sepia tones.

What I do know, having watched it unfold through adult eyes, is how dramatically this country has eroded since my childhood. We've recreated the yawning socioeconomic chasm of the last Gilded Age, our middle class crumbling like an ancient bridge. The spirit of cooperation in the public square has withered, replaced by a polarization so fierce it tears families apart. Community ties have unraveled like a sweater caught on a nail, leaving us isolated in our individual bubbles. Our culture celebrates a rampant individualism—narcissism, really—that treats the common good as an outmoded concept, like manual typewriters or party lines.

I remember watching JFK's inaugural address, his words crackling through our television set as he called for Americans to elevate shared interest above self-interest. Even to my teenage ears, it sounded like reveille for a new era of collective achievement. He painted a vision of a country that could accomplish anything through cooperation and shared purpose. *Beat polio? Done that*, his confidence seemed to say, *and you ain't seen nothing yet.*

But looking back across six decades, I realize he was unknowingly sounding taps for an era about to sunset. Since then, America has transformed from a "we" society into an "I" society, like a photograph slowly fading to its negative image. What a shame. Now we're reaping what we've sown, and we're choking on the chaff.

And Amy—my brilliant, passionate daughter who's given so much of herself to this town—what's happening to her terrifies me more than I can express. I see it in the shadows under her eyes, in the way she flinches at unexpected sounds, in how she obsessively checks the locks before bed. The spark that's always defined her—that fierce determination to do what's right —is being slowly extinguished by fear and exhaustion. Each morning, I watch her steel herself just to walk out the door, and my heart breaks for her a little more.

She tries to hide these emotional bruises from me, of course —she's always been protective of me that way, just like her mother was. But I hear her pacing late at night when she thinks everyone's asleep. I notice how her hand trembles slightly when she checks her phone, dreading what new threats might await her. Yesterday, she jumped when Annabelle barked at a squirrel in the yard, and for a moment, I saw raw panic in her eyes before she could mask it.

And Will—that good man who's been nothing but a blessing to our family—suffering from a fractured jaw and a severe concussion, all because he tried to protect my daughter. Amy and I went to visit him this morning. The interaction between them was the exact opposite of their typical flirty banter. She looked at him with eyes that were haunted and worn down. He put on a brave face, but his own eyes were full of pain and anger. Not just physical pain, I suspect, but probably deep frustration at knowing that Amy isn't safe—and at being temporarily sidelined in his efforts to protect her. And, perhaps this is projection on my part, but I believe I see disappointment there, too—a sadness that she persists in this volunteer service to the community, despite the danger.

Sometimes at night, when my joints ache too much for sleep, I lie awake wondering if I should beg Amy to resign from the school board. The thought of it galls me. I raised her to stand up for what's right, to never back down from bullies. But what father wouldn't consider it, watching his child suffer like this? Then I remember the steel in her spine, inherited from her mother, and I know such a conversation would only add to her burden. She'd see it as one more person she's letting down, one more reason to doubt herself.

All these aren't the nebulous worries of an aging father about society's decline. These are visceral fears that wake me in cold sweats: Will the next attack be worse? What if they come to our house? What if next time, Will's injuries are more severe, or Amy's? What if Matty gets caught in the crossfire? The weight of these fears presses against my chest like a physical thing, making it hard to breathe. But I have to stay strong for Amy, have to be her safe harbor in this storm, even as I wonder if I'm watching my daughter's spirit being crushed by the very community she's trying to serve.

Chapter Thirty-Four

Amy

Will's injuries weigh on my conscience like a stone. He's badly hurt because of me. And every time he brings up the subject of my service on the school board, I dance away from the topic like it's a burning coal. Truth is, I don't need his tirades to make me think about leaving. Matty's obvious misery has already done that. Maybe it's time to hang up my cleats. I have a full enough life without the board. And I certainly don't need this fear, this aggravation, this harm to those I love.

These thoughts circle my mind like restless birds as I pull up to Agnes Moore's house. I'd spent yesterday afternoon fine-tuning my plan to keep her in her home, emailing the details to her son Raymond with a heads-up about today's visit.

Agnes answers the doorbell but keeps the security chain fastened, peering at me through the narrow gap, like I'm a door-to-door criminal.

"My Ray isn't here yet." That signature wheeze whistles through the crack.

"What's the problem, Agnes?" I ask.

"Problem?"

"Why aren't you opening the door?"

"I have opened the door."

"Enough to let a fly in. How about enough to let *me* in?"

Another wheeze, this one carrying an odor like bad fish or rancid cheese. "I don't know that I can trust you. You're that school-board woman."

"Agnes, I'm your occupational therapist. I'm here to help you." A car crunches into the driveway behind mine—a beat-up, sun-bleached Nissan Versa. A tall, thin man in his late forties unfolds himself from the driver's seat, his longish brown hair, with wispy lines of gray, hanging limp around a weathered face. His clothes speak of someone long acquainted with hard times.

He ambles up the walk, offering a wave and smile that seem oddly bright when juxtaposed with his own appearance and the paranoid greeting I just received from his mother. "Ms. Wilson," he says. "Welcome."

I swallow my suspicion of his incongruous warmth and opt for professionalism. "You must be Ray. I'm Amy Wilson, the OT. Nice to meet you." I extend my hand, which he takes. "I'm glad you could join us today because I want to move your mother further down the path of staying here in her beautiful home."

We're still on the porch, Agnes fortified behind her chain like it's razor wire. He peers through the crack in the door. "Mom," he calls through the crack, "how about letting us in?"

"Raymond, are you sure we should let this evil woman in?"

He chuckles. But then, as if chagrined by her comment, turns to me and says, "I don't know what's gotten into her. Sorry." Then back to his mother: "Yes, Mom. Please open the door."

Agnes slides the chain free with glacial slowness. Ray makes a gallant gesture for me to enter first. "Please."

Inside, he says, "Thanks very much for the 'Stay In Your Home' plan you emailed me, Ms. Wilson."

"Please call me Amy. I'm glad you—"

Agnes cuts in like a dull knife. "I bet you don't let them call you 'Amy' at those school-board meetings. I hear you think you're the Queen Bee."

"Mom, let's not be unkind."

"Raymond, you're the one who said—"

"You know what, Amy?" Ray interrupts smoothly. "Let's go through the house together and discuss your suggestions, so I can be sure I understand what you're thinking. Mom, you stay here. No need for you to traipse around behind us." Agnes harrumphs and drops into a kitchen chair like a sulking teenager.

We tour the house, discussing safety modifications. Ray blanches at the costs but shrugs. "It's her money. She can decide how to spend it." Under his breath, bitterness seeping through, he adds, "God knows she doesn't share it." Later, he asks how I like my OT work.

I give him my standard response, words worn smooth from repetition: "... fulfilling ... enjoy helping others ... blah, blah, blah ..."

"How about serving on the school board?"

I pause, but his interest induces me to lower my guard. "I liked it fine until Covid came along and we were thrust into decisions beyond budgets and personnel. None of us wants to be setting policy about school closings, masks, or—god help us—vaccinations. I hate knowing so many people in the community are deeply unhappy with our decisions. The thing is, I'm not some crazy ideologue. I don't have a liberal agenda I'm trying to ram down people's throats. I'm just a citizen, doing a job, trying to make the best decisions I can with the information available at any given moment."

His expression shifts, surprise and confusion dancing across his features. After a pause: "Well, you're right: there are a lot of angry people out there. ... That must scare you."

Something in his voice—empathy, maybe—or just the fresh memory of beer in my face and Will's head hitting pavement,crumbles my professional walls. I tell him about the harassment, the words spilling out like water through a broken dam. "Honestly, it's pretty awful. I don't understand how people can do this to someone over a policy disagreement. It just seems crazy to me. Anyway, I'm sorry to go on about it."

"No, that's fine. I asked." We're downstairs again, about to rejoin Agnes in the kitchen. "Does all this make you feel like quitting? Make you want to just walk away from it all?"

I stop, studying this stranger who's drawn out what I haven't told even those closest to me. "Yeah. I'm seriously considering it. I'm thinking of quitting."

The words hang in the air between us like smoke, and I'm struck by how easily they came out—not to Will or Dad or

Jack, but to this man I don't even know, in his mother's living room on an ordinary Tuesday morning. Something about that feels wrong, like I've given away a piece of myself I didn't mean to share.

Chapter Thirty-Five

Ray

The empty beer bottles multiply on Marty's coffee table as our Thursday evening meeting drags on. His second-floor apartment smells of stale cigarettes and the microwaved burritos he offered us earlier. Klover isn't here—the walk-up stairs are too much for him—but his gravelly voice crackles through the speakerphone placed in the center of the table like some kind of technological tabernacle.

My knee bounces with excitement as I wait for my turn to speak. The news I have about Amy Wilson feels like a firecracker in my chest, ready to explode.

"You guys aren't gonna believe this," I burst out finally. "Our efforts with Wilson? They're working."

Marty leans forward in his leather recliner, his eyes sharp. "What makes you say that?"

"Because she told me so herself." The words tumble out, proud and eager.

"When was this?" Marty's voice has that precise quality it gets when he's really interested.

"A few days ago. I did what we discussed—went to my mother's house when Wilson was there for an appointment."

"What, exactly, did she say?" Each word comes out measured, careful.

The overhead light casts harsh shadows across Marty's face as I explain how I'd played it casual, asking about her work and the school board. "She said she used to like serving on the school board before Covid started. Then she talked about how many angry people there are out there and how she's being harassed." I can't keep the satisfaction from my voice. "I asked something like 'does that make you feel like quitting?' And she said, 'Yeah. I'm seriously considering it. I'm thinking of quitting.' She meant it, too. You could see it in her eyes."

"That's very good news. Very good." Klover's voice crackles through the phone's speaker, distorted but pleased.

The praise warms me. "Yeah, and I should thank you guys for suggesting that I not fire her but try to talk with her instead. Turns out, that was a good idea."

Marty's fingers drum against his armrest. "Do you think it would seem unusual if you were there again at some future appointment?"

"No, I don't think so." The possibilities spiral out before me.

"Good. This is great having a direct line into her head. What a lucky break."

The meeting shifts as Klover's voice cuts through our satisfaction. "What about you, Dwayne? Any news to report?"

Dwayne shifts his bulk on the sagging couch, and something dark flashes across his face as he starts talking about following Wilson's car to a restaurant. My stomach tightens as his voice grows animated when he describes what happened next,.

"So, we're sitting there, my buddy Jerry and me, having a couple of beers, keeping an eye on Wilson and her companion. We can see them, through the door to the patio." He grins, showing tobacco-stained teeth. "Jerry says to me, 'You know what would be funny? How about I go toss a beer in her face?'"

The room temperature seems to drop as Dwayne continues. "We both start laughing, thinking about Wilson sputtering and blubbering after she's drenched with a beer. And, before I know it, Jerry is on his way across the dining room to where they're sitting, just through the door to the patio.. Sure enough, he throws his beer in her face. Yells something like, 'Too bad you're not wearing a mask, bitch,' which I thought was a nice touch."

The change in Marty is instant and violent. He explodes from his recliner, face flushing crimson under the harsh lighting. "Jesus Christ, Fowler." His voice bounces off the thin apartment walls. "You should have told us about this sooner. Nobody authorized you to personally accost Wilson. Throwing a beer on her is assault and battery. That's a crime, you idiot. It's not just some funny joke."

Confusion clouds Dwayne's face like a child who expected praise and got a slap instead. "What's the problem? Isn't everything we're doing a crime?"

"None of it has been where people could see you, you idiot."

Marty's knuckles whiten as he grips the back of his chair. "I assume there were other people in this restaurant?"

"Yeah."

"That means there are people who could identify you."

"I got out of there when Jerry threw the beer."

"Okay, but you said you sat there long enough to have a couple of beers. That's plenty long enough for people to have taken notice of you. And let's just say you have a fairly memorable appearance."

The air grows thick with tension as Dwayne bristles. "What's that supposed to mean?"

Marty waves the question away, his jaw clenched. "So, who is this Jerry?"

Dwayne, defensive, says, "Just a friend of mine."

With a tone I recognize as forced amiability, Marty says, "And what does Jerry think about what we're doing to Wilson?"

Dwayne, letting his guard down, smiles and says, "Oh, he thinks it's really cool. He says he wishes he'd been along for some of the other things I did."

Marty explodes again. "Dwayne, you idiot. That means you've been telling him. You're not supposed to talk about what we're doing with anyone. Don't you realize you've now compromised all of us by blabbing to this guy?"

"Aw, Jerry wouldn't squeal. He's a good guy."

Marty just stares slack-jawed at Dwayne. Finally, he rubs his face with both palms, sighs, and says, "Tell me what happened after Jerry threw the beer on her."

"Her black boyfriend got up and kicked Jerry to the floor."

But I barely hear the rest of the exchange because of this bomb Dwayne has just dropped. Wilson has a black boyfriend?

194

What the fuck? This revelation hits me like a physical blow, but Marty just pushes on with his interrogation about the incident. My mind spins as Dwayne describes the fight, the knockout, the hasty escape.

I tune back in when Dwayne is saying, "Out in the parking lot, I hit him. Knocked him out cold, I think. He wasn't moving and—"

"Dwayne. Are you out of your mind?" Marty puts his palms to his forehead. "What then?"

"Jerry was struggling with someone trying to hold him by the door. I yelled to him to run. He managed to break free and both of us ran to my truck and got out of there."

"They see your truck?"

"Probably. But the parking lot was very dark, so I doubt they got a good look at it."

"Police?"

"Someone must have called them. We heard a siren in the distance."

Klover, who's been silent through all this, says, "This is most disconcerting. Dwayne, you can't go rogue like this. You can't just go around pulling a major stunt like this without discussing it with us first."

"Yeah, yeah. Okay, I get it. Okay?"

Klover asks, "Has your GPS tracker placed Wilson anywhere unusual since ... when was it this happened?"

"Thursday night."

"Since then?"

"Not that I've noticed."

"Not the police? Not the *Sentinel's* office?"

"No."

Marty says, "The tracker's working normally? No sign that they found it and removed it?"

"Nope. It's working fine."

"Jesus. Okay. Well, as Klover says, don't do anything to Wilson except track her, unless you clear it with the squad first. Okay?"

"I *said*, okay."

"And don't keep shooting off your mouth to this Jerry about our operation."

<hr>

THE DRIVE HOME to my trailer in Loma gives me twenty minutes alone with my thoughts, and they're darker than the winter night around me. The image of Amy Wilson with a black man burns in my brain like acid. I'd started to soften toward her when we met—she hadn't seemed like the left-wing zealot I'd imagined. But this? This confirms every suspicion, every fear.

Memory takes me back to North Park Hill, where I learned about s early. Back then it was still a decent, white working-class neighborhood in Denver, the kind of place where kids played outside after dark and nobody locked their doors. Then they started moving in. First just a few families, then more and more. My dad, who sorted mail at the central post office for thirty years, would come home talking about how the neighborhood was "changing." Mom was more subtle about it—she just started driving me to a school across town and warning me away from certain blocks, certain people.

Then Marie got mugged. My sister was seventeen, closing

up at the Dairy Queen on Colorado Boulevard, near what the city renamed Martin Luther King Blvd. That tells you something, right there. Some kid—couldn't have been more than fifteen—stuck a knife in her face and took everything. When she got home, mascara streaking her face, I watched my quiet, careful father turn purple with rage. "This is what happens," he kept saying. "This is what they do." Marie was never the same after that. None of us were.

Dad was right about North Park Hill. Within ten years, our neat little ranch houses with their perfect lawns had turned into Section 8 rentals. The park where I used to play baseball became a hangout for druggies. Mom started finding needles in her flower beds. Our white neighbors fled one by one, but we couldn't afford to move. Every morning, Dad would look out at the neighbor's sagging chain-link fence and say, "They're destroying everything." They destroyed him, too.

The gas gauge needle hovering near empty forces me to pull into a station halfway between Mesa Vista and Loma. There's another car at the pumps—a BMW. Its driver is black, and I somehow recognize him. It comes to me that he lives in Loma too, not in the trailer park but in a neat little yellow house with a patch of lawn that reminds me of my childhood home. The kind of place I should have had.

He has the nerve to smile at me, like we're neighbors or something. Like he belongs here. And something in me just ... snaps. Here I am, scraping by in life, living in a trailer, doing under-the-table IT work, while this guy's living the life that should've been mine. Driving the kind of car I used to have in Denver.

I follow him when he leaves, keeping my lights off until we

hit that dark stretch of road near the creek. What happens next ... well, let's just say he won't be smiling at white folks anymore. Won't be driving that BMW for a while either.

Back in my truck, my boots are sticky with evidence that'll need dealing with. I should burn these clothes, get rid of these boots, too. Some stains never quite come out, you know? But they're my lucky boots, been with me since Denver. Besides, nobody out here's gonna be looking too hard into the assault of a black guy. Some people need to learn their place in this world, need to understand they can't just walk around like they own it. Like they earned it.

The porch light of my trailer casts weak yellow shadows as I sit in the idling truck, letting the engine's rumble match the dark rhythm of my thoughts. Maybe we're wrong to rein in Dwayne. Maybe we should just let him do what comes naturally to him. He's itching to go after Wilson. Now, I bet he'd love to go another round with that black boyfriend of hers, too. Maybe we should let him. Move things along.

The familiar weight of my lucky boots feels different now as I climb the trailer steps. Maybe what happened at that restaurant ... maybe that's just the beginning of what needs to be done.

Chapter Thirty-Six

Amy

The morning sun streams through my kitchen window as I spread out today's *Daily Sentinel* on the kitchen table. But my suddenly darkened spirit has sucked out all the light, like a black hole. My coffee has grown cold and bitter beside me. A shocking story claims the front page, the bold text seeming to vibrate with sensationalism.

TARRANT INJURED WHILE EVADING PURSUERS—
BOTH ASSAILANTS DIE AT SCENE

My hands shake slightly as I reread the article, the words blurring and sharpening as I try to focus:

Diana Tarrant, the deputy director of the Mesa County Public Health Department, was severely injured in a three-vehicle crash Thursday night at the intersection of North Avenue and First Street in downtown Mesa Vista. Her husband was driving their Ford Fusion when it collided at high speed with a Honda Civic. Police say the Tarrants were being chased by two men in a pickup truck who had harassed them earlier in the evening at a restaurant east of where the crash occurred.

The story unfolds like a nightmare. I can picture every detail of it all too clearly: the Tarrants trying to enjoy a quiet dinner at The Winery, their walk across the darkened parking lot, the sudden appearance of two men from a white pickup truck. The image of them spraying Diana with urine from a Super Soaker makes my stomach turn.

The rest of the article reads like an action movie script gone horrifically wrong—David Tarrant racing through red lights, the pickup repeatedly ramming their car, forcing it into a crash with the Honda at North Avenue and First Street. I know that intersection well; I drive through it almost daily. The article's clinical description of the pursuers being struck by an SUV as they tried to flee across the broad intersection and into Lilac Park barely masks the horror of what happened there.

I have zero interest in my coffee now as I sit back, trying to process the tangle of emotions coursing through me. First and foremost, there's gut-wrenching anguish for Diana and her family. I know exactly what it feels like to look over your shoulder constantly, to wonder if every stranger might be a threat. But Diana and her husband experienced what I only have feared—actual violence, the sickening crunch of impact.

Then there's the selfish thought that creeps in, unwanted

but persistent: it easily could be me in that hospital bed at St. Mary's. I see myself in Diana's place, Will in David's, fleeing through the dark streets of Mesa Vista with unknown assailants on our tail. The thought makes me shudder.

And then still another emotion surfaces—relief. If these were indeed the same men who've been harassing me—and both the tactics and the white truck make me think that's the case—then maybe this is the end of it. With both men now dead, it could be all over. But what if the well of hatred runs deeper than that and there are more of them out there?

Chapter Thirty-Seven

Marty

The evening news drones in the background as I pour myself another bourbon and drop in fresh ice. On the screen, they're showing footage of the crash scene again—twisted metal under harsh emergency lights, the white pickup truck crumpled like paper. What a clusterfuck.

I've known since day one that Dwayne was a liability. Men like him, all muscle and impulse, they're useful up to a point. But they're like attack dogs—sometimes they slip the leash. And when they do, well ... the wreckage at North Avenue and 1st Street speaks for itself.

The cubes clink against my glass as I check Signal for the hundredth time today. Klover and Ray are as paranoid as I am. We're each trying to assess the damage, figure out if Dwayne's stupidity has put us in jeopardy. Ray, ever the technical mind, maintains we're clean. His message glows on my screen: *Signal encryption is unbreakable. And we've had no direct comms outside the app—no calls, no emails, no texts. We're ghosts.*

He's right about our protocols. From the beginning, we've been meticulous—no contact information stored on our devices, no paper trails, no digital breadcrumbs. But Dwayne? The same man who, not two weeks ago, stood in my living room swearing he'd never pull another stunt like the *Le Merise* incident with Amy Wilson? The same man who then went and escalated with Diana Tarrant? Hard to trust that he followed any protocol at all.

I drain my glass, the bourbon burning less than the memory of that night. We'd read him the riot act, made him understand —or thought we had—that personal confrontation wasn't part of the plan. Now he's dead, smashed like a squirrel by an SUV on a highway median, and who knows what kind of trail he's left behind that could lead back to us?

The news switches to footage of Diana Tarrant being loaded into an ambulance, then cuts to a clip of Amy Wilson talking about the harassment she, too, has faced. This morning's *Sentinel* confirmed Tarrant won't be returning to her position. Mission accomplished with Tarrant. Broke her fast, even if our methods were messier than planned. But Amy Wilson has made no such announcement. She seems determined to persist.

My phone buzzes—another Signal message to us from Klover: *It's time to go dark for a while Let the heat die down. Let the police chase their tails, let the media circus move on to the next sensation.*

I text back that I agree. It feels hot out there. We'll lay low.

Chapter Thirty-Eight

Jack

Twenty-three years as a cop teaches you things about human nature that you can never unlearn. There's a particular smell to evil—not physical, but something you sense in your gut when you're circling close to it. I've spent too many nights studying case files, building profiles of the people who let darkness win, trying to understand why some cross that line while others pull back from the edge.

In the days following the Tarrant incident, I fall back into old habits, working my contacts, piecing together the puzzle of what happened. The familiar rhythm of investigation feels both comforting and troubling—comforting because I know how to do this, troubling because this time it's personal.

The first piece comes together quickly: Dwayne Fowler, one of the dead men. Former professional wrestler, local rabble-rouser, a man who seemed to feed off chaos. The kind of guy who showed up at every public meeting just to cause trouble, more interested in the spectacle than the issues. In the photos my contacts shared with me, Fowler's damaged ear and flat nose tell the story of too many fights, both in and out of the ring.

The second piece is Jerry Sanford, the other deceased. A police source—let's call him Rick—meets me at our usual spot, a dim corner of Everyday Joe's Coffee House. Steam rises from his cup as he describes Sanford as "pure poison, but smart enough to stay just this side of prosecutable." A vandalism case against him for attacking a judge's home fell apart because, as Rick puts it, we have "a timid-shit district attorney who wouldn't take it to court without DNA and three eyewitnesses."

But it's what Rick tells me next that gets my attention. They found a sophisticated tracking device in Fowler's mangled truck. And there in the back right wheel well of the Tarrants' Ford? A matching transponder. Rick doesn't need much convincing—just the promise of two tickets to an upcoming concert at CMU his kid wants to see—to confirm what I already suspected: the tag on Amy's car was linked to the same system.

Later, when I show Amy the photos, her hands shake slightly as she confirms what I assumed: Fowler and Sanford were the men from *Le Merise*, the ones who attacked her and Will. More disturbingly, she recognizes Fowler from countless places around town—school board meetings, the grocery store, the hospital cafeteria. Too many places for it to be coincidence.

The vandalism, the doxxing—it all fits their profile. But

proof? That's another matter. Fowler's phone is a dead end, locked down tight with Signal's encryption. The browser history, emails, texts—all clean of anything involving Amy or Diana Tarrant. No messages to confederates, no smoking gun leading us to others involved. Even the search of his apartment turns up nothing but protein-powder containers and a disturbing collection of conspiracy-theory books.

Sitting in my home office late at night, studying the photos spread across my desk, I keep coming back to Kelly Albertson's statement about the men at Bin 707. Fowler was definitely one of them—she confirmed that when I showed her his picture. But Sanford wasn't there that day. I'd stopped by the restaurant with the photos, and Kelly was certain: he wasn't at that table.

The math is simple and troubling: at least two other men were involved in this campaign against Amy, and probably against Diana Tarrant too. At least two men—maybe more— are still out there, still free to act on their hatred.

Maybe I'm overthinking it. Maybe Fowler and Sanford were the entirety of it. But twenty-three years of investigating hasn't just taught me about human nature—it's taught me to trust my gut. And my gut says this isn't over.

Chapter Thirty-Nine

Tom

Peggy's absence from the PPS group's previous meeting seems to have made her more determined now to regain control of the group's dynamic. "Sorry I missed the last session," she says, straightening the collar of her powder-blue cardigan. "I understand it was excellent. Why don't we pick up where you all left off. Earl, let's hear from you."

Earl's power chair whirs softly as he adjusts his position. The sound has become as familiar to us as breathing. "At our last meeting, Tom talked about how dealing with the unexpected is part of a polio survivor's routine. Well, I'm gonna tell you a story about this power chair of mine." He pats the armrest. The chair gleams under the ceiling lights—a testament to how well he maintains it, how much it means to his independence.

"This was a couple years ago now. I'd just returned home

from a couple of weeks at a rehab center where I'd been evaluated by a PT, an OT, and my personal physician—all of whom concluded that I needed a power chair." His voice takes on a harder edge. "The longtime weakness in my legs makes it difficult for me to walk around the house. And increasingly this post-polio business has left me with arm weakness, too. So, a power chair is in order. The folks at the rehab center contacted a power-chair supplier and arranged for them to meet with me to figure out the right chair for me."

Earl's eyes flash with remembered indignation as he continues. "So far, so good. After I was home and using the rented power chair, I engaged a home-health agency to send around a PT that the doctor had ordered. That's when the trouble started." His knuckles whiten on the armrests. "This PT, having seen me only once, called the power-chair supplier, without consulting anyone else, and declared that only a manual chair was indicated for my level of arm weakness." He looks around at each of us, his gaze challenging, daring anyone to question his narrative.

The tension in the room rises as Earl's voice grows stronger. "I'm here to tell ya that we do not have to sit by passively and watch as so-called experts take over our lives. I told that whippersnapper PT, 'Look, I'm in charge here. Not you.'" He punctuates each word with a sharp rap on his armrest. "I sent him packing and I fired the home health agency. Then I set about hiring a new one that would honor the evaluations I'd already received."

His face reddens as he builds to his point. "What I'm getting at with this story is that we have to understand that our health-care decisions are up to us. We should not casually hand over our authority to every individual who stumbles into the picture." He folds his arms across his chest and releases a kind of "hmph" that seems to vibrate through the room.

Peggy shifts in her chair, her silver bracelet catching the light. "Well that's an interesting story, Earl, but it doesn't tell us how you *feel* about your post-polio syndrome. Can you reach a little deeper and tell us some of the emotions involved—like Tom apparently did at the last meeting?"

The change in Earl is immediate and stark. He glowers at her as if she's suggested that he pull down his pants and let us all have a good long look at his genitals. The muscles in his jaw work visibly before he speaks. "I just *did* tell you how I feel about it. I feel it's important we don't let so-called experts make personal decisions for us."

The pause that follows is heavy with unspoken tension. When he resumes, his voice rises like a gathering storm. "There's too damn much of that in this society. We've got that damn Fauci at the national level telling us we should plan to get vaccinated, and you have that damn governor of ours, that Polis fella, closing restaurants and churches according to his whims." His words bounce off the institutional walls, making several group members flinch. "The county public-health department and the damn school board here in Mesa Vista order masks and social distancing and are considering mandating vaccines. Where does it all end? This is America. We're supposed to be a free people. But then we let these public officials—nitwits, all —make decisions for us. It's appalling. Just appalling. It's got to stop."

I feel my pulse quickening, in light of Amy sitting on that very school board. The irony of Earl's ignorance about this fact isn't lost on me, but I keep that knowledge tucked away. Still, I can't let his tirade go unchallenged.

"Earl," I say, keeping my voice measured despite the heat rising in my chest, "there are perfectly good reasons for all those public-health measures relating to Covid. What makes you think the officials behind them are intent on restricting your freedoms?"

His response comes like a whip crack. "Because they don't care about normal citizens. All they care about is what they can do with whatever power they have. They're all like a little boy with a hammer to whom everything looks like a nail." Spittle flies from his lips as he speaks, his face growing redder by the second. "It's some sort of mental sickness they have. And we, the people, have let them get away with it for too long. If this country's gonna survive as a democracy, it's gonna require that the people stand up and take matters into our own hands and say, 'Enough. *We're* in charge here, not you.'"

"How does wearing a mask restrict your freedom?"

"Cuz I *don't want* to wear a mask."

"Does it bother your face? Make your breathing difficult?"

"No."

"Then what's the problem? You don't want to wear one just because some so-called expert or person in power says you have to?"

He pauses and appears to think about it. "Well, yeah. That's right. Who are they to make personal decisions for me?"

"They're not. The mask is to protect others. Those officials are making decisions for society—for the good of all. That's their job. To look out for the public interest."

"Oh, bullshit. You've bought into the notion that those

people can identify problems and solve them. I'm telling you, they can't. They *are* the problem. And let me tell you something else. Sofia here steered me to some ancestry websites she finds useful. And I did some genealogical research on you and your family. I know who you are, Franklin. And I know about your daughter."

"Oh, really, Earl? And, pray tell, what amazing information have you uncovered?" My sarcasm stems from the fact that It would take a brain-dead squirrel all of two minutes to find out about me and Amy.

"I know that your daughter is Amy Wilson, who has a seat on the school board here. She's one of the undesirables on the board, in my opinion. And I know about you. I know you were the head of the state's department of public health for some years."

The revelation about Amy draws little reaction, but the mention of my former position sends a ripple through the room. Heads turn, and I can see the recalculation happening behind their eyes, their perception of me shifting in real time.

Peggy's eyes widen. "Is that so, Tom? And you didn't tell us? Why not? You were hiding your light under a bushel."

I meet their gazes steadily, having anticipated that this moment might come at some point. "Well, it didn't seem appropriate to bring it up. We don't talk about our past work lives in here. And I didn't want anyone to think I believed my opinions or views should carry any more weight than anyone else's just because of what my career was." Several people nod, but Earl's cold stare bores into me.

"But telling us might have helped us understand why you're so hyped up about governmental power," he says, each word dripping with disdain. "And it would have been good to know that your opinions on things like vaccines and face masks reflect a professional bias."

I return his stare, feeling the weight of decades of public service behind my words. "I don't see how it would have benefited you to know, Earl. You don't like my views anyway."

"You're right. I certainly don't."

When Peggy finally intervenes, her voice cuts through the tension like a knife through butter. "Gentlemen, I think it's time to move on." The collective relief in the room is palpable, evidenced by the vigorous nodding of heads around the circle.

Through the remainder of the meeting, Earl's words and the look of contempt on his face burn in my mind like an afterimage. And the familiar weight of public scrutiny settles back onto my shoulders, a burden I thought I'd left behind when I retired. Some things, it seems, never change.

At the hall's exit door after the session's end, Earl and I somehow find ourselves in an Alphonse-and-Gaston routine. I gesture for him to motor through first on his scooter. He insists that I go ahead, but I demur. He insists more firmly. I again sweep my arm forward, urging him ahead. He doesn't budge. Tired of the performance, I move forward, and before I know it, Earl has crashed into me, sending me in a tumble to the floor. I'm dazed, but—I think—not harmed. Others hurry over, such as they can, solicitously asking if I'm injured. Two of the more able-bodied folk help me up and brush off my clothes. Earl's face shows no concern whatsoever. All he says is, "Oh, what a shame."

Chapter Forty

Tom

The last month has been pure peace. The harassment against Amy dried up virtually overnight. The death of the thugs who'd been tailing and harassing Amy and Diana Tarrant seems to have brought an end to it all. And you can't begin to imagine the sense of relief we've all felt. It's as if we can breathe again, as if lead weights had been pressed against our chests for months and then finally lifted away.

But that's not the only development of recent weeks that has brought joy to my heart. Remember that morning a couple months ago when Hannah came into the kitchen and opened her robe to me? Instead of returning to Denver that afternoon as planned, she stayed another four days, each morning beginning with that same deliberate opening of her robe, leading to the kind of pleasure I'd resigned to memory. My aging body awakened to possibilities I'd tucked away in some dusty corner of my mind.

Even after she returned to Denver, the magic didn't fade. Our phone calls punctuated each day like heartbeats—morning, afternoon, evening. She's driven out here each weekend since then, her car appearing in our driveway every Thursday evening like a promise kept. The house seems to brighten when she's here, as if it welcomes the life she brings to it.

But yesterday? Well, yesterday brought news that truly knocked me sideways.

It started innocently enough. Hannah called to tell me about having lunch on Tuesday with John Kirby, the executive director of the Mesa County public-health department, who was in Denver for a meeting of county health executives. She and John go way back—the kind of easy friendship that grows from long toil in the same field. She'd reached out to him, ostensibly to catch up on shop talk and discuss how he was getting by without someone in his deputy position. Just two old colleagues sharing war stories over lunch.

Here's what left me gobsmacked: John called her yesterday morning and offered her the deputy position. And Hannah—my Hannah —said she'd accept, pending my approval.

When I heard that, my hand stopped midway on its mission to bring the coffee cup to my lips. "You'd give up your job as deputy of the state agency to become deputy of a county agency?" The words came out of me, stretched with disbelief.

"Sure. Why not?" Her voice carried that smile I'd grown to know so well. "I've held the state job for plenty long. The county job would be fun, like returning to my roots."

"Well, I don't know about 'fun.' You might—"

214

"Anyway, dopey," she cut in, using an affectionate nickname that somehow made me feel both ancient and seventeen again, "the job is just a pretext. What I really want is to move out there permanently with you."

The world seemed to tilt on its axis. "You do?"

"I do."

"Why?"

"You really want me to answer that?"

"I do." My voice had gone soft, uncertain.

"Okay ..." She paused, and I could picture her gathering her thoughts, the way she always touches her left ear when she's about to say something important. "Because I like Amy. And Jack. And Matt. And Will. And Annabelle. Because I like Mesa Vista when I'm not there ..." Another pause, this one weighted with decades of history. "And because I love you. Always have, always will."

The morning sun streamed through my kitchen window, catching the steam rising from my coffee cup, and I realized I was grinning like a fool. Eight decades on this earth, and here I was, feeling like a teenager who'd just been asked to the prom by the prettiest girl in school.

Chapter Forty-One

Amy

Life has a way of writing stories you'd never try to pitch to a fiction publisher. Roughly three months ago, I was about to close the door on public service, almost driven from the school board by horrific threats and harassment. Now, I'm sitting at our expanded kitchen table, gently arguing with Hannah—who somehow went from Dad's old flame to our permanent houseguest—about whether she and Dad should be taking on local public-service jobs themselves.

Hannah is two weeks into her new role at the county Department of Public Health, despite my best efforts to talk her out of it. Not the moving to Mesa Vista part—I'm still giddy about having her here—but the job? After what happened to me and the near-fatal pursuit of Diana Tarrant? The top jobs in public health make school-board service look like a church picnic these days.

"Look," Hannah had said when she took the position, "I'm not a newbie, not a spring chicken. I can take whatever they throw at me." Her confidence had been both admirable and terrifying. "And if I can't—or if the seat gets too hot or too dangerous—I'll quit. Easy, peasy. I'm close to retiring anyway. But I think I can do this for a few years. It's not like there's a steep learning curve for me with this. I could do this job in my sleep. Besides, I think the worst of the Covid conflicts are over. They're behind us. The harassment campaign targeting you has ended. I'd be surprised if there's any more of that—against you all in education, or against us in public health."

What does one say to that level of self-assurance? I had no good argument in reply. I'd pretty much kept quiet. But now life's taking another wild turn, and my self-restraint is breaking.

The county public health department is managed by its executive director and deputy but overseen by a five-member volunteer board. These Board of Public Health members serve five-year terms, appointed by the county board of commissioners. Now Hannah and her boss, John Kirby, have somehow convinced the commissioners to appoint Dad to fill a vacancy on that public health board.

"There isn't a better person in the whole state—much less, Mesa County—to serve in that position," Hannah declares, sliding a stack of pancakes onto Dad's plate with the air of someone who's already won the argument.

"But he's 75!" The words burst out of me, carrying echoes of all our recent family traumas.

Hannah's eyes narrow as she sets down the syrup. "So what? He still has all his marbles. And it's just a volunteer gig, not like restarting his career or anything. The other board members all have demanding, full-time jobs in addition to this board service. Besides," she adds with a triumphant glance at Dad, "he wants to do it."

I turn to Dad, who's been suspiciously quiet throughout this whole exchange. "Do you?"

He looks up from his careful study of pancake architecture, a hint of mischief in his eyes. "Oh, how nice that somebody has decided to involve me in this delightful conversation! Thank you!" His sarcasm drips like syrup. He gives me a direct, pointed look. "Yes, I would like to do it. I agree with Hannah that it wouldn't be heavy lifting, and I think it would be interesting. Plus, I feel I still have something to offer."

This runaway train clearly left me behind long ago, but I can't help trying to throw one last obstacle on the tracks. I raise an eyebrow at Hannah. "Don't you think it will be unseemly—and potentially scandalous—that there's a close personal relationship between the agency's second-in-command and the new member of its supervisory board? The public may not like the whiff of that!"

Hannah actually snorts. "Oh, please," she says, settling into her own chair. "One in four Americans can't name a single branch of the national government. They certainly aren't going to be attuned to the personnel details at DPH."

"They will be if the *Sentinel* decides to make an issue of it."

"Let them try." Hannah's voice carries the calm certainty of someone who's already thought ten moves ahead. "Your Dad and I have already talked to the county attorney's office about it. They had no concerns, since your father won't be my direct superior and will share general supervisory responsibilities with four other people. Plus, he can recuse himself from any decisions specific to my position, such as salary." She pauses, her expression softening. "Look, Amy. Your Dad has a wealth of expertise to share. If he wants to do it, we shouldn't stand in his way."

I look at Dad, really look at him. His face has that eager expression I remember from my childhood, the one he'd get before starting a new project or solving a particularly thorny problem. It reminds me of Annabelle as a puppy, all enthusiasm and optimism. Something in my chest loosens.

"Okay." I reach for the syrup. "Public service is a noble calling. Go for it." It takes every ounce of my self-restraint to keep from adding, *But don't be surprised if someone keys your car or throws a beer in your face at a restaurant.*

Chapter Forty-Two

Tom

The morning sun catches the newsprint as I spread the *Daily Sentinel* across my kitchen table. There on page three, nestled between ads for local car dealerships, sits a small article about my appointment to the Board of Public Health, complete with a photo that makes me look more distinguished than I feel. The piece mentions my years leading the state's public health department, and to my surprise, deeper in the paper, there's even a short editorial praising the commissioners' selection of me. Somehow, I hadn't expected such public fanfare.

When I arrive late to the post-polio support group meeting, applause catches me off guard. The air in the familiar institutional room seems more charged today—the circle of faces turned toward me with varying degrees of approval and, in Earl's case, barely concealed disdain.

"In case any of you don't know," Peggy announces, her silver bracelet catching the fluorescent light, "that applause for Tom is in response to the news that he will be serving on the county board of public health. Congratulations, Tom." Another round of applause ripples through the room. "Why don't you tell us what you see as some of the agency's immediate challenges."

Earl's face is a mask of shock and outrage. His frustrated sigh cuts through the applause like a knife. "Must he?"

Several people shush him, and I feel the familiar tension that always accompanies my interactions with him. Still, I forge ahead, trying to keep it brief but substantive.

"I think what the pandemic has shown is that our nation's local health departments play a critical role in protecting the public's health." The words feel weighted with my decades of experience. "But decades of under-funding and under-staffing have stretched local public-health infrastructures to their limits. During Covid, agencies were forced to de-prioritize essential services—environmental health, maternal and child health programs—exacerbating existing social inequities. The same with substance-abuse disorders. We watched the overdose crisis quietly escalate during the pandemic."

Earl's dramatic groan echoes off the institutional walls.

"Also," I continue, watching his face redden, "the rampant politicization of Covid protection measures made local public-health responses challenging. Around the country, workers on the front line experienced widespread harassment and threats from within their own communities. We witnessed that vividly right here in Mesa Vista with the horrific intimidation campaign against Diana Tarrant."

Earl's arms cross his chest like armor and he releases an

angry harumph. "So, let me get this straight. Peggy asked you about 'immediate challenges' the agency faces. And you've replied exactly as I would expect you to." His voice drips with contempt. "First, you whined about not having enough money, enough taxpayer dollars to spend as you like. Second, you whined about having critics, fellow citizens who exercise their constitutional right to disagree with what you're doing. How precious. Jesus, you people really are something."

The familiar anger rises in my chest, but I measure my response carefully. "Earl, conservatives have been trying to starve all levels of government of needed resources ever since the Reagan era. You've done a good job of it. Too good."

Then something snaps, and I lean forward in my chair, pointing directly at him. "And it's appalling that you sit there and describe the near-fatal harassment of a public official here in Mesa Vista as a form of 'disagreeing' that is protected by the Constitution. That's appalling, sick, and ignorant."

The circle erupts in supportive murmurs and scattered applause. Earl's face flushes deeper, his breathing heavy and labored, eyes darting around the room like he's a cornered animal.

Sofia breaks the silence. "Tom, you mentioned our weak public-health infrastructure. From what I see, the Covid response —federal, state, and local—was purely *ad hoc*. Is anything being done to prepare for the next pandemic? Bird flu, or worse?"

"No, and it concerns me deeply." I glance around the circle. "I've dominated the conversation today, but I'm curious—how many of you have seen the news about mpox cases appearing in places like the UK, where it's not endemic?"

Steve, Sofia, and Minnie raise their hands. Sofia leans forward. "I was thinking of mpox when I asked my question."

"There's no reason for great alarm yet," I say, meeting her eyes. "This strain appears to spread through sexual contact, making it different from—and likely less dangerous than—Covid's airborne transmission. But if that changes—if it starts spreading through surface contact, for instance—we'd be facing a very different threat."

Steve shakes his head. "Americans, especially our politicians, can't see beyond the current crisis. Once it's over, we pretend nothing like it will ever happen again. We forget the lessons—and the victims."

A heavy silence falls. Then David, who usually stays quiet except when discussing his military model collection, clears his throat. "Like polio survivors being forgotten once that war was 'won.'" His voice catches. "As veterans of other wars have learned, the public doesn't like to be reminded of the wounded and dead after the victory parade."

After the meeting disperses, Sofia holds me back, her face unusually serious. "Tom, I have something to tell you. I probably should have shared this with you long ago." She glances around the empty room. "I was reminded of it again today when Earl unleashed some of his animus against you."

"What is it?"

"Remember a few months ago when Earl revealed he'd done genealogical research on you?" She pauses, choosing her words carefully. "A few weeks later, he told me he'd discovered your father-in-law was Walter Ward."

The name hangs in the air between us.

"Earl holds him directly responsible for contracting the polio virus through the vaccine."

The fluorescent lights suddenly seem too bright. "What?"

"Was your late wife's name Laura Ward?"

"Yes." My mouth goes dry.

"Her father worked for Cutter Laboratories in California in 1954." Sofia's voice is gentle but firm. "He was their director of medical research when Earl got polio from a Cutter vaccine."

The room seems to tilt sideways. "I ... I don't ... I've never heard anything about Walter being at Cutter. I only knew about his years at Stanford Medical School. By the time Laura and I met, both her parents had died."

Sofia reaches into her bag and withdraws a manila envelope. "Look, the only reason I'm bringing this up is that Earl has a few screws loose, in my opinion, and his hostility toward you worries me. I wanted you to know why." She hands me the envelope. "This will tell you what I've found about Walter Ward." She looks at me closely. "I'm guessing you'll find this surprising and enlightening."

The envelope feels heavy in my hands, weighted with information that could reshape my understanding of my father-in-law—and of Earl's antagonism toward me.

Chapter Forty-Three

Earl

Steam swirls up from the bowl of soup that Doris made for my lunch. I wheel my mobile chair up to the kitchen table and spread out the *Daily Sentinel,* which I hadn't had time to read before going to this morning's PPS meeting. I search for the article Peggy mentioned, the one about Franklin's appointment to the health board. As my eyes scan the headline, my heart begins to race, my hands trembling against the newsprint. With bile threatening to surge in my throat, I read the short piece and the editorial, too.

Jesus Christ! I sweep my arm across the table in disgust, accidentally knocking my glass of water to the floor with a crash, and slopping soup all over. In seconds, Doris is in from the living room, her face tense with alarm.

"What in God's name—"

"Don't start, Doris. Don't even start."

"But, what—"

I know she won't leave this alone without an answer, so I say a name that I hope will tell her all she needs to know. "It's Tom Franklin."

Her expression changes from agitation to confusion. "The man in your PPS group? The father of—"

"Yeah, the father of that Wilson woman."

"What about him?"

I sigh and gesture to the newspaper that's now soaked with minestrone. "There's an article in there that says he's been named to the county health board."

Whatever else I might say about Doris—and, believe me, after forty-five years of marriage, I have plenty to say about Doris—she's exquisitely attuned to me and knows all my triggers. She knows they're like land mines. She's heard all about Tom Franklin. She knows he sends me into fits of rage. The way he sits there in our group meetings, all high and mighty, pontificating about government and public health. Talking about what "reliable" chemicals we must allow to be pumped into our veins. If we leave things to people like Tom Franklin and his daughter Amy Wilson, we're all doomed.

Doris has been by my side over the years—sometimes literally—as I've researched everything I could find about how and why I got polio. How Walter Ward, Cutter Pharmaceuticals, and their federal government cronies screwed up and shot live polio virus into children across the American West. How they sentenced people like me to a lifetime of paralysis. How they destroyed our futures with their arrogance and negligence.

And she was by my side a few months ago, when I used what Sofia from the PPS group had taught me about genealog-

226

ical research to find out what I could about Amy Wilson's family.

She was by my side the moment I discovered that Amy Wilson is Walter Ward's granddaughter. That Mike Franklin is Walter Ward's son-in-law.

And she was there to get me my nitroglycerin when, the instant of that discovery, my angina flared so severely I thought I was having the big heart attack that would finally carry me away.

You won't understand how I could have such a deep, visceral response to that shocking news—and now, this morning, to this news about Ward's son-in-law being appointed to the county health board—unless I tell you the story. So I will. Let me back up and explain why this matters so much to me. Some truths, after all, demand to be told.

Spring, 1954. The National Foundation for Infantile Paralysis launched what they called the largest human clinical test in medical history—field trials of Jonas Salk's miracle polio vaccine. Over 1.8 million children participated, their parents' hopes riding on every needle. A year later, on April 12, 1955, they declared the vaccine safe with great fanfare. "Powerfully affirmed," they said, as if volume could substitute for vigilance. The shots began flowing immediately.

Two weeks. That's all it took for their house of cards to start crumbling. Five cases of paralytic polio reported in children who'd just received the vaccine. All five had gotten their shots from batches made by Cutter Laboratories in California. The government finally requested Cutter recall their vaccine, and sure, they complied—after the damage was done. The "Cutter Incident," they called it, like it was some minor traffic accident instead of a catastrophe that spread across 25 states, paralyzed 260 people—including me—and killed 11 innocent children.

I was seven years old when that needle went into my arm. Seven years old when the virus they promised would protect me instead stole my legs forever.

And at the center of it all? Walter Ward. As Cutter's director of medical research for human products, his signature touched every step of their polio vaccine production. He reviewed the protocols for growing the virus, examined the graphs showing virus inactivation, supervised all safety tests. Every lot of vaccine and every safety protocol needed his approval. He was the spider at the center of the web, the only person at Cutter who saw the whole picture—and chose to stay silent.

Can you understand that I am trembling—actually shaking with outrage—as I relate this tale to you?

Ward *knew* that Cutter's processes showed a lack of sufficient regard for Jonas Salk's protocols for inactivating the polio virus in the vaccine. He *saw* the evidence that nine out of twenty-seven lots failed safety tests. He *watched* them ignore the problem, sweep it under the rug. And what did he do? *Nothing*. Didn't warn Cutter's executives, didn't alert federal regulators. Just let it happen.

If I'm being generous—and god knows that's hard when it comes to Ward—I'll admit he wasn't the only villain in this tragedy. Take William Workman, director of the U.S. Laboratory of Biologics Control. He suspected the testing protocols weren't up to snuff, ignored warnings from his own staff about flaws in Cutter's process. But Ward? Ward knew everything and chose to do nothing.

So, now, reading in this morning's *Sentinel* that Walter Ward's son-in-law has been named to the county health board, I am so livid I can barely hold the phone as I text Marty Stauffer and Ray Moore to set up a call. The squad has laid low long enough. It's time to revive our campaign—Franklin needs to understand that his family's legacy of medical tyranny won't be tolerated here in Mesa Vista.

WE'VE BEEN on the Signal call for ten minutes already. I'm somehow not making myself understood to Marty.

"If you're so exercised about this connection that Wilson and Franklin have to Ward, why didn't you ever say anything about it before?" Marty asks.

"Because I only discovered it after Dwayne's crash and our decision to lay low."

There was a long pause. Finally, Marty's voice crackled through the phone speaker. "Look, Klover, I'm sorry, but I just don't see how it has any relevance to our concerns about Amy Wilson."

I stare at my phone in disbelief. *No relevance? No fucking relevance! It's not relevant to "our concerns" about Amy Wilson that she's a direct descendant of the man who caused my paralysis? What the actual fuck?! It's sure relevant to my concerns.*

Marty prattles on. "And I don't understand why you're so exercised about Wilson's father getting a seat on the health board. You know that board doesn't really make the decisions.

"Marty," I snarled, "for months I thought Dwayne was the stupidest member of this squad. But you've just taken the trophy from him."

There's a hostile silence until I break it. "Ray, what do you think?"

Ray clears his throat with his usual phlegmy cough, the legacy of too many years of smoking. Then he says, "I'm with you on this, Klover. I think we've laid low plenty long enough. Maybe too long. We were *so close* to pushing Wilson over the edge, Marty. I told you what she said to me that day at my mother's house. And then we stopped."

Marty tries to interject. "Ray—"

"Yeah, yeah. I know we had good reason to stop, Marty. I'm not saying we were wrong to do that. But it's now time to finish what we started."

Marty hems and haws. "But both the school board and the health department have decided that vaccinations will only be recommended, not mandatory. The whole thing's less urgent."

I smile, knowing that was the wrong thing to say to Ray.

Ray's voice is suddenly full of rage. "The school board is still guilty of all this race stuff, Marty. You know that!" He takes a deep breath. I can tell he's trying to calm down. Eventually, he adds, in a lower voice, "And it pisses me off that you don't care about that. Just as I can tell it pisses off Klover that you don't care about Tom Franklin and this whole Ward thing."

Finally, Marty says, "What is it you guys want to do about all this?"

I say, "We need to ramp up the harassment again to finish the job. Drive Amy Wilson out of office. And now Tom Franklin, too."

"Really, Klover? I can't believe this is a high priority for you." The derision in his voice is thick enough to spread on toast.

"Marty! Have you been drinking? What's wrong with you?! You used to be the front line of defense against these statist assholes!"

"I still am, Klover. I am. I just have a lot on my plate at the moment."

Ray jumps in, clearly having hit his limit with Marty's pussyfooting. With a tone that would scare Al Capone, Ray says, "Marty, you're the one who recruited us for this work. You convinced us this is war. A war for the soul of our country, for our freedoms. Now, you want to pack it in because you have *a lot on your plate*?" His voice drips with contempt. "No. We keep going. We keep after these liberal bureaucrats who are threatening our way of life."

"The thing is, without Dwayne, who's gonna do the dirty work?" Marty asks, as if he hasn't heard a thing Ray just said.

I can't believe what I'm hearing. I finally say, "You know what, Marty? Forget it. We'll take care of this ourselves." I jab so hard at the end call button on my phone that I break a fingernail.

Almost immediately, Ray sends me a text: *You're absolutely right. Now is not the time to let up. We're almost there with Wilson. You and I will take care of this.*

Ray's courage and spirit give me a jolt of reinvigoration. *Yes,* I text back. *We keep going until Wilson and her father leave office, broken like Tarrant or dead like Dwayne.*

I stare out the kitchen window, trying to get my heart rate under control. It suddenly hits me that Marty never gave a damn about my polio, probably never cared about vaccines at all. For him, it was just another issue weapon in his culture-war arsenal, another cudgel for bludgeoning liberals.

It was never personal for Marty. Not in the way it is for me. The way it is for Ray.

What I know is that Walter Ward's son-in-law has no business making health policy decisions for Mesa County. If Marty doesn't want to help me with that problem—and help Ray with the Wilson problem—that's okay. Sometimes, to fight monsters, you need other monsters on your side. Other times, you just need to become more of one yourself.

Chapter Forty-Four

Amy

The scent of barbecue smoke drifts across the patio as the sun sinks toward the horizon, spraying the wispy clouds with deep oranges and purples. Will's arm brushes mine as he helps me arrange plates on the outdoor table, while Jack tends to the spareribs on the grill. The tangy lemon meringue pie I made cools on the kitchen counter inside, next to Hannah's potato salad. Dad's documents about my grandfather are scattered across the far end of the table, the pages lifting slightly in the evening breeze.

Will catches my eye and squeezes my hand, sensing my unease about the family revelations. He's been quiet but supportive since I showed him the documents earlier, letting me process this strange piece of family history at my own pace.

"Do you think Mom knew about this?" I ask Dad, settling

into my chair. Will takes the seat beside me, his steady presence grounding me.

Dad's face is thoughtful in the golden light. "I assume not. If she had, I'm sure she would've shared that information with me. I can't imagine she'd keep that to herself."

"Unless she just found it too embarrassing to deal with," I suggest, running my finger along the rim of my wine glass.

"I suppose that's possible." Dad's voice carries a note of uncertainty I rarely hear.

"How do you feel about this? Are you upset?" Will asks, directing the question to both of us.

I consider this, feeling the weight of everyone's attention. "No, I don't think I'd say I'm upset about it. I just find it peculiar and awkward to have this remote association with someone involved with the polio vaccine." My voice sounds steadier than I feel.

Dad leans forward, his elbows on the table. "Same for me. I also feel at a disadvantage now vis-a-vis Earl, this guy in my PPS group who's always clashing with me. He got polio through the Cutter vaccine and is pissed about it. And now he knows of our family connection to all that."

"He knows about Walter?" Jack asks, flipping the ribs with practiced precision.

"Yeah, but his animus toward me was obvious before he found out about Walter." Dad's fingers drum against his glass. "And it has increased over time. He's a very bitter guy. Angry at government, at the political system, at scientists, at pharmaceutical companies. And at me."

Hannah sets down her drink, ice cubes clinking. "You know I'm the last person who'd be sympathetic to someone who is virulently anti-government. But I find myself wondering how I'd feel if I got polio because somebody messed up and distributed vaccines containing live virus. I think I'd be pretty bitter."

The muscles in Dad's jaw tighten visibly. "More bitter than if you got polio because some infected kid at your school sneezed or coughed and you got droplets on your hands and then touched your mouth or breathed in the droplets? More reason to be bitter?"

Will shifts in his chair, and I catch the concerned look he shoots my way. He knows Dad well enough now to recognize when something has struck a nerve.

"More of a *right* to be bitter?" Dad's voice has that careful precision that signals his irritation.

Hannah sets her glass down with deliberate care. "Tom, it's not a contest. I have led a charmed life, so what the hell do I know? I can't fathom how *anyone* afflicted with a dread disease doesn't become bitter and angry. But *you* didn't. And that's greatly to your credit."

The tension in the air is palpable until Hannah continues, "I guess all I'm saying is that maybe people who know exactly how they got some horrible virus react differently from people who got the same virus but don't know how they contracted it. Maybe the former are more prone to anger and bitterness. Possible?"

I watch the stiffness slowly leave Dad's shoulders. His face softens into a grin. "I see what you're saying. And, yes, I suppose that's possible."

"They say knowledge is power," I interject, grateful for the lightening mood. "And they say power corrupts. So, by some mathematical property I no longer can name, you could say knowledge can corrupt. In this case, this guy's knowledge of how he contracted polio has really warped or twisted his brain. He's become corrupted—infected, contaminated—by his knowledge."

Will nods thoughtfully. "Like a feedback loop of bitterness," he adds, and I squeeze his hand under the table, grateful for his support.

Dad beams at us both. To the others, he says, "That's my smart baby girl and her equally smart boyfriend talkin' right there."

Jack raises his glass to me. "Are you a beaver? Because, dam."

Hannah snorts, nearly choking on her drink. "Oh, good god, Jack. I bet that's a pickup line you've used on women for years."

Jack springs to his feet with theatrical indignation, almost knocking over the bottle of wine Will brought. "I was just trying to compliment my amazing niece. And I don't need pickup lines, Hannah. I'm naturally charismatic and alluring. But I do have a repertoire of put-downs I've used for years on judgmental people like you. Want to hear some of them?"

Hannah's eyes sparkle with mischief. "Hit me with 'em, you sleazy geezer."

"Try these on for size, Miss Deputy Director."

Dad groans and drags his palm down his face. "No, please, Jack, no. For the love of god, no." But I can see a smile trying to break through.

Jack assumes an exaggerated pose, hands clutching invisible

lapels, chin tilted skyward. *"Are you always such an idiot, or do you just show off when I'm around?"*

"Ooooohhhh," Matt says appreciatively, nearly knocking over his soda in his enthusiasm.

Will leans close to whisper in my ear, "Is your uncle always this ... theatrical?" His amused breath tickles my neck.

"Just wait," I whisper back. "It gets better."

Jack winks at Matt. *"Sorry, I don't understand what you're saying. I don't speak bullshit."*

Matt howls with laughter, and Dad's attempt at disapproval crumbles completely.

"The Jerk Store called. They said they're all out of ... you."

Now, we're all laughing, the earlier tension completely forgotten. Will's shoulders shake next to mine as he joins in.

"If ignorance is bliss, you must be the happiest person on the planet."

Matt's practically crying with laughter.

Dad wipes tears from his eyes. "Oh, my god, Jack. Just stop."

"Just one more, dear brother." Jack turns to Matt. "Drum roll, please, my good man."

Matt produces a surprisingly authentic drum-roll sound from his mouth.

Jack clears his throat with theatrical flair, then delivers his coup de grâce: *"Look, if I wanted to hear from an asshole, all I had to do was fart."*

Matt collapses in helpless giggles, and my dignified, intellectual father is laughing so hard he's silent, shoulders bouncing as he claps like an overexcited seal. With the smell of slightly charred ribs floating overhead, Will wraps an arm around my shoulders as we watch my family's antics.

Chapter Forty-Five

Amy

Having promised Matty I'd grocery shop on my way home from my OT appointment, I navigate the aisles at Sprouts, trying hard to remember what he told me he wanted me to pick up. Seems like several times a day, Matt lobs a reminder at me about whatever he fears he's running low on— potato chips, peaches, ice cream, Goldfish, cheese sticks ... Mind you, he's seldom actually running low. It's the fear he'll be without comfort snacks that matters.

The supermarket is oddly quiet for mid-afternoon, my footsteps seeming too loud against the polished floors. I've been here maybe seven minutes when my phone rings. The screen reads "Unknown Caller." Those assholes who tormented me in the fall used burner phones that showed up that way. But I haven't received a call like that in months.

I know I shouldn't answer it. But I do.

"I'm watching you." The male voice slides through the speaker like oil. It sounds familiar somehow.

Ice water floods my veins. "Who is this? Why are you doing this? What do you want?"

"I just want to watch you." His breath catches with something like pleasure. "You're in the baking and spices aisle at Sprouts. You're wearing dark jeans and a light blue sweater. Looks like soft cashmere. Very nice, Amy. I bet you'd be huggable—maybe even fuckable—if you weren't such a bitch. Does that black boyfriend of yours fuck you, Amy? Does he bend you over your kitchen counter and slam into you from behind?"

My heart hammers against my ribs as I scan the store, spinning in place. The spice bottles blur into a kaleidoscope of colors. I only see two men, both focused on their work behind the meat counter. Then I realize the aisle I'm in is visible from the parking lot. The voice continues to slither through the phone, but I terminate the call, my finger shaking as it hits the screen.

The grocery list in my hand has become a crumpled mess. I grab what I need with mechanical movements, constantly looking over my shoulder. The checkout feels endless, each beep of the scanner marking another moment I'm exposed. In the parking lot, I scan the area and see no one, no drivers sitting in their cars. Nothing suspicious. It seems whoever it was is gone. But my keys leave marks in my palm from gripping them so tightly.

The drive home is a blur of checking mirrors, looking for vehicles that follow too long. I see no one, but the feeling of being watched clings to me like a second skin.

At home, I pull into the driveway, scanning the street one last time before gathering the grocery bags. The familiar routine should be comforting, but the caller's words still echo in my head, making everything feel off-kilter.

A sharp yelp from the backyard freezes me mid-step. I drop the bags and run toward the sound, my heart in my throat. Annabelle lies in the grass, her massive body wracked with spasms, foam gathering at the corners of her mouth. Next to her, half-eaten chunks of raw meat scatter the ground like evidence at a crime scene.

"Oh god, no no no." I fall to my knees beside her, hands hovering helplessly over her convulsing form. Her eyes roll wildly, unfocused and terrified. The smell of vomit mingles with something chemical—something wrong.

I fumble for my phone, dialing the emergency vet with trembling fingers. As I wait for someone to pick up, movement catches my eye. Looking up, I see Matt's bedroom window has been shattered—again!—the curtains fluttering at the broken pane.

The voice on the phone snaps me back: "Valley Emergency Veterinary Clinic."

"Please," I choke out, one hand buried in Annabelle's fur. "Someone's poisoned my dog. They threw meat into my yard. She's having seizures. I need help."

"Get her here immediately. Do you need the address?"

"No, I know where you are." I end the call and struggle to lift Annabelle's deadweight. She's too heavy—I can't do this alone.

My phone is already dialing Jack even before I consciously decide to do so. "I need you," I say when he answers. "Someone's poisoned Annabelle and broken into the house. Please come. Please hurry."

As I wait, holding Annabelle's head in my lap, trying to soothe her tremors, I realize this is different from the previous harassment. This isn't just about frightening me anymore. They're escalating—moving from threats to action, from property damage to causing real harm. And they're targeting the ones I love.

What terrifies me most isn't the violence of it, but the calculation. The careful staging: the phone call to establish they were watching, the poisoned meat, the rock through Matt's window. Each piece designed to show me nowhere is safe—not the grocery store, not my yard, not even my son's bedroom.

I press my face into Annabelle's fur, breathing in her familiar scent beneath the acrid smell of poison, and wonder how much more of this I can take.

Chapter Forty-Six

Hannah

The sunlight slants through my office window at a low angle this time of year. It catches the figure of John Kirby, who stands in my doorway. No greeting. No small talk. His face is grave as he steps inside and closes the door with a soft click that sounds like trouble.

"Somebody tipped off Gloria Snyder at *The Sentinel* about you and Tom being romantic partners. They're running the story tomorrow and want the agency's comment."

I feel my spine stiffen but keep my expression neutral. We'd prepared for this moment, had known it was coming. Some people get their kicks from manufacturing drama out of other people's happiness, finding scandal in the mundane. The Venn diagram between gossipmongers and troublemakers is basically a circle.

"We already talked about this, John," I say, my voice steady.

"Just tell the *Sentinel* what we worked up in advance: there's nothing improper; no supervisory or direct work relationship; the county attorney cleared it; it's a nothing-burger."

"I know. And that's what we will say." He shifts his weight, and I notice the newspaper tucked under his arm. "I'm not worried or upset about this. I'm only here to let you know that it will be in the paper. Didn't want you to be taken by surprise."

"Thanks. That's considerate. I appreciate you."

"But there's a more urgent reason why I'm here." There's something in his voice that makes my stomach clench.

I look up from the stack of reports on my desk.

"Did you see today's *New York Times*?" he asks.

"Not yet. Why?"

He unfolds the paper like he's handling evidence at a crime scene. "A young man in Rockland County, just outside New York City, went to the hospital two months ago. Stiff neck, pain in his back and abdomen, gradual weakening of his leg muscles." He pauses, and I can see him steeling himself. "Lab tests confirmed it was polio."

The word hits me like a physical blow. "Really? That's highly unlikely." My mind races through the statistics—three known polio cases in the U.S. in twenty years, all cases imported.

"I know. But here's where it gets worse." John leans against my desk, his shoulders tight. "CDC, New York health department, Rockland County—they all jumped on it. Started testing wastewater. Found the polio virus had been circulating in Rockland since May. Then they found it in Orange County. And New York City."

"Oh, god." The implications unfold in my mind like a

nightmare origami. Thousands of infected people, most protected by vaccines but serving as unwitting carriers. The unvaccinated walking through an invisible minefield where one in two hundred of them could become paralyzed.

And Rockland County—my brain connects the dots before John can lay them out. Ultra-Orthodox Jewish communities. Rock-bottom vaccination rates. A perfect storm that's been brewing for years.

I push back from my desk, needing to move. "The anti-vaccine groups targeted them deliberately, you know. They're smart—they look for communities with strong values about bodily purity and personal liberty. It's not just Orthodox Jews. It's Amish communities in Ohio and Pennsylvania. Somali refugees in Minnesota." I pause by the window, watching the morning traffic crawl past. "Hell, you even see the same patterns in some wealthy liberal enclaves in Marin County and Portland."

The irony would be amusing if it weren't so dangerous. "A whole generation of parents who've never seen these diseases firsthand. They're more afraid of the vaccines than they are of the viruses because the vaccines did such a good job of getting rid of the diseases." I turn to my computer, intending to pull up the *Times* article, but the damn machine is going through some update sequence. I turn back to John. "My computer's updating —what does the *Times* say about the source? Those cases in Jerusalem and London were vaccine-derived."

"This one was, too. Genetic testing confirms it. Someone brought it in from abroad, probably had no idea they were carrying it."

I press my fingers to my temples. "The media's going to have a field day with this. Just what we need—more fuel for the anti-vax fire."

John slumps against the wall, looking suddenly older. I can read the weight of responsibility in every line of his face. Covid still raging, mpox spreading, and now polio rising from its grave like some medical zombie. Being a county public health director these days is like juggling chainsaws while walking a tightrope.

"I'm sorry, Hannah, but there's more." His voice is heavy with fatigue. "CDPHE just sent the latest mpox numbers. We're at 157 cases statewide."

The numbers march through my head for each of the previous three months—2, then 6, then, 74. Now 157. The exponential curve makes my chest tight. "What's our count in Mesa County?"

His wince tells me everything before he speaks. "Eight. All here in Mesa Vista. Seven at CMU."

The numbers hit me like body blows. Seven cases on campus. "Jesus, John. We need to move. Fast."

The rest of the afternoon becomes a blur of crisis management—the kind of coordinated chaos that public health departments handle best. Setting up testing protocols, contact tracing, vaccine distribution. Careful outreach to gay organizations at CMU and in the community, walking the delicate line between alerting and alarming, informing without stigmatizing.

By the time I push open our front door at home that evening, my shoulders feel weighted with lead. Usually, Annabelle is the first to greet me. Tonight, it's Tom, waiting with a hug and a perfectly chilled martini.

"God. I need a little more of both," I murmur into his shoulder.

His chuckle rumbles against my cheek. "Neither is in short supply."

"Praise the Lord." I sink onto the couch, the leather cool against my back. I'm surprised that Annabelle's not already here, shoving her velvet muzzle under my arm with enough enthusiasm to splash Tanqueray across my skirt.

"Where's my Bellie girl?" I call, laughing as I anticipate Belle bounding into the room. "Bellie want some Tanqueray? Bellie's a gin girl. Yes, she is. A good gin girl. Bellie, Bellie, Bellie!"

Tom gently eases himself onto the couch beside me, his movements careful in the way they always are by day's end. He takes my hand and says, "I have some bad news. Annabelle is sick ... but the vet thinks she'll be okay." And then he explains that the nightmare has resumed.

Chapter Forty-Seven

Ray

The past couple weeks have been like waking from a bad dream. Lying low after Dwayne's death had felt like surrender—something that goes against everything I believe. But now, I'm back in the fight, and it feels fucking glorious.

I check my secure Signal app to find a new text from Klover: *"Ding dong, the witch is rattled."*

I smirk, leaning back in my chair, savoring the moment. Klover's been relentless in his own way. His radio broadcasts are reaching more patriots than ever, and his new, more vigorous doxxing campaign has gathered momentum like a boulder rolling downhill. He did something last night he hadn't done before—shared Wilson's number with his listeners—hardcore types who know what to do without explicit instructions. My phone pings with another message: *"Sent an ambulance to Wilson's house today. Gave me such satisfaction."*

I laugh out loud. Emergency-services swatting is elegant in its simplicity—anonymous calls, impossible to trace, draining resources while making Wilson look unhinged. We'll keep it up, and eventually, the services will stop responding so quickly. Then she'll be truly vulnerable.

And that GPS tracker has continued to be a goldmine. I know when Wilson's at work, when she's shopping, when she's meeting her boyfriend. Knowledge is power, and we hold all the cards now. Watching her become increasingly paranoid, constantly looking over her shoulder, has been deeply satisfying.

Don't I feel bad about it sometimes? Hell, no. People like her, like her father, have been destroying this country for years while claiming it's for our own good. They force their "protections" on us whether we want them or not. They divide communities with their equity bullshit and gender politics. They undermine parental authority, corrupt our children, and then have the fucking audacity to act surprised when we push back.

This isn't some political game—it's war for the soul of America. Wilson and her father are casualties in that war, collateral damage in a battle that's much bigger than them.

With Dwayne gone, I've had to step up. The poisoned meat for the dog and the rock through the kid's window were my doing—a message that nothing's safe, no matter how precious to her. And no place is safe. Not the grocery store, not the car, not the house, not even their kid's bedroom. I've watched enough horror movies to know that true fear comes from the knowledge that danger could be anywhere, anytime. Wilson needs to understand that this will keep happening to her—life will be a living hell—until she leaves office.

My phone buzzes again—another text from Klover: *"Love having Tom Franklin in our sights now, too."*

Makes total sense to me. I'd never understood Klover's anger about vaccinations. But I finally got it when he told me all about Walter Ward and how his negligence at Cutter Laboratories sentenced Klover to a life of paralysis and pain. Ward's not around to pay for that sin. But his son-in-law's right here. In our town. Why shouldn't he be made to pay?

I pause my train of thought to focus on my next move. Tonight, I'll make another round of anonymous calls to Wilson's number. Nothing explicit—just enough heavy breathing to keep her on edge. Maybe I'll drive by her house later, too. There's something primal about stalking your prey, watching them, knowing where they are.

As I sit in my darkened trailer, watching occasional headlights from the highway sweep across my ceiling, I think about Wilson and her father. I think about how they must feel right now—scared, isolated, helpless. I think about the constant tension of waiting for the next attack, never knowing when or where it might come from.

And I smile.

We're going to break them both, one piece at a time. And when we're done, when they're finally driven out, we'll move on to the next battle. Because this war won't end with Amy Wilson or Tom Franklin. It will only end when America is restored to its rightful place—when people like me are back in control.

I drain my beer and reach for my phone. Time to rattle the witch.

Chapter Forty-Eight

Tom

The church basement's garish lights cast their usual unflattering glow as I wheel in late to the PPS meeting, the last to arrive. My damn car chose this morning to play dead, forcing me to call Jack for a ride. These meetings feel more like an obligation than a necessity these days, but I can't bring myself to abandon them completely. Some of these people have become genuine friends—particularly Sofia. I like and respect her and am beholden to her for all the useful information she gave me. But looking now at Earl's scowling face across the circle, I'm reminded why these gatherings sometimes feel like an exercise in patience.

Minnie's gentle voice fills the room as she discusses how each of us needs to conserve our energy, her silver hair catching the light. "We have to pace our physical activity and rest frequently to reduce muscle fatigue. And if you can get physical therapy, that's great. It's important to find exercises that can strengthen your muscles without fatiguing them." Her face brightens with a smile that makes her look decades younger. "I consider myself really lucky that I can do water aerobics."

The conversation drifts to pain management, a compare-and-contrast of various over-the-counter pills that have people nodding in recognition at familiar names. Several voices rise in praise of gabapentin, sharing stories of how it's helped with both nerve pain and the depression that often accompanies chronic conditions.

Then, like a storm cloud passing overhead and blocking the sun, the mood shifts. I feel it coming before anyone speaks—the inevitable discussion of the New York polio outbreak. Peggy, sweet and naive, voices what many are thinking: "I just don't see how this can happen in this day and age with the availability of vaccines."

Earl pounces so fast Peggy's head spins. "It's the damn vaccines that are responsible!" His voice carries the triumphant tone of someone who's been waiting all morning to spring this trap.

Peggy physically recoils, her hand flying to her throat. "What do you mean, Earl? What are you talking about?"

Earl's eye roll and body twist remind me of when Amy was in the most dramatic phase of her teenage years. Horrid. "Jesus Christ, Peggy!" he says. "Do you ever read beyond the headlines? If you did, you'd know that the original source of the virus that's spreading in New York—and in London and Jerusalem—is the vaccine itself!"

Sally's nose wrinkles like she's caught a whiff of something rancid. "What are you saying, Earl?" She draws out his name like it's a curse word that she's trying not to fully pronounce.

"I'm saying the viruses detected in all three countries are 'vaccine-derived,'" Earl's fingers make aggressive air quotes, "meaning that they're mutated versions of a virus that originated in the oral vaccine. It's basically what happened to me." He slaps his unresponsive legs. "People have been given a form of the live virus and now they're dying or suffering paralysis. It's confirmation of what I've been trying to tell you people all along: vaccines are dangerous!"

Steve leans forward, his usually peaceful face hardening. "Earl, I think that's not the right lesson to take from this outbreak."

"Oh, really, why not?" Earl's voice drips with contempt.

What follows is a masterclass in patience, as Steve explains the difference between the injectable vaccine used in the U.S. and the oral vaccine, used around much of the world because it's cheap and easy to administer. "Unlike the injectable, that oral vaccine contains a weakened form of the live virus. What's happened in this case is that the weakened virus has mutated into a more dangerous form and sparked outbreaks, especially in places with poor sanitation and low vaccination levels."

"Okay, smart guy. Then how does it end up in the United States?"

Now, when Steve replies, there's a level of contempt in his own voice that matches Earl's. "If *you* read beyond the headlines, you'd know that the kind of outbreak that has occurred in New York typically begins when people who've been vaccinated shed live virus from the vaccine in their feces. From there, the virus can spread within the community and, over time, turn into a form that can paralyze people and start new epidemics. That's why public-health officials are alarmed about this." He turns to me. "Am I correct in what I've said, Tom?"

I smile, grateful for his precise explanation. "You gave a perfect summary of the situation, Steve."

"Oh, god, now Mr. Let's-Vaccinate-Everyone-For-Everything is entering the discussion." Earl's voice rises an octave with mock horror.

The explosion is sudden and simultaneous. David and Sonia, who've been sitting in tight-lipped silence, erupt like a pair of synchronized volcanoes:

"Oh, be quiet, Earl. You're—"

"Earl, you are so ill-mannered!"

"—a real pain in the ass. You don't have a decent bone in your body. I, for one—"

"You don't know how to engage in civil conversation."

"—don't want to hear another word from you."

When the dust settles, I force my voice into neutral territory, a measured tone. "Earl, it is you—not I—who has positioned himself as a vaccine expert. And, unfortunately for you, the facts of this case belie your beliefs about vaccines. The area of New York that's in jeopardy from this outbreak is in danger precisely *because* the people in those communities have refused to get their children vaccinated against polio. In areas with high vaccination rates, there's no danger at all."

Then Minnie—tiny, gentle Minnie, who probably apologizes to houseplants when she prunes them—delivers the coup de grâce: "Earl, I urge you to take in those facts Tom just offered you. But I think you'll have to shove them up your ass, because your brain is clearly already full of shit."

The stunned silence that follows is absolute. Then, like a dam breaking, laughter erupts. From all except Earl, who sits rigid in his power chair, his face darkening to match the crimson of its cushion. His arms cross over his chest as he surveys the room, jaw working silently. Without a word, he powers up his chair and flees, the door slamming behind him with a hollow bang that echoes in the basement.

Minnie's hands flutter to her cheeks. "My goodness, I don't know what came over me. I don't think I've ever spoken to someone like that in my life."

The rest of the meeting dissolves into a post-mortem of Earl's behavior. Outside, everyone else already having departed, I wait for Jack in the empty parking lot, my mind elsewhere. watching autumn leaves skitter across the pavement. Jack's Mustang announces its arrival with a roar, executing a sliding 180-degree turn on the gravel that shows off both his skill and his complete lack of adult judgment.

He pops the trunk for my walker, grinning like a teenager who's just stolen his dad's car. "I've still got it, eh? A far better driver than you."

"We'll never know. I don't compete in the 'Dumb Asshole' division."

"Is that any way to greet your chauffeur?"

"I don't know how you've lived as long as you have. Between the way you drive and your propensity for Laphroaig, you should have been dead years ago."

"Laphroaig is the only thing that has kept me alive. And you're not exactly Mr. Carrie Nation yourself."

"True. In fact, I could use a drink and a sandwich right now. You have time?"

"Yup."

"Let's go to Marley's."

As we head into town, I recount the morning's drama. Jack's response surprises me: "So, this Earl left the meeting early?"

"Yeah, he was really pissed."

"Do you know what kind of car he drives?"

The question seems odd, but I answer: "Yeah. A silver, side-entry wheelchair van. A Ford Explorer, I think. Why do you ask?"

Jack's face takes on the focused expression I recognize from his investigative days. He says, "When I was driving out of the parking lot this morning after dropping you off, I noticed that van. It has the license plate 'KL3VR. The van wasn't there when I came back to get you at the end of the meeting."

Something in his tone makes me sit up straighter. "That's definitely Earl's van. What would make you notice the van and its license plate?"

"The tag rang a bell. I went home and looked through my notes. Just as I thought, someone with the handle K3LVR was one of the people posting lots of shit on the internet about Amy .I suspected him at the time of being one of the ringleaders behind the initial round of doxxing, but I couldn't find a way to discover who the person was. It was a lead that went cold."

The pieces click into place with an almost audible snap. "Well, I'd say it's not cold anymore. His first name is Earl, but I don't know his last name. We don't use last names at the PPS group."

Jack's fingers tap the steering wheel thoughtfully. "I'll call one of my friends in the state patrol. He'll run the license plate.

We'll get Earl's full name and address. And then we should be able to get other information about him, too. It was a lucky break that your car didn't work this morning and you needed me to take you to the meeting. We might never have put two and two together otherwise."

As we pull into Marley's parking lot, Jack adds: "Is there anything else you can tell me about this guy?"

I think back through our meetings. "At one session, people talked about their hobbies. Earl said he uses the internet, especially social media, to 'educate people about their governmental oppressors. And he runs a ham radio station where he does the same thing."

"Really?" Jack's eyebrows rise. "I wonder if K3LVR is his ham-radio call sign. I bet it is. If so, we'll have to figure out how to tune in to find out the kind of thing he says."

"I have a pretty good sense of the kind of thing he says." The morning's confrontation replays in my mind. "But I agree. We should do that. Right now, though, I need that Laphroaig."

As we head into the restaurant, I can't shake the feeling that what started as a simple support group confrontation has just opened up into something much darker. The coincidence of my car breaking down has helped pull back the curtain on the identity of one of the people still harassing my daughter.

Chapter Forty-Nine

Jack

My state-cop friend's text about the K3LVR license plate hits my phone at 3 AM. I'm already awake, nursing a glass of scotch and staring at my laptop screen. Finally, a name to go with the poison pen. Earl Phillips, age 73.

The scotch burns my throat as I start digging. Dawn creeps in through my study windows, painting my walls the color of old bruises as I follow digital breadcrumbs. The official footprint of "Earl Phillips" is surprisingly small for a man who's spent seven decades on Earth. Former accountant. No civil suits. No criminal record. Clean as fresh snow—on paper.

But "K3LVR"? That's another story entirely.

I crack my knuckles and dive deeper, methodically working through K3LVR's social media presence. Instagram. Twitter. Parler. Each platform reveals another layer of hate, like peeling back the skin of an onion made of pure bile. I've seen the older posts before—they're burned into my memory from when Amy was being targeted before. But there's a lot of new content to wade through.

My old friend Derek from the cyber crimes unit in Denver has walked me through accessing the darker corners of the web where K3LVR really lets his freak flag fly. The stuff I find there makes his social media posts look like nursery rhymes. By hour four, my eyes are burning and my soul feels like it needs fumigation. I pour another finger of scotch, but it doesn't wash away the taste of what I've been reading.

Fifteen years of working cases has taught me what a prosecutor needs to make charges stick. K3LVR wasn't clever enough—his digital fingerprints are all over the doxxing campaign. He fired up a little army of keyboard warriors. The evidence against him in Amy's case is solid. Maybe not absolutely iron-clad, but close.

I should feel satisfied. This is what I've been looking for—ammunition to bring some justice to bear against the people who harassed Amy.

Instead, my stomach churns as I click through his most recent posts.

"Longtime Bureaucrat Noses Into County's Health," screams one headline, accompanied by a grainy photo of Tom, clearly taken without his knowledge.

"Tom Franklin, Father of School-Board Nazi, Wants to Control Your Body," declares another, this one featuring a poorly photoshopped image of Tom in a Nazi uniform.

"Beware of New County Health Board Despot," comes with a rambling manifesto about government overreach and medical tyranny.

My hand tightens around the glass. Going after Amy was bad enough. But attacking Tom? My brother has spent his entire life trying to help people, working through his own challenges to make sure others don't have to suffer like he did. After everything he's been through, he doesn't deserve to have this snake targeting him.

I slam the glass against the desktop, sloshing scotch over the rim. This isn't just about gathering evidence anymore. If K3LVR thinks he can come after my family like this, he's about to learn a harsh lesson about consequences—and that there are worse things than government overreach. Like having a pissed-off former cop with nothing better to do dismantle your life piece by piece.

I pull up a blank document and start organizing the evidence I've collected about Earl, my fingers striking the keys with military precision. The last of the scotch burns going down, but not as much as the anger burning in my gut. Family is everything. And nobody messes with mine

Chapter Fifty

Amy

The floodgates of harassment have fully reopened.

Yesterday started early with Engine 4 from the Mesa Vista Fire Department screaming up our street, followed by two ladder trucks and the chief's SUV. They'd received a report of smoke pouring from our basement windows. As the firefighters searched the house in full gear, I stood on our front lawn in my bathrobe, arms wrapped around myself against the morning chill, watching neighbors peek through curtains at the commotion.

Three hours later, an ambulance responded to a call about my father having a stroke. The EMTs found him calmly reading the newspaper in his favorite chair, bewildered by their arrival. Late afternoon, three police cruisers converged on our house—someone had reported hearing gunshots and a woman screaming. Each time, I had to explain that we were victims of false reports. Each time, I watched the responders' faces shift from concern to frustration to barely concealed anger at having their time wasted.

The pattern was clear: someone wanted to make us feel vulnerable while exhausting the goodwill of emergency services. The strategy was working on both counts. After the third incident, I heard one of the younger officers mutter something about "crying wolf" as he left.

The hospital administration wasn't any more sympathetic when they called me in this morning. Dr. Reeves, head of rehabilitation services, sat behind his desk with three manila folders laid out before him like tarot cards predicting my doom. "These complaints are ... troubling, Amy." His eyes wouldn't quite meet mine as he detailed the allegations: deliberately causing a stroke patient to fall, ignoring safety protocols with an elderly client, roughly handling a child with cerebral palsy.

"That's ridiculous," I protested. "Check the documentation. Ask my colleagues. Ask the patients themselves!"

"We *are* investigating," he said carefully. "But you understand we have to take such accusations seriously." The unspoken message was clear: where there's smoke, people assume fire. My carefully built professional reputation was being smeared by invisible hands.

Now I sit in our darkened living room, my laptop's screen casting shadows on the wall as I obsessively check our security camera feeds. At exactly 9:47 PM, all six cameras went dark simultaneously, their feeds replaced by error messages. The security company claims there are no technical issues on their end. Someone has blinded our electronic eyes and ears, leaving us vulnerable in the growing dark.

These people have the ability to take control of our security system. That explains why the cameras didn't catch any sign of someone poisoning Annabelle and throwing the rock through Matty's window. The system was one of the few things that helped make us feel safer. Knowing now that they can hijack it with the ease of flipping a switch feels like a betrayal and adds to our feeling of vulnerability. I check the feed again. Still nothing.

Matt appears in the doorway, his pale face ghostly in the blue glow of the phone he holds in front of him. He looks younger suddenly, more vulnerable, like the little boy who used to crawl into my bed during thunderstorms. "Mom? I got another one." He holds his phone out to me, his hand trembling slightly. The message is simple but devastating: "Ask your mom if you're worth it."

I pull him close, feeling his heart hammer against my ribs. The scent of his shampoo brings back memories of easier days —bath times and bedtime stories, skinned knees and "monster checks" under the bed. Now the monsters are real, and I don't know how to fight them. "I'm so sorry, baby. So sorry." The words feel useless, inadequate against this rising tide of terror.

A sharp sound from the backyard makes us both jump. Probably just Annabelle chasing raccoons, but we can't be sure. We can't be sure of anything anymore. Every creak could be a footstep, every shadow a threat.

Dad shuffles into the room. "We should call Jack," he says quietly.

I shake my head, though the temptation to lean on my uncle's strength is almost overwhelming. "He's already doing everything he can." My voice cracks. "They're trying to make us feel like nowhere is safe."

"They won't succeed." Dad's hand finds mine in the darkness, his grip still strong despite everything the years have taken from him. "We're stronger than they know."

But as another unseen sound makes Matt flinch against me, I wonder if that's true. The walls feel like they're closing in, every shadow holding potential threats. Our home has become a fortress under siege, and I don't know how much longer we can hold out.

Chapter Fifty-One

Jack

The ham radio receiver sits on my desk like a piece of evidence, its vintage dials and meters a window into Earl's twisted world. Two hundred bucks at the secondhand electronics store, and suddenly I'm privy to Mesa County's underground frequency of hate. I may be a total doofus when it comes to amateur radio, but I've got buddies who aren't. That's my superpower—being just "likable enough" (as Obama described Hillary) to maintain a network of people who'll give me a hand when I need it.

My cop friend Rick, also a radio enthusiast, had smirked when he saw K3LVR's call sign. "He's showing off," he'd said, adjusting the frequency dial with practiced precision. "Telling his ham-radio pals that he's a lover of the K3 transceiver from Elecraft. High-end equipment. Your boy Earl wants everyone to know he's got the fancy toys."

In the week since I started listening, I've discovered that amateur radio makes the darknet look tame. Earl's voice crackles through my speakers at all hours, a fountain of bile spewing into the airwaves around Mesa Vista. He's got opinions about everything—college football, the space program, Chinese food —but it's when he turns to politics and public health that the real poison flows.

Tonight, I sit in my darkened study, tape recorder running, as Earl launches into another tirade about "the great vaccine con." The ice in my scotch has long since melted, forgotten as I document his ramblings. His logic isn't always coherent—the who and why behind his grand conspiracy theories shift like desert sand—but the hatred in his voice comes through crystal clear.

"They want to push their needles into your body, like the Roman bureaucrats who pressed that crown of thorns down on the brow of Jesus Christ," he growls, and I resist the urge to go shower off the metaphor.

The guest segments are worse. "Raymond," a regular caller whose voice drips with malice, spins theories about vaccines being weapons in some "Great Replacement" plot. My pen scratches across my notepad as he elaborates: "White women are being sterilized through vaccines, and white men are being injected with carcinogens that will lead to death. Anyone who agrees to be vaccinated is an idiot."

Earl's voice cuts in, feeding off Raymond's energy: "And now, right as their government-hyped Covid hysteria is dying down, they find another reason to vaccinate you—mpox. Don't fall for it, people. Don't fall for their great, evil hoax!"

My hand tightens around my glass as he shifts targets.

"Right here in Mesa County, we have to worry about Hannah Matthews, the deputy director of the county health department. And, of course, her loverboy, Tom Franklin, whom she managed to get appointed to the board that oversees her office!"

Then come the phone numbers, Earl's voice rising with malicious glee as he encourages his listeners to harass Hannah and Tom. The threats he suggests make my stomach turn, but I keep recording. Each word is another nail in his coffin.

Interesting that he's keeping this off the internet, I think, noting the time and date. Earl probably figures radio leaves no digital fingerprints. He doesn't realize he's got an audience member who's collecting evidence instead of inspiration.

But recorded proof of his broadcasts isn't enough. I need more, and I know how to get it. As dusk settles over Mesa County, I drive out to Canyon Creek Drive in the Redlands, where the hills rise up west of town. Earl's residence announces itself before I see the house number—that radio tower must be seventy feet tall, a metal finger pointing accusingly at the sky. From this hilltop perch, his signal can reach every bitter, paranoid soul in the valley.

The GPS tracker feels heavy in my pocket as I park down the street, waiting for full darkness. The street is quiet, just crickets and the occasional distant coyote. Earl's silver van sits in his driveway like a sleeping beast. One minute. That's all I need.

My boots make no sound on the asphalt as I approach. The tracker attaches easily underneath the van—I've done this enough times to know all the best spots. As I straighten up, the tower looms above me, silhouetted against the stars. All that hate, broadcast from this peaceful hilltop.

Driving home, I check my phone. The tracker's signal

comes through strong and clear. Now it's just a matter of following Earl's movements, building a complete picture of his activities. He thinks he's safe behind his microphone, spreading poison through the airwaves. He has no idea he's giving me exactly what I need to bring him down.

The night air coming through my car window carries the scent of sage and juniper. Somewhere out there, Earl's voice probably churns through that same air, but his days of spreading hate are numbered. I've learned patience in my years of investigation. The evidence builds, piece by piece, until there's nowhere left to hide.

Let him keep talking. Every word brings him closer to consequences.

Chapter Fifty-Two

Jack

As it turns out, Earl doesn't go out much. From what I've seen so far, he mostly just goes to the grocery store or drug store. But right now, I'm a few cars behind him as he winds his way out of the hills and onto Rt. 6. When he pulls into IHOP's parking lot, I ease into a spot with a clear view of his van. The hydraulic whir of his wheelchair lift breaks the dawn quiet as his scooter descends to the pavement.

Inside, the lights over each table battle the grey morning pressing against the windows. A rail-thin woman with silver hair escorts Earl to a table near the door, showing him where to park his power chair. When she turns to seat me, I request a booth deeper in the restaurant, positioning myself where I can watch Earl without being obvious about it.

I've only been there a minute or so, when a voice greets me.

"Been standing over there wracking my brain trying to

remember how I know you. ... Finally hit me—you're that fella who came in late last summer wearing a 'Grandpas for Liberty' t-shirt. With that handsome guy who had a walker." Becky Dubrovsky fills my coffee mug with practiced precision, though a few drops escape onto the formica tabletop.

I slip into my Texas drawl like a comfortable pair of boots. "Why, you sure are right about that, Miss, uh, Miss ... Becky! That's it. Miss Becky! Told you I'd never forget that pretty face of yours, and dang it, I didn't."

She giggles, her uniform fitting looser than I remember. "You sure didn't. And I didn't forget your name either, Jack. Same as my first boyfriend." She actually bats her eyelashes at me, and I hide my amusement behind my coffee mug. "And I even remember what we talked about—that awful Amy Wilson woman and who might have been vandalizing her property. Right?"

"Why, I reckon you're correct about that, Miss Becky. You're right as rain!"

She takes my order to the kitchen, and when she returns she asks me why I'm so interested in "Mr. Grumps."

"Who?"

"The guy you've been keepin' a close eye on."

I grin. "Why *Mr. Grumps*?"

"He's one of the crabbiest people I've ever waited on. And that pair of 'em—him and the depressed, greasy skeleton he's with—have been coming in here regularly for a year or so." Leaning close enough that I catch a whiff of vanilla perfume, Becky confides, "Our other name for Mr. Grumps is 'Grabby Paws,' because he's a big-time fondler."

"Anybody else ever with them?"

"Used to be two others who joined them, but those two stopped coming."

"You know any real names?"

"One of the ones who stopped coming was Marty Stauffer. I remember mentioning him to you when you was in here before."

"What about Grabby's current tablemate? Know his name?"

"Actually, I know his first name. Ray." She glances at Earl's table. "Grabby Paws always orders for him—'Bring my friend Ray some orange juice,' or 'Ray needs his coffee refreshed.'"

The name clicks into place like a puzzle piece. Ray—the same Raymond from Earl's radio broadcasts, spewing theories about vaccine conspiracies and race replacement. The web of connections grows tighter.

When Becky returns with my Denver omelet, I steer the conversation toward the missing fourth member. Her description paints a picture of Dwayne that's unmistakable—huge, bald, damaged ear, uneven gait, sloppy dresser. The timing of his disappearance fits perfectly with what I know about the group's activities. I'm congratulating myself on how well this morning mission is going when Becky surprises me again. She shows me a photo she's just snapped of Earl and Ray, then hands me her phone. "Punch your number in here, Jackie, and I'll send you the pic."

"I'm mighty happy to have your phone number, Miss Becky, but what makes you think I'd want a photo of them?"

Her eyes narrow playfully. "Cause you are super interested in them for some reason. And I like you, Jack. So I want to help you out, whatever it is you're up to."

"Well, now, can't a fella just be curious?"

"Oh, you're way beyond curious, my Texas friend. Way beyond. And just so you know, I think you're some kinda cop. But I'm happy to help you anyway, 'cuz I've never liked that group of men."

She's sharper than I gave her credit for. I try deflection through humor.

I say, "Busted. I'm a Texas Ranger, and those guys are drug lords we've been after for years."

She crosses her arms and rolls her eyes. "Uh, huh."

"Okay, I'm FBI, and we think those guys are part of Hillary Clinton's ring of pedophiles."

She grins. "A bit closer to believable."

"Okay, okay. I'm a Mesa County undercover detective. Those guys have been taking two samples from the cheese counter at Sprouts, when the sign clearly says, *ONLY ONE*."

Now, she giggles. ""Look. I don't really care what it's about. I just don't want you thinking I'm some sort of clueless moron, too stupid to see what you're doing."

"Becky, I never—"

"Shhhh." She presses her index finger to my lips. "Don't ruin it, Jack. Now, if you sit there a minute, I'll be right back with something else I know you'll like."

I finish my omelet and drain my coffee mug.

Becky returns with a Polaroid photo, which she snaps down on the table in front of me like it's the ace of spades. "And *here's* a picture of all four of 'em."

"Wow! How do you have this?"

"As we were talking, I remembered that this photo was on a bulletin board in the employee break room. Last year, we offered all-you-can-eat pancake breakfasts and took photos of anyone who ate more than twenty. The big goon with the funny ear ate a mountain of 'em." She flips the polaroid over and points to "29" written on the back. At the bottom, I notice a date: August 11, 2021. The four of 'em. Together. In 2021. Documented in this photo that's worth its weight in gold.

I grasp Becky's hand. "Miss Becky, you are a force for good in this world. How can I ever repay you?"

She considers this, a smile playing at the corners of her mouth. "Take me out for a drink sometime, Jack. You have my number."

Watching Earl and Raymond hunched over their table, presumably plotting and strategizing, I make a silent vow. If Becky's assist helps me nail these bastards, I'll not only take her for that drink, I'll be her love slave for the rest of my life.

Chapter Fifty-Three

Amy

When I get home from the weekly meeting of the OT staff, I check to make sure Annabelle is okay, then go through my usual routine: groceries away, washed dishes back in cupboards; laundry folded; bag of soup—today, Blount Clam Shack Gumbo—in boiling water. The routine of all this should be comforting, but it feels like I'm merely performing normalcy.

I check the mail slot by the front door. Nothing. Lately, Dad and I have been racing each other to be the first to collect the daily mail—each trying to protect the other from seeing what it contains. Yesterday, I came up behind Dad at the kitchen table, his hands trembling as he read a letter that had arrived. He tried to hide it, but I caught a glimpse: "Your daughter should have listened. Now your whole family will pay."

I open my laptop to check personal email, and my performative facade crumbles. Almost a dozen emails. They pour out of my inbox like wasps, with wishes for my rape, my death, my family's destruction, Will's maiming. One particularly creative writer with mangled grammar suggests, "Your lucky someone hasn't killed you and your whole family. It'll probably happen. Save us the trouble. Buy a gun and a bullet. Put the barrel into your mouth and pull the trigger. I guarantee not one person on planet earth will miss you."

The subject line of another declares, "Your about to get ruined." The contents swim before my eyes: "Get ready. We are coming for you. Your a hateful, evil monster. I hope this is a nightmare to you're life." Different address, same atrocious grammar and punctuation. One person with multiple accounts, or a crowd of equally illiterate haters?

The sudden angry hiss of boiling water hitting the stovetop jolts me back to reality. The gumbo! I rescue what I can, pouring half into a bowl. Annabelle appears at my elbow, her nose twitching hopefully for a bite of chicken or uncured sausage from the soup. "Not yet, girl. Too hot still." She settles at my feet, head on paws, but her eyes never leave me.

My phone, when I check it, has exploded with voicemails. I hear heavy breathing, laughter, threats whispered in electronically distorted voices: "We're watching you." "Your son walks to school alone." "Quit or else."

The texts are worse—graphic descriptions of violence, photos of my house taken from different angles, images of me going about my daily routine that I never noticed being captured. The last one stops my breath—a photo of me, blown up to almost life-size. Looks like it's mounted on foam board.

And it's riddled with what look like bullet holes. Each dark perforation looks like an eye staring back at me.

My legs give out. I slide to the floor beside Annabelle, who immediately places her paw on my leg. She whines softly as my body begins to shake, pressing against me as if trying to hold me together.

Those bullet holes transform in my mind—no longer just dark circles on a photo, but windows into a terrifying future. What if next time it's not a photo? What if it's actually me? What if it's Dad, slowly making his way to his car, or Matty heading to soccer practice? Will, forced off the road into a ditch? The thoughts send another violent tremor through my body.

Annabelle's warmth against my side grounds me, but my mind spirals deeper into the horror of what could happen. These people, whoever they are, they know where we live. Where I shop. Where Matty goes to school. Where Will works.

And Dad—sweet, stubborn Dad, who's already been through so much. He's finally finding his rhythm again after Mom's death, finally learning to navigate his new limitations, finally finding joy with Hannah and his new work. The thought of him becoming a target because of my choices ... A sob catches in my throat. He's always been my fiercest defender, my strongest supporter. How could I live with myself if something happened to him? because I was too proud, too stubborn to back down?

They're all vulnerable because of me, because I've believed in serving my community, despite the cost. But *this* cost?

My fingers find Annabelle's fur, gripping perhaps too

tightly, but she doesn't complain. She just presses closer, her steady heartbeat a counterpoint to my racing one.

Chapter Fifty-Four

Tom

This morning, I found three more letters in the mailbox. Same frenzied handwriting, same bile-filled messages. I threw them away before Hannah or Amy could see them, just like I do every day now. But I can't throw away social-media posts about "wasted money" on polio testing. I can't make the anti-vaxxers who've made the Department of Public Health their second home disappear. Can't erase the shadows their protest signs cast across the building's entrance. Their crusade feels like waves lapping at my feet, growing stronger each day.

I can't quite imagine how Amy has been able to stand this kind of abuse for so long. Hannah and I have only been targets for a few weeks, and at nowhere near the level Amy has experienced. But I see the toll it's taking on all of us—the worry lines deepening on our faces, shadows under our eyes, worse than they were three weeks ago. In all our years at the state health agency, neither Hannah nor I ever faced anything like this.

I already had an aversion to leaving the house, pinned here by the psychological exhaustion of thinking about all the hurdles of the physical world. But now, it's not just the normal, everyday, tiresome people one might want to avoid, but actual hostiles, people who might want to do me harm. Needless to say, that reality has elevated my disinclination to venture out.

But out, I am. Looking back on my decision, I'm not certain why I agreed to give this lecture tonight at CMU. I guess because I believe I still have things to say and—let's be honest—still have the kind of ego that enjoys having been invited.

The lecture went well. The public policy students seemed genuinely interested in the parallels and contrasts I drew between polio and Covid, the different societal responses to the diseases and to the vaccines. A few students even stayed after to ask questions about my years running the state health department. Now, heading home, I feel drained but satisfied.

The first hit comes just after I turn off 27th onto Hawthorne Avenue—metal screaming against metal. I'm driving Amy's car, and it lurches left, tires squealing as they search for grip. Through the side mirror, I see a silver van emerge from the shadows. It accelerates, rams me again. The impact shoots up my spine. My heart hammers. The weakness I usually manage to ignore now terrifies me—will my legs respond if I need them?

The van drops back slightly. In my rearview mirror, a street-light illuminates the driver's face. Earl from the PPS group. His features are twisted into something feral, hungry. He comes at me again, striking the right rear panel. The car fishtails wildly. I fight to maintain control, but my arms are already trembling from fatigue.

Earl pulls alongside on my left. He cranks his wheel hard right. The van's front quarter panel slams into my driver's side door. Metal shrieks. My side mirror explodes in a shower of glass and plastic. I try to accelerate, but Earl matches my speed. He rams me again. And again. My arms are shaking so badly now I can barely hold the wheel. I've lost all feeling in my legs. The van hits me one final time. My right front tire catches the curb. The steering wheel jerks in my hands. As if in slow motion, I watch the light pole rush toward me, see the front end crumple around it, the white mass of the airbag filling my vision. Then blackness.

Chapter Fifty-Five

Earl

I'd thought about doing it for weeks. Ever since I discovered who he really was—the connections, the lies, the years of pushing poison on children. The betrayal festered like an infection.

He'd been using his daughter's car a lot. Something must be wrong with his own. But that's only made it easier for me to track him. Tonight, knowing that he'd just been in Dominguez Hall, spreading his vaccine propaganda to a university audience, I finally snapped.

My hands were steady on the wheel as I accelerated. Calm. Focused. The first hit was almost gentle—just enough to let him know what was coming. His car swerved, then righted itself. Beautiful, how the metal screamed when I rammed him again. Harder this time. Lovely, the way his tires fought for grip.

Amusing, thinking of his weakened body having a hard time responding.

The light pole bent like a broken crutch. Poetic, really.

I should feel something—guilt, remorse, triumph. Instead, there's just a hollow emptiness, like all those support group meetings where we were supposed to share our feelings, work through our anger. What a joke. Tom Franklin sat there, session after session, pretending to understand our pain while hiding who he really was. Some things don't get "worked through". Some debts have to be paid. The hard way.

I hit the gas harder now, heading for the highway. Behind me, sirens begin to wail, but I barely hear them over the sound of my own breathing. The night air rushing through my broken side window tastes like victory. Like justice.

Chapter Fifty-Six

Tom

Consciousness returns gradually. The side of my face throbs where it hit the window. Warm blood trickles down my neck. The acrid smell of the airbag's chemicals burns in my nose. Finally, the realization that I'm alive.

I try to move but can't tell if my good leg is responding. The door is crushed inward, pinning my left arm. Over the airbag, I peer through the cracked windshield and see the light pole I hit, tilting at a crazy angle. My phone has fallen somewhere out of reach.

Somewhere distant, sirens. Then closer—voices, running feet. A face appears at my window.

"Sir? Sir, can you hear me? I'm a paramedic. Try not to move."

The words float past me. Through the haze of shock, one

thought crystallizes: Earl. How could he be so angry, so unhinged, that he would do this?

The paramedics work to stabilize my neck, to cut away the crumpled door. I hear them discussing my condition in the clipped shorthand of their profession.

Jack arrives as they're extricating me from the car. His face is ghost-white. "A witness saw it, Tom. Got the van's license plate. It was Earl... I'm so sorry, bud. I took my eye off the ball one night. And he got to you."

"Yes ... Earl ..." I try to tell him but my voice isn't working right. He grabs my hand and squeezes. The adrenaline is wearing off, and pain floods in to replace it. I close my eyes.

The last thing I hear before the ambulance doors close is Jack on his phone: "Amy? They're taking him to St. Mary's. No, I don't know how bad... Yes, he was conscious... forced off the road into a lamp post ... It was Earl Phillips, the angry polio guy."

Earlier tonight, I told those students how fear and misinformation about vaccines cost lives. I should have told them something else: that hate, once unleashed, doesn't stay theoretical. It doesn't remain confined to angry Facebook posts or protest signs. It comes for you in a silver van on your way home, metal striking metal, until everything goes black.

Chapter Fifty-Seven

Amy

I've spent most of the day at St. Mary's, watching Dad sleep between tests and examinations. Will isn't Dad's assigned hospitalist, but his friend Dr. Crenson doesn't mind Will checking in frequently and keeping us updated. The diagnosis is almost absurdly good, given what happened: severe bruising, and a head laceration that isn't even as bad as when Annabelle knocked him into the coffee table last year. Sometimes miracles come disguised as mere luck.

I'm heading out through the main entrance when I spot Danny coming in, clutching a bouquet of grocery-store flowers. He stops, waiting for me, shifting his weight from foot to foot like he used to do when he was nervous about telling me something.

"Those for me?" I ask, attempting to lighten the moment.

His smile is tentative. "If you want them. Otherwise, they're for your dad ... How is he?"

I cock my head. "How did you know?"

"Grapevine."

He guides me gently away from the flow of foot traffic, his voice dropping. "I was hoping I'd find you here." His usual cockiness is conspicuously absent. "I overheard something last night at a bar in town. Something you need to know about."

The gravity in his voice makes my stomach clench. "Okay. What was it?"

"I was at Dwellington's. There was this drunk guy, about our age, bragging to another guy about being a 'prominent anti-government activist.' Boasting about running a campaign of intimidation against a school-board member and a public-health official."

My pulse quickens. Danny has my attention in a way he hasn't managed in years. "And?"

"Well, the younger guy he was drinking with kept pressing for details. So, he laid it all out: doxxing, vandalism, stalking. The works."

"This is incredible. What did you do?"

"Nothing, except edge closer and listen harder. Then he said something about members of his squad targeting 'a couple of crazy, pro-vax health officials,' trying to drive them out of office, too."

My hands find the doorframe, steadying myself. "Did you get his name?"

He nods. "According to the regulars, he's Marty Stauffer. Local far-right zealot." Danny hesitates, a slight flush creeping up his neck. "He was talking to a CMU student. Kid named Lucas Murdoch."

"At Charlie Dwellington's?" I raise an eyebrow, thinking of the rainbow flags adorning the bar's windows. "I thought Quincy's was more your scene."

A ghost of his old grin appears. "Can't a guy branch out?"

The moment of levity evaporates as I process what he's told me. "Why are you sharing this with me, Danny? We haven't exactly been on good speaking terms."

His eyes soften, catching me off guard. "Your dad was always good to me, Amy. Even after ... everything. He never judged, never treated me differently. I was really sorry to hear what happened to him." He looks down, then meets my gaze again. "And I was sorry about all you went through, too. I hope you're okay."

For the first time since our marriage imploded, I feel a flicker of warmth toward my ex-husband. "Thank you," I say, meaning it.

<hr />

HOURS LATER, I'm at the kitchen table with Hannah and Jack, our long-cold coffee replaced by stronger drinks. Jack has played recordings of Earl's vitriolic broadcasts, and we've been piecing together the evidence against Earl, Marty Stauffer, and Ray Moore.

Jack turns to me, wonder in his voice. "It's wild that you actually met Ray. What are the odds?"

I study the faces in the photo Becky Dubrovsky texted to

Jack. "Yep, met Ray and encountered the big guy. Two of the four in this rogues' gallery."

Hannah's voice is tight with worry. "You think the cops have enough to nail them?"

Jack says, "More than enough on Earl. Marty's case may hinge on Danny and the CMU kid testifying. Ray ..." He pauses, weighing his words. "Ray will be the hardest to get. Unless ..."

"Unless what?" I prompt, though something tells me I already know.

Jack's eyes gleam with possibility. "Unless Earl decides to save his own skin."

Chapter Fifty-Eight

Earl

Detective Taylor doesn't waste time with niceties. He takes the seat opposite me at the police station's little interview table like he's settling in for a long night of poker. One by one, he begins laying out papers on the table, each document another card in a hand he knows will win. Printouts of my broadcasts. Screenshots of posts I'd made in dark corners of the internet where I thought no one was watching. Everything I'd done to Wilson, Tarrant, Franklin, and Matthews—the harassment, the vandalism, the fear campaigns—spread out in black and white like a confession I never meant to write.

It's funny how the mind works. You do something wrong once, get away with it, and it gets easier to do it again. The second time barely registers. Do it enough times without consequences, and you start thinking maybe it wasn't even wrong after all. Or, you think maybe you're special, immune to the rules that govern everyone else. I knew, somewhere deep down, that what we did to those officials crossed lines. Every kid learns that bad deeds deserve punishment. But every kid also learns that sometimes you get away with it. Until you don't.

I still can't figure out how they pieced it all together. But there it is: evidence linking me to Marty and Ray, and—Christ almighty—proof of our connections to Dwayne right up until his death. I keep my mouth shut, just like they do on TV. No lawyer, no talk.

Taylor tells me I'm being arrested for assault with a deadly weapon—the van, he says—and criminal harassment. Then he recites my rights like he's reading ingredients off a cereal box. Another cop—probably been watching through that one-way mirror—enters to take me into custody.

Taylor starts to leave the room, then turns back. "Just one more thing," he says, like he's Columbo. Something in his tone makes my skin crawl. "Do you know a Becky Dubrovsky?"

The name means nothing. I see no harm in saying so. "Don't think so, no."

"She's employed as a waitress at the IHOP in town."

Oh, I think. *Becky at IHOP*. "Yeah, I know who she is, yes." My mouth suddenly goes dry as sand. "Why?"

Taylor's eyes, cold and calculating, never leave mine. "She claims you sexually assaulted her last year on three different occasions by placing your hand on her bottom and cupping her cheek. Says other servers saw it happen and are willing to testify to it." He pauses, watching me like a cat at a mouse hole. And with a vague mistiness worth of Peter Falk, he says, "I'm just wondering, Mr. Phillips, sir, if any of that rings a bell."

The bile rises so fast I can taste it, bitter and burning.

Through the acid in my throat, I manage to spit out three words: "That fucking bitch."

The corner of Taylor's mouth twitches, just slightly, and in that moment, I realize I've just given him the final card he needed for a Royal Flush, an absolutely unbeatable hand.

Chapter Fifty-Nine

Tom

The last thing I want right now is to be in a restaurant. My body aches for my recliner, for the quiet of home, but sometimes being part of a family means showing up when you'd rather not. So here I am at Spoons Bistro, my walker parked beside me like a silent dining companion at our cobbled-together table for six.

The warm glow of victory fills the air around us—Hannah, Amy, Will, Matty, Jack, and me—as animated conversation spills over our water glasses and mingles with the clink of silverware. They've been talking non-stop since we got here, riding the high of the arrests: Earl Phillips, Marty Stauffer, and Ray Moore, all finally in custody.

Jack sits across from me, wearing what I've come to think of as his "aw shucks" expression while the others shower him with praise. The way they're carrying on about him, he might as well be wearing a cape and mask.

"No, no, no," he protests, waving off their compliments with his bread roll. "It's not brilliant detective work at all. I'm telling you, ninety percent of the time, solving a crime comes down to blind chance or dumb luck." He leans forward, warming to his theme, crumbs scattering across his plate. "Someone glimpses something they barely remember until later. Someone catches a snippet of conversation that clicks only because they recognize a name. An unusual license plate number sparks attention. A restaurant manager snaps a photo because some fool wolfs down twenty-nine pancakes. A flirtatious waitress opens up to a customer who's clearly not what he seems."

"Oh, come on, Jack. You're too modest," Amy insists, the candlelight catching the animation in her face, the shadows of worry finally lifting from her eyes.

"No, I'm telling ya—it's people talking, people listening, people sharing what they've seen or heard. That's the real detective work." He turns to Matty, his voice softening. "Little buddy, remember when I told you the superhero I'm most like is Captain America? How he brings down bad guys without superpowers?"

Matty nods, a half-eaten french fry forgotten in his hand.

"My power—my ordinary, everyday power—is listening and observing. That's all you need to be good at this job."

"I don't want to be a cop," Matty declares without hesitation. "Most cops are assholes. Sorry. Not you, Uncle Jack. But most of 'em."

Jack's laugh booms across the table, drawing glances from nearby diners. "Can't argue with that, my man."

My grandson—wise beyond his years in that way kids sometimes are—furrows his brow and says, "But I'd guess being observant and a good listener are good traits to have for almost any line of work."

Amy beams with pride, reaching over to ruffle his hair. "Yup, buddy. Even better than math skills."

He squirms away like she's attacked him with a cattle prod. "Personal foul!"

Hannah sets down her wine glass, her expression turning serious. "Jack, help me understand something. I get what the police have on Earl. But how did they nail Marty Stauffer?"

"Earl flipped on Marty like an egg going over easy." Jack's eyes twinkle at his own metaphor.

"Flipped?" Matty asks, confusion creasing his forehead.

"It means Earl sang like a canary," Jack explains, buttering another roll. "Gave the police evidence against Marty, probably in the hope of earning himself a lighter sentence. It happens all the time with these types—they talk tough until they're facing real consequences. Then they'll throw anyone under the bus to save their own skin."

I lean toward Matty and, in a stage whisper, say, "That's a highly sophisticated analysis by one of America's leading law-enforcement experts."

"Eat my shorts, Tom. Eat my shorts," Jack says.

Matty's guffaw explodes like a firecracker, drawing more glances from nearby tables.

"Did Earl turn on Ray too?" Amy asks, dragging us back to the matter at hand.

Jack's expression darkens, his playfulness evaporating. "Yes, but that's not even the worst of Ray's problems. Word from the county prosecutor's office is he's about to be charged with aggravated assault in a different case."

The clatter of silverware stops dead. All eyes lock on Jack, waiting for more.

"A year ago, out in Loma where Ray lives, a man was badly beaten and left by the side of the road. Earl's testimony about Ray's racist views got the cops looking harder at the cold case. And at Ray. They found physical evidence in Moore's trailer linking him to that assault. Apparently, a pair of boots."

Hannah's voice is barely above a whisper. "Good lord. These are truly awful people."

Amy releases a long breath, like she's been holding it for months. "That's for sure. But they're all getting their comeuppance now. Criminal harassment charges against each of them. Earl also gets charged with sexual assault and assault with a deadly weapon, Ray with aggravated assault." She pauses, considering. "Seems like only Marty Stauffer is getting off easy."

Jack's smile spreads slow and wide. "Oh, I wouldn't say that."

Amy leans forward. "Really? Tell us!"

Jack can barely contain himself, like a kid with the world's best secret. "Marty has mpox."

The burst of startled laughter around the table feels a celebration of justice served with a side of karma.

Epilogue

Five Months Later - Halloween, 2022

Amy

A titanium wheelchair arrives for Dad. After months of Kaiser Permanente's endless bureaucratic dance, Dad finally has easier mobility, and he's making the most of it. The old walker stands abandoned in a corner while he zips through the house like a Formula One driver, Annabelle barking joyfully in his wake. When he announces he's "going for a spin," I hold my breath. But, honestly? After everything we've been through, seeing him enjoy it makes my heart soar.

Yesterday, he confessed to feeling guilty about his satisfaction with our enemies' misfortunes. "I know I should be above feeling *schadenfreude*," he said, fingers drumming on his armrest. "Being glad they're facing justice for what they did to us is one thing. But finding joy in their extra problems?" He shook his head. "Not nice of me."

I reached over, rubbing his forearm. "Look, it's not like you're cackling over the misfortunes of saints here. These are genuinely awful human beings who tried to destroy us. Besides," I squeezed his arm, "you can't control your feelings. You feel what you feel!"

His smile spread slow and warm, like honey in sunlight. "I guess you're right. Thanks." We sat in comfortable silence until he asked, "Where's Matty? Haven't seen him today."

"Working on his Halloween costume. Says this will probably be his last year trick-or-treating, so he wants to make it special."

"Do you know what he's going as?"

"Nope. He's being all mysterious about it. He got Jack to take him to Home Depot and Petsmart. Jack just laughed when I asked what they bought." I straightened some magazines on the coffee table. "Can I make you lunch?"

"No thanks. I'll get something later. ... Say, do you still have Matt's old stuffed animals?"

"Yeah, they're in a big bag up in the attic."

"Would you bring them down when you get a chance?"

"Sure. Anything specific you want?"

His eyes twinkled. "Yep, but I'm not telling. It's part of my costume."

We'd all promised to dress up this year, marking Matt's self-proclaimed finale. The plan: meet in the dining room at six sharp, costumed and ready for a light dinner before Matt heads out with his friends.

Now, I'm the first in the kitchen, juggling salad bowls from the fridge. Between work and everything else, I'd barely had time to think about a costume. Mine's pathetically simple: black leggings and a black T-shirt and a witch's hat. As I say, pathetic.

Hannah enters wearing a brassy yellow wig, her face painted in garish clown makeup, with an "MTG" brooch pinned to her chest.

"Marjorie, darling," I call out, "how nice of you to pull your head out of your ass for dinner!" I reach for the wine. "Drink?"

"God, yes. Impersonating this twat requires alcohol."

The doorbell announces Jack's arrival. Hannah ushers him in, doubled over with laughter. He's squeezed himself into a Captain America costume, the polyester tights leaving little to the imagination.

I raise my phone for a photo. "Jack! You actually went all out. How much did this set you back?"

"Let's just say I have to get at least five years' use out of it." He brandishes his shield proudly. "This alone was forty bucks."

The clickety-clack of Annabelle's nails heralds her entrance. She pauses dramatically in the doorway, tail wagging at our applause. Her Underdog costume—complete with red shirt, white U, and flowing blue cape—transforms our Great Pyrenees mix into a furry superhero.

"Your doing?" I ask Jack, nodding toward Bellie.

"Matty's idea, my purchase. Superheroes need allies."

Dad wheels in next, his hair styled back to look wind-swept, thick-framed sunglasses perched on his nose. We're all puzzling over his costume until he reveals the stuffed penguin in his lap —Opus from "Bloom County."

Jack nearly splits his tights laughing. "Oh my god, you're Cutter John! That's perfect, Tom!"

"Indeed I am, good sir." Dad affects confusion, scanning the room. "Now where's my raven-haired girlfriend, Bobbi Harlow?" He rolls toward Hannah. "You seen her, blondie?"

Hannah grabs his chin, plants a kiss on him. "Forget Bobbi. You're mine now, buster."

A kazoo fanfare announces Matty's entrance. He's wearing a Central High baseball cap and a white bib labeled "Pee and Poo Here" with an arrow pointing down. Around his neck hangs a tray that sticks out in front of him, in the fashion of a "cigarette girl" of the 1940s who plied their wares in restaurants. The tray holds about a one-inch layer of kitty litter, the front emblazoned with a little sign that says, "For Furry Use Only."

"What happens if someone actually tries to use it?" Dad asks when he stops laughing.

"Hadn't thought about that," Matty says. "I suppose I could take Underdog for protectio,."

Jack fist-bumps him. "Major chops, man."

"Think people will get it?" I ask, studying the costume.

Matt adopts the tone of a stuffy professor. "Subtlety is a virtue. Most people won't get it, but the ones who do will absolutely love it. They're my target audience."

The doorbell interrupts. "Sorry," Matt says, "can't stay for dinner. Amber and Jason are early."

We crowd the doorway to see his friends. Amber's Lauren Boebert is pitch-perfect: black latex probably repurposed from a

Catwoman costume, holstered Glock (please let it be fake), MAGA hat, performative gum-chewing.

Jason'a wearing a Marie Antoinette ball gown, towering platinum wig with ringlets, rouge, crimson lipstick, and dramatic eyebrows. His choker reads "Dr. Oz." He flourishes a piece of broccoli like a scepter. "Crudité, anyone?"

We wave goodbye to the three of them, then settle in for a steady stream of trick-or-treaters, starting with younger kids whose costumes are fairly predictable—princesses, fairies, superheroes. As evening deepens, the demographics shift from tots to teens, mostly girls—a parade of seductive Taylor Swifts, naughty nurses, raunchy cowgirls, French maids, and Hooters waitresses.

I swallow a fun-sized Milky Way, channeling my inner mom. "What's with teenage girls these days? Why all the skank worship?"

"Oh, come on, Amy," Jack drawls. "Don't be such a prude. Inside every madonna is a whore, waiting to burst out."

Hannah and I pelt him with candy. "Take that back, caveman!" She looks to Dad for backup. "Control your Neanderthal!"

Dad chuckles. "Jack's beyond redemption, I'm afraid."

The doorbell chimes again. "God, isn't it getting late?" I groan.

Jack checks his watch. "That's probably my date." He heads for the door.

"Some of the political costumes gave me hope," Hannah muses. "Maybe this town isn't completely lost."

"What, like Matty and his friends?"

"Well, yes, and those girls who came as Serena and Venus!"

Dad's smile is indulgent. "Honey, I'm not sure blackface counts as progressive. And did you notice all the stumbling Joe Bidens? The villainous Faucis and Pelosis? The triumphant Trumps?"

Jack returns, arm draped over a short, plump woman. Her red cap proclaims "Let's Go, Brandon!" and her matching outfit includes a T-shirt declaring, "Forget dogs and cats! Spay and neuter LIBERALS!"

"Hi, y'all," she chirps. "I'm Becky!"

The room goes silent. In that moment, watching Jack's triumphant grin, I realize this final twist is either cosmic justice or the universe's darkest joke. Maybe both. And somehow, that feels exactly right.

The End

About the Author

Thank you for reading *Extreme Malice*.

Reviews are crucial for authors. If you enjoyed this book and have a few moments to spare, please post a brief, honest review. That would be enormously helpful in connecting this novel with more readers.

J.T. Tierney writes fiction in several genres. His first novel was *Love, Literally*, a contemporary smart romance set on Cape Cod. His second, *The Butcher on Colfax*, is a historical novel that immerses readers in the lives of Irish immigrants in Denver in the 1890s.

Midsummer of 2025 will see the release of his comedy about convention coordinators in New York.

A retired professor of American government, Tierney's writings include academic books and journal articles. He was a contributing writer for *The Atlantic* for several years after he left academia. He later turned his attention to writing fiction. He resides outside Chicago with his wife of 43 years and their dog.

To sign up for his newsletter and be the first to hear about upcoming releases, news, and special offers, please provide your name and email address on the subscription sign-up form at jttierney.com. Thanks again.